MW01199442

A PLACE IN
THE SUN

USA TODAY BESTSELLING AUTHOR
R.S. GREY

Published: R.S. Grey 2016
authorrsgrey@gmail.com
Editing: Editing by C. Marie
Proofreading: Jennifer at JaVa Editing
Cover Design: R.S. Grey
ISBN: 1537776746
ISBN-13: 978-1537776743

Dedication

To every gelatician (master gelato maker) in Vernazza, Italy. You are the real heroes.

Chapter One

Georgie

HOW WAS NO *one else seeing this?*

The two middle-aged tourists in queue to enter the Colosseum were going at it like randy teenagers. The woman had her leg coiled up around her lover's waist and his hand had disappeared beneath her skirt fifteen minutes ago—the thing hadn't come up for air since.

She moaned into his mouth and fingered his hair. He growled like an undersexed werewolf, and then went back in for another snog with enough tenacity to suck her lips off.

I sat ensconced from my vantage point a few yards away, picking at a croissant and pretending to pay attention to a travel podcast about the Colosseum. In the last few minutes, the spirited performance had completely stolen my focus. Surely their oxygen levels were getting pretty low.

In all my twenty-six years, I'd never once kissed someone the way they were kissing each other. It was as if they were newlyweds on a transatlantic flight and the pilot had just announced that they'd lost both engines. God, if they went at it like that in full public view at the foot of a crusty old ruin, what on Earth did they do in private?

I blushed just thinking about it.

Eventually, a security guard with a red, pudgy face and an awkward manner asked the couple to politely refrain from boning in line, or so I imagined—his words were in Italian, so I couldn't be sure. The unflinching lovebirds disappeared inside the Colosseum and I was left with my pastry once again. *It's just me and you, carbs.*

"Seat taken?"

I glanced up to find a devastatingly handsome Italian man with cool trainers and slicked-back hair. He was smiling down at me, pointing to the bit of stone to my left. I tossed my croissant aside and yanked my earbuds out so quickly they nearly took my ears with them.

In front of the Colosseum, there's not much in the way of seating. It's all brash vendors peddling plastic crap, pale-thighed sightseers running after their bored children, and pushy groups of veteran tourists spilling out of buses with expensive cameras around their necks. I'd sought refuge from the swirling sea of humanity on a distant rock in the only bit of shade I could find.

"Oh, yeah. All yours," I said with a big smile.

The man sat down beside me, pulled out a water bottle, and took a long swig.

"*Bellissima*," he said, tipping his water bottle in my direction, and for one tiny moment, my heart leapt. I didn't know much Italian—nearly none in fact—but every woman on Earth knows that word.

I blushed and opened my mouth to thank him before he pointed to the Colosseum. "It's beautiful," he repeated, this time in thickly accented English.

Oh.

Of course. *The crumbling heap.*

"It's all right," I grumbled, glancing back to the Colosseum so he wouldn't see my frown. Truthfully, it wasn't what I had expected. The street was crowded, the sun was blazing overhead, and the street performers waltzing around in skimpy gladiator outfits for photo-ops weren't half as sexy as I'd assumed they'd be. The latter was the issue that bothered me the most.

"You aren't going in?" he asked, tilting his head to the queue spiraling around the base of the building.

I scrunched my nose. "It seems fairly self-explanatory from the outside."

"You're missing out," he said before stuffing his water bottle back into his backpack and turning his full attention to me.

I shrugged. Maybe I was cheating myself, or maybe I was smarter than the sweaty masses filing in. Perching on my rock with my croissant and my podcast had been pretty nice up until the canoodlers had distracted me with their tonsil tennis.

"How long are you in Rome?" he asked, flashing a wide smirk in my direction.

This man was handsome, *really* handsome, and though I was due to leave the next day, I was hesitant to tell him that. If he wanted to sweep me off my feet and put his hand up my skirt while we stood in line at the Colosseum, I'd consider extending my stay.

"Well, actually I…"

My sentence faded out as a glamorous woman appeared behind him. The sun shaded her face so I couldn't really make her out until she'd bent low and wrapped a possessive

3

arm around the Italian man's shoulders. There, with his head shading her face, I suddenly saw her dark eyes narrow into little slits right at me.

"Luciana, look, I've found us a new friend," he smiled.

Luciana didn't share his excitement.

I'll spare the superfluous details and cut to the chase: Italian man had a girlfriend. The good ones always do. After a few minutes of terribly awkward conversation in which I tried to pretend Luciana wasn't wishing me a swift, sudden death, my phone rang on my lap and I seized the excuse to flee. I scooted off the rock, gave my spot to Luciana, and promised to come back after I'd finished my call. It was a lie—there was a better chance of me sacrificing myself in the arena.

I curled around the side of the colosseum, using the massive structure to shade me as I answered the call.

"Georgie, finally!"

My brother sounded exasperated.

"Hello ol' chum. What do you want?"

"When will you be at Mum's? We're waiting for you before we sit down for dinner."

Oh, oops. Had I forgotten to phone and cancel?

"Don't bother waiting for me, Fred. Eat up."

"You aren't coming? Mom's expecting you." He sounded a bit sad about it, which made me feel good. He used to find me so annoying when we were younger, but he was finally coming around. *As he should.* I was (objectively) the only person in our family with any personality.

"No, I'm not coming. You go on ahead."

A group of young, rowdy American tourists ran past me then, shouting and pretending to be gladiators fighting one another. I tried to muffle the sound of their shouts through the phone, but it was no use. Freddie heard them.

"Georgie, where are you?"

"Oh, well actually…"

I glanced around me, trying to conjure up the name of a street back home in London. I'd lived there my whole life but my brain wasn't cooperating.

"Georgie."

"Well, as a matter of fact, I've gone to Italy."

A massive moment of silence hung between us before he flipped out.

"*Italy?!* Since when?"

"Just yesterday. I meant to tell you."

"Georgie, have you gone insane?"

I smiled. "No, brother. All is well."

"Then why on Earth are you in Italy?"

"To find love, of course."

• • •

I found myself in Italy the way I find myself in most places: by chance. The week before, I'd been sitting in a restaurant in London, partaking in another miserable blind date set up by my mother. The man sitting across from me was chewing with his mouth open. His massive chompers were spewing steak at a rate that concerned me—and the diners sitting within a five-yard radius.

In a moment of panic (I was particularly worried I'd become a new statistic taught to medical students: the first case of mad cow disease transmitted by sirloin to the eye), I realized I couldn't allow my mum to control my love life any longer. She was concerned for me, laboring under the outdated perception that if I were to remain single past twenty-six, I'd be branded a hopeless spinster, destined to spend my days scouring the streets for love.

Unbeknownst to him, Chompers served as a perfect example of why I needed to take my love life into my own hands. He was nearing forty in both years of life and strands of hair. His job was something like "insurance for insurance" and though he tried to explain it to me while chewing, after thirty minutes, I still didn't quite understand any of it.

It really wasn't fair to poor Chompers. He hadn't chosen to be the latest in the long string of terrible blind dates my mother had forced upon me, but in that role, he suddenly had to bear the cumulative weight of disappointment of all those who'd come before him. There was Mitch—the gouty muppet who had the personality of a dull housefly, Thom—my brother's naff friend who smelled perpetually of tuna fish, and Celso—a Spaniard who, despite looking fairly tidy, wouldn't let go of my hand through the entire dinner. I made it through the appetizers all right, but when I'd tried to cut my chicken one-handed, I only succeeded in flinging it off my plate and onto his lap.

The real problem lay in the fact that my brother—the golden child of our family—had found love and married years ago. He and his wife, Andie, had three chubby-cheeked children, and thus my mother was able to focus the full power of her matrimonial death beam onto me.

"You're in your prime, Georgie!"

As if this was the seventeenth century.

"You're getting older every day!"

She'd said this to me at my twentieth birthday party, just before gifting me an actual antique hourglass, making sure to emphasize the symbolism by flipping it upside down in my hands.

"You really ought to loosen your standards. That man who comes round your house every now and then is so handsome and in quite good shape."

She'd been referring to the postman.

A few years ago, fearing that my status as single was a permanent problem, my mum had started enlisting the help of her friends and their "eligible" sons. I'd been a good sport about it, going on dates with men from nearly every county in England, but in the years since then, the novelty had lost its luster. Though I was no closer to marrying, I *had* developed a very clear list of requirements in a future husband. For instance, he must chew with his mouth closed. He must wash a few times a week and be taller than he is round. I used to think a sense of a humor would have been nice. I wasn't asking for a Russell Brand or a Ricky Gervais, just a man who wasn't a complete bump on a log. But those days were coming to a close—if my mother had her way, I would settle down with a well-meaning bump on a very average log.

After my date with Chompers, I'd left him on the curbside after dodging—*you guessed it*—an open-mouthed kiss. I took the long way home, puzzling over my problem. I wanted to find love as much as my mother wanted it for me. At twenty-six, I *obviously* wasn't a spinster, but I was becoming a bit lonely. I hadn't ever experienced a gut-clenching, obsessive, swoony kind of romance.

Obviously, it was time for a change.

But the need for change wasn't new. After each of these bad dates, I'd head home, working out how I'd break the news to my mother: no more dates. No more matchmaking. A week or two would pass, she'd bat her eyelashes, and I'd cave. I always caved, but not this time.

I knew if I was really going to make a change, I had to

get out of London. My mother, bless her, would never leave me alone as long as I stayed within her reach.

So I'd done what any rational girl would have.

I spun a globe in our estate's library and promised myself I'd travel to whichever country my finger landed on. The globe's colors had blended together in a mess of blue and green and then I'd dropped my finger, abruptly stopping its rotation.

Syria.

Er, right. Minor hiccup.

I spun again and *voila!*

Italy!

Specifically, *Vernazza.*

• • •

Even though I'd never heard of Vernazza and needed a magnifying glass to see it on the map, I didn't spin the globe for a third time—I didn't want to get on destiny's bad side. Instead, I wrote down the name and rolled it over my tongue to get a feel for the pronunciation.

After a bit of research, I learned that Vernazza is one of five seaside villages that make up Cinque Terre. All five of the centuries-old villages are tucked into the rugged Ligurian coastline, and are only easily accessible by train—lovely, considering motion sickness was my fiercest enemy.

In an effort to break up the trip and spare my poor stomach, I'd flown into Rome first and planned a day of exploring the ancient city. After escaping the Colosseum, I walked along the cobblestone streets, turning the paper map in my hand and trying to maneuver around the crowds. I saw all the important sights that day. I stood in the center of the Pantheon under the massive oculus, boiling. It was noon and the sun was right overhead, blinding everyone in the room.

"Not incredibly practical to cut a hole in the roof if you ask me," I deadpanned to the ten-year-old beside me.

She sighed heavily and rolled her eyes, walking away with *Architecture of the Italian Renaissance* shoved underneath her arm. Very cultured, these kids today.

After that, I toured the Vatican and got in trouble for talking in the Sistine Chapel. They shuffled a thousand of us into the room at once, told us to zip it, and threatened to start chopping fingers if we tried to take photos. Still, an elderly Italian woman prodded my arm with her cane and pointed at her iPhone like she wanted me to help her take an illegal photo.

"Oh, I don't think you're allow—"

A baritone voice boomed overhead. *"SILENCIO! SIIIILLLEEENNNCE."*

I'd jumped a mile in the air, assuming it was the voice of God himself.

My final stop of the day was the Trevi Fountain. I chucked a euro over the crowds, but my aim was crap, and it ended up striking a woman in the forehead as she stood for a photo-op in front of the fountain. I shrugged—my wish had been to make the crowds disappear, and as the woman hurried off angrily, I counted it as a win.

Confident that I'd consumed the best bits of Rome and also anxious to flee the area in case the woman with the coin-shaped bruise on her forehead came back looking for vengeance, I turned back for my hotel. The sun was setting and my feet were aching.

In the morning, I would head to Vernazza and see what

fate had in store for me.

• • •

In true Georgie Archibald form, I slept right through my alarm the following morning. It BEEPED BEEPED BEEPED over and over again and my brain—still exhausted from traveling—had assumed it was some annoying Italian songbird outside my window. Eventually, my subconscious brain realized that birds don't even sound remotely like alarm clocks, and I shot out of bed.

I looked at the time. "Arse! Bugger! SHITE!"

If I missed my first train of the day, I'd have a hell of a time making my connections. I tossed anything and everything into my suitcase, nearly taking half the hotel room with me. The train station was only a few minutes away, so I didn't bother with a cab. I shot across streets without looking both ways, nearly collided with a few cars, and made it past security with ten minutes to spare before the train departed.

It was an 11:20 AM departure for Pisa, packed with families on holiday. I took a deep breath, telling myself, *I made it.* I stowed my luggage then wandered down the aisle, glancing at the numbers posted above each seat. I was assigned to 11A and when my eyes landed on my backward-facing seat, I groaned. It wouldn't do; I had to face the direction the train was moving or I'd get sick.

I glanced around for an opening, but my late arrival had ensured that every last seat on the train was full except for mine.

"Sir," I said, turning to the distinguished-looking man sitting in 11C. His seat was opposite mine, facing the right direction. It was a small move, but it would ensure I didn't spew up the granola bar I'd stuffed down my throat on the way over from my hotel.

He tilted his head up, a bit annoyed to be pulled out of his crossword.

I offered him a massive, pleading smile. "Is there any way I could convince you to swap seats with me? I get motion sickness on trains and I—"

He shook his head before I'd even finished.

"This is my assigned seat."

"Of course, and I'm assigned to 11A."

I pointed between the two seats as if trying to convince him of how small the distance was. He'd just have to pop up, rotate that impressively large bottom of his, and plop back down across the gap. Easy peasy.

"Then 11A is where I suggest you sit."

On that note, he held up his crossword to cover his face.

I moved on to my next target: the woman sitting in 11D, but unfortunately, she was snoozing against the window, a bit of drool already rolling down her chin. I could have forced her awake and asked her to swap seats, but it seemed like bad form.

I tried one last glance around the train, displaying the most desperately tragic face I could muster, but everyone turned away, avoided eye contact, or offered up a blatant shake of their head.

Fine.

I sat down in 11A, dropped my backpack between my feet, and yanked out the supplies I carried with me whenever I traveled: chewing gum, ginger candy, peppermints, and Dramamine. I began to fortify myself for my impending doom, but it was no use.

By the time we'd chugged away from the station in

Rome, dizziness had taken hold of my head and wouldn't let go. I squeezed my eyes closed, willing the sensation to pass, but it only grew worse. I managed to make it to the toilet before throwing up the first time, but the second time, I made sure to look right in 11C's eyes as I hurled into the paper bag. *See? See what you've done to me?*

Fortunately for me—and everyone else assigned to my car—I had a forward-facing seat for the next leg of the journey, from Pisa to La Spezia, but it didn't matter. By that point, my head was swimming and my stomach was rejecting everything I put in it. I considered stopping in La Spezia for the night, but it was still early afternoon and I'd intended on making it all the way to Vernazza before calling it quits for the day. I wanted to crash, but a bigger part of me just wanted to get the journey over with. I wanted a hotel room. I wanted a proper shower and a bed to collapse into.

Unfortunately, I'd underestimated how difficult the final leg of my journey would be. It was a short train journey between La Spezia and Vernazza, but the regional train was small and all the seats were full by the time I lugged my suitcases onboard. I was forced to stand, packed like a sardine, in the small compartment between two cars. My body was crushed against the side door, facing out. I desperately willed my nausea to pass; I'd used my last sick bag on the train to La Spezia and I really didn't want to traumatize the family of five laughing behind me.

The small train sped along the coast of Italy, through long, dark tunnels cut through rock. I caught my own reflection in the door's window and cringed. My brown eyes, usually bright and lively, had heavy circles beneath them. Strands of my long chestnut brown hair were coated with sweat and stuck to my cheeks. All color had faded from my face and the bit of throw-up crusted below my bottom lip served as the *pièce de résistance* to my entire haggard appearance.

I nearly caved then. It would have been so easy to call Freddie and beg him to come collect me, but in the blink of an eye the tunnel broke open and my vision was filled with an expanse of turquoise water.

It was blue in every direction, different hues painted across the landscape as far as my eyes could see. A cloudless sky met crystal clear waters. Angry waves crashed against the shore, spilling white sea foam over massive granite rocks that had tumbled down from the mountains over the centuries. I pressed my hands to the glass, leaned forward, and gasped, nearly lost in the beauty of it, right before another bout of motion sickness overtook me.

Oh bloody hell.

"Mom! The crazy lady just threw up on me!"

Chapter Two

Gianluca

I PULLED MY baseball cap off my head and wiped my forehead on my shirt sleeve. It was dirty, just like my forehead was dirty, but it seemed better than nothing. I'd been out on the water all morning and had a boat full of fish to deliver to Massimo. He'd smile when he saw the sea bass; it was the biggest one I'd caught in weeks. He'd coat it in olive oil, bury it in a mound of sea salt, and bake it for some lucky tourist in his restaurant. I'd have envied them if I didn't have half a dozen fish to keep for myself.

I cranked my motor up another notch, slicing across the sea on my way back home. The waves were choppy, sloshing water up over the sides of my small fishing boat. I could feel the winds changing; I'd felt them all morning, playing with the currents and riling the sea. I'd almost skipped the trip out on the water, but I'd compromised instead, staying close to the shore in case things went south.

As Vernazza's tiny harbor came into view on the

horizon, I let out a breath I'd been holding all morning, grateful to the sea for delivering me back home in one piece. The painted village stretched closer and I maneuvered my boat around the granite breakers. Of all five Cinque Terre villages, Vernazza boasted the largest true harbor. Even still, it could only fit a couple dozen fishing boats at once, nothing more.

My cousin was waiting for me on the breaker, smiling at the lot I'd brought back for him.

"*Buongiorno, cugino?*"

I threw him the line. "*Molto buono.*"

It was Saturday and the village was already bustling, alive with chatter. Life in Vernazza was centered around the restaurants in the heart of the village. Five of them dotted the perimeter of the square, carving out space of their own with wide-brimmed umbrellas. Tourists gathered underneath them, enjoying their lunches with enough wine and bread to last them well into the evening. Massimo and I worked together to unload the fish into a small cart. He'd roll it up to his restaurant—not one of the lucky five located on the square—and I'd head back up to my house and shower off the stench of fish and foam.

"Watch it!" I said, scolding the group of children running around the harbor, daring one another to jump into the water. It was safe to swim there; the water was calm thanks to the large partial seawall the village had built a decade earlier to shield itself from the power of the ocean.

The boys weren't tourists. I'd watched them grow up for the last few years.

"And stay out of my boat, or tomorrow I'll use you as shark bait!" I shouted over my shoulder before they'd run too far. I knew from their giggles it had been years since they'd taken my threats seriously. It didn't matter; I had the boat's key, so they couldn't get into too much trouble.

"They call you the village grump, y'know," Massimo said, nudging my shoulder.

I smiled, despite myself. "Good."

The title fit.

"Have any plans tonight? *Appuntamento romantico?"*

I let go of the cart, no longer in the mood to help him push it up the square. "Enjoy your fish, Massimo."

He groaned. "Aw, c'mon. S'only a joke! One of these days the answer will be yes, and I want to be the first to know!"

I'd have flipped him off if there weren't so many children milling around. Instead, I walked away.

"Hey! Help me with this cart!"

I turned around to tell him off, but a sight over his right shoulder caught my attention instead. A woman had just stepped into the square from one of the side streets. She looked like most tourists did upon their arrival to Vernazza—a little frazzled and tired from lugging their suitcases on the train for so many hours—but there was something off about her. She paused and squeezed her eyes closed, leaning against the building behind her. For a moment I thought she just needed to catch her breath, but then I watched in slow motion as she tottered on her feet and, as if all her bones had been zapped from her body, collapsed to the ground.

"Shit!"

I ran for her, sidestepping chairs and tables and tourists.

"Move!"

A woman huffed as I collided with her shoulder. I threw an apology over my shoulder but kept running. No one else had seen the woman faint. There was too much going on in the square.

By the time I reached her, she was laid out on the ground, her brown hair covering her face. Her backpack had protected her head from the stone, but she hadn't regained consciousness yet. Massimo was right behind me by the time I reached her.

"What happened? What do we do?" Massimo asked, wiping his hand down his face.

I stepped forward and put my cheek right over her nose. When I felt her breath hit my skin, I exhaled.

"Well, she's breathing."

"And her pulse?" he asked.

I brushed some strands of brown hair off her neck and pressed my fingers to the soft skin below her chin. It was steady.

"What the hell happened to her?"

I swallowed down my panic and shook my head. I had no clue.

A small crowd had gathered around her by then.

"*È morta?!*"

"I don't think she's breathing!"

It wouldn't be long before the entire square had gathered to ogle her.

"She's probably just dehydrated. Let's take her in there," I said, pointing to the building behind us. It was a lucky break, her passing out right in front of the building our family had owned for as long as anyone could remember. My grandmother had operated it as a bed and breakfast. Now it was abandoned, but it was out of the sun and the view of tourists, and we could call the doctor once we were inside.

Massimo unlocked the door, using one of the keys on his jingling chain.

We carried her in together, careful to keep her head

steady as we pushed boxes and cobwebs out of the way. There was a bed in the bottom bedroom, one the manager had used when the bed and breakfast was still open. I shook out the bedding, checking for bugs, and watched as dust flew into the air. It wasn't clean, but it was better than putting her down on the wood floor.

Massimo and I maneuvered her onto the bed and stepped away, giving her space. She looked like hell. Her hair was matted around her face, sweaty and stuck to her cheeks. Her skin was sickly pale.

"I'm going to go grab her stuff before someone nabs it," Massimo said, darting out of the room and back out onto the street.

I knew I needed to move, to go find a doctor and help figure out what was wrong with her, but my feet were rooted in place. It'd been five years since I'd seen a woman lying on a sick bed, but the memories came flooding back all at once.

"Luca, come help with this bag!"

Massimo's voice snapped me out of my memories. I spun away from the bed and ran out to help him gather her things. The amount of luggage she'd carried with her could have filled four wardrobes. Massimo lugged the suitcase inside and I grabbed her backpack, which weighed more than she did.

"No wonder she passed out," Massimo laughed, groaning with the weight of the suitcase.

We were outside her room, dropping her things against the wall when I heard a rustling on the bed followed by an exasperated English accent.

"Oh my Liam Neeson. I've been *taken!*"

Chapter three

Georgie

I'D SEEN MOVIES; I knew this was just what the gritty underbelly of the European sex trade must look like. I'd woken up disoriented in a dusty room. Very little light passed through the boarded-up windows and the stench of mildew hung in the air.

I'd known it was bound to happen eventually. My mother had given me great bone structure, and growing up with naff brothers had forced me to cultivate a fantastic (and apparently, highly abductable) personality. I supposed that even with the smell of sick clinging to me, my raw sexual aura had shone through, and now rogue sheikhs and warlords were in the other room trying to outbid one another for me. To save myself, I'd need to somehow dampen my agreeable nature during auction.

Voices sounded out in the hallway, hushed tones I strained to hear. I tried to sit up and then groaned at the effort. They'd likely already put something in my system, possibly via poison dart on the train. I wasn't tied down or anything, so they'd have taken chemical precautions to ensure I didn't run away.

When two men rushed into the room, I pushed myself back against the wall and held my hands out to stop them from getting any closer.

"I don't know how much you've paid for this— *millions*, I'm sure—but my family is very wealthy, and they'll double it for my freedom."

It was true: my family was from old English money, the kind that seems to grow no matter how much you spend.

The two traffickers glanced between each other, confused, and I sighed. Of course, they wouldn't understand English well.

I leaned closer and spoke very slowly with dramatic gestures. "You haaaavvve to let meee gooooooo."

The shorter one propped his hands on his hips and turned to his friend. "What is she going on about? And why is she speaking as though we're mentally ill?"

I clapped, excited. "Oh good, you speak English! That should make the whole ransoming bit much easier. Shouldn't you two be busy cutting letters out of magazines?"

The taller bloke in the baseball cap bit down to conceal a smile. "She thinks we've kidnapped her, Massimo."

Massimo blanched and whipped his head back to me. "No! No, you passed out in the square outside. In Vernazza. We carried you in here because everyone was gawking and…"

It took a bit more information before the pieces of my day started to settle back into place. The sick feeling on the train, how lightheaded I'd felt as I'd tried to maneuver my way down to the village square. At some point I'd blacked out, and now I was there, in a dusty room with two Italian men. Now that I was fairly confident they weren't sex traffickers, I let myself mull over their features. They were *very* handsome, especially the taller one. I didn't know his name yet, but I kept slipping quick glances his way as Massimo chattered on about my passing out and how I could have died, yada yada. He lingered in the door of the room, happy to let Massimo take the lead, but I wanted him to step closer and introduce himself, peel the cap off his head so I could see his face properly. From what I could see beneath it, he was beautiful. Golden from the Italian sun. Tall and muscled beneath his rolled long-sleeve shirt and jeans. I scanned higher, up to his defined jaw. He was studying me just as intently as I was studying him, and instead of looking away when our eyes locked beneath the brim of his cap, I smiled.

I was in Italy to find love, after all. How convenient that this romantic-looking man, out of *every* man in the village, had been the one to rescue me.

"Are you feeling okay now? Should I call the doctor?" Massimo asked, stepping in front of his friend and cutting off our intense staring contest. I nearly shifted my head around him, but he was being kind and I didn't want to snub my nose at his hospitality.

"Honestly, I think I just need a few hours of sleep. I've had a rough day and I'm still a bit dizzy from travel."

Massimo nodded. "Right, well—"

"What is this place?" I cut in, glancing around the room. Sure, it was dusty, but the bones of the room were nice. The window, though boarded up, was large, and beneath the layer of dirt, I could just barely make out pastel yellow paint on the walls. It reminded me of sunflowers.

I'd wanted the tall one to answer, but Massimo replied

23

first. "It's an old bed and breakfast. Our grandmother took care of it when she was alive."

I grinned. "Perfect. I'd like to rent a room here, please."

The man leaning against the door jamb laughed. "In case you hadn't noticed, the place isn't exactly operational."

His voice shook me. There were layers of depth there, a proper English accent at its base with a rich Italian layer up top. I suspected he'd spent a good deal of time both in England and Italy.

Massimo turned back and addressed his friend in rapid-fire Italian. I ached to cut in and ask him to translate, but I held my tongue until they were finished.

Finally, he glanced back to me and clapped his hands as if the situation was settled. "There's a place across the square. They should have a room available."

I nodded, though a part of me wanted to struggle, to insist on staying in the dark room. There was something wonderful about it, the history of its walls, the mysteries that filled the boxes stacked in the corner.

"Are you okay to walk?" Massimo asked with a worried expression.

Truthfully, I still felt terrible, but I didn't want to take up any more of their time. I'd force my dizziness aside and let them lead me across the square. As soon as I made it to my room, I could crash.

With the promise of sleep on the horizon, I leaned forward and dropped my feet to the ground, testing the waters. I still felt ill, but not nearly as close to passing out as I had earlier. I put my weight into my feet and was about to stand from the bed when the man from the doorway stepped forward and gripped my forearm to steady me.

I stilled for the briefest of moments, shocked by his

touch. It was warm and unwavering. He wasn't worried that he'd overstepped his bounds, not like English blokes would have been, teetering in their boots with shaky, nervous voices. This man had rushed forward to help me with a pragmatism that showed he wasn't just a gentleman when told to be.

"Steady," he said, helping lead me through the doorway of the room. He reached for my backpack with his other hand and slung it over his shoulder like it was filled with cotton candy. Massimo reached for my suitcase, turned down my offer of help, and then the three of us headed back out the door toward the square. I glanced behind me one last time, saying goodbye to the old, abandoned bed and breakfast before Massimo locked the door behind us.

"I'm Georgie by the way," I said, chancing a quick glance up to the man whose grip was still around my forearm.

He offered a curt nod and continued to lead me across the square.

When it was clear he wasn't going to offer up his name on his own, I asked.

"And what are you called?"

"Gianluca."

The name slipped off his tongue so beautifully, I nearly asked him to say it once more, just so I could listen to his accent.

"But his friends call him Luca," Massimo filled in, rushing forward to catch up to us.

Luca. I rolled the name around my head, testing it on his tall frame. It fit perfectly.

• • •

The door to my room was barely locked before I lunged for the twin bed and collapsed on top of the sheets. I'd meant to rest there for only a moment before getting up to wash, but my body had other plans. A short nap turned into the longest, deepest sleep of my life. I didn't wake until the following morning, disoriented and so hungry I was nearly delirious. It'd been over twenty-four hours since I'd had a meal.

I blinked my eyes open, rolled to sit up, and waited for the dizziness to overtake me again.

It didn't.

Which meant it was time to show Vernazza my good side—that is, the one *not* covered in vomit.

I threw off my soiled clothes from the day before and hopped into the shower. My room was barely more than a broom cupboard, but it was cheap. Plus, the woman who'd checked me in the day before had promised I could stay as long as I wanted, though I suspected she'd have said anything to elicit a smile from Gianluca. I toweled off and inspected my surroundings. There was the small bed, the sheets still mostly in place despite my having collapsed right on top of them, and a small wicker chair resting in the corner of the room. The plaster walls were painted a light blue and a small painting of the choppy sea hung on the wall over the bed.

I turned to the door, where Massimo and Gianluca had dropped my luggage the day before. They'd ensured I made it to my room all right and then they'd nearly sprinted away, no promise of meeting up or seeing me again. *Oh god, who'd blame them.* I'd accused them of kidnapping me! It was all a bit depressing. Gianluca was one of the most handsome men I'd ever met and I hadn't even properly seen him, not with the cap on. In all likelihood, I probably wouldn't get another chance. He'd seen me at my absolute worst, bits of dried throw-up and all.

I sighed and dragged my suitcase across the floor, deciding to forget about my embarrassing arrival. Sure, it would have been lovely if Gianluca had insisted on staying the night and nursing me back to health (with his mouth), but there would be other men in Italy, other deliciously handsome men—I was sure of it.

I propped my suitcase open on the wicker chair and started to flip through my clothes. It was early summer in Italy, chilly in the mornings and evenings but warm and sunny in the afternoons. I rummaged around for a simple white sundress and was about to drop my towel when a loud gothic bell rang out in the square behind me, reminding me where I was.

Vernazza.

I grinned and flew to the window, flinging it open with enough gusto that the shutters slapped against the plaster walls inside my room. It punched me right in the gut, the *beauty* of the place. The main square was surrounded on three sides by pastel buildings: small hotels, rooms, apartments, restaurants stacked up three or four stories high on the mountainside. They were all varying shades of pink and light red, yellow and green, cast in early morning light. The sun had barely begun to rise over the terraced hills surrounding the small village. The sea air swelled past the window, blooming goosebumps across my exposed shoulders. I clutched my towel around my middle and leaned out, glancing to the left and inhaling the harbor and sea that lined the village on the fourth side. It was just as spectacular as the view from the train: turquoise water and bright blue skies stretched out to infinity.

The church bells rang seven times in total, a beautiful sound that I mourned after they'd finished, but then I remembered that they'd only just begun. The day was young. I left the windows open, enjoying the cool breeze as I dressed for the day. I didn't bother fixing myself up. After a day of suffering, I wanted to get out and explore. Besides, my stomach was grumbling so loud I feared I would wake up the other guests staying in the building.

I flung on a pair of leather sandals, stuffed the small room key in my purse, and set off down the narrow staircase. The woman who'd checked me in the day before was already set up behind the counter on the ground floor. She glanced up and smiled when she saw me approach.

"Feeling better?" she asked with a thick Italian accent.

I nodded. "Yeah, sorry about all the drama yesterday. I didn't plan on arriving so close to death."

She laughed and stood up, reaching across the counter with her hand. "It's…" She paused for a moment, trying to find the right English word. "Normal?"

I nodded. "Ah, well that's reassuring."

"I'm Chiara."

I grinned. "Georgie."

She was younger than I'd thought at first, about my age or maybe a year or two older. Her long hair was darker than mine, nearly black, and her eyes almost matched.

"Are you having breakfast now?" she asked.

"Yeah." I smoothed a hand against my stomach. "I'm starved."

"There is a place," she said, turning and pointing through the front door of the hotel. "Just up the road. The Blue Marlin. Tell Antonio that Chiara sent you."

My stomach grumbled loudly then, as if wanting to answer her itself. Chiara laughed and waved me off, promising to see me when I returned to my room later.

I stepped out of the hotel and my sandals clapped against the stone walkway. I'd been in the square the day before, but this felt massively different. Then, not only had I been sick and disoriented, I'd arrived in the middle of the day when the square was crowded with tourists. Now, as I stepped away from the hotel and stood on the perimeter of the square, I felt like I was seeing a new side of Vernazza, a secret, quiet side. The tables and umbrellas used for the square's restaurants were closed and pushed to the side, stored up until they needed them for lunch service later in the day.

An old man with thinning white hair swept out a doorway, nodding to me as I passed. Boats bobbed in the harbor, and this early, there were no children splashing in the water, no teenagers sunbathing on the large rocks. A few extra boats sat in the center of the square, stored with thin cloth covers over the top of them. I passed a sleepy cat relaxing in the center of one and it coaxed me closer with a few cheeky meows. It was fat and happy, most likely the result of daily scraps from pliable tourists.

What a lovely life, I thought, petting under its chin before my stomach reminded me for the twentieth time that I was nearing death if I didn't feed myself soon. I turned from the cat, resisting its meows of protest, and turned in the direction of The Blue Marlin.

There was only one main street in Vernazza, the Via Roma. It wound straight from the village square up to the train station and the narrow lane was mostly meant for foot traffic, but that morning, a few motorized carts ran alongside me, making early morning deliveries. I walked along the side of the road, inspecting the shops as I passed them. They weren't open yet, but I peered through the windows, admiring the things inside. Most had kitschy trinkets and cheap t-shirts, of course, but a few of them stocked specialty handmade pastas and local olive oil, bottled pesto and lemon candies. I memorized the name of one I wanted to visit later and continued my walk, all but salivating as I grew closer to The Blue Marlin and smelled the first sign of breakfast.

I dreamt of having a proper meal, one filled with croissants, sausage, and eggs. Oh, and toast and milky tea! When I strolled through the open door of the restaurant and saw the overflowing pastry case propped on the counter, I knew I wouldn't be disappointed.

"*Buongiorno*," greeted the man wiping down the top of the counter. He had lovely kind eyes rimmed by deep-set wrinkles.

I smiled and greeted him with a meek hello. My knowledge of the Italian language was abysmal, and even though I knew he'd just wished me good morning, I was too nervous to try the greeting on my own tongue. I didn't want to sound like a silly oaf.

"English?" he asked, taking my shyness to mean I hadn't understood him.

"Please," I said as I breathed out, relieved.

He chuckled and slid a menu across the bar. "We don't start serving eggs until 8:30 AM, but I can get you a coffee or pastry."

With that, he went back to work and gave me a few moments of peace to review the menu and peruse the pastry case. I was deciding between an almond croissant or a plain one when four older tourists strolled into the restaurant dressed in proper hiking gear. They had on hats, boots, and industrial-grade sunglasses, and they even had walking sticks folded up and stuffed into the side pockets of their small backpacks. They passed behind me and waved to the man behind the counter. Without a word, he started whipping up drinks for them, a ritual they all seemed comfortable with.

"I think we should take the train to Monterosso and then hike back from there," one of the American men said, addressing his group. "Everyone says that's the best view. It's the one you see on postcards."

"It's also the hardest trek though," one of the women warned.

"Then we should do it while it's cool out."

The four of them were working out whether or not it was a good idea when I stepped forward and cut in.

"You can hike between the villages?"

Four pair of eyes sliced over to me.

"Of course!" one replied, seemingly shocked by my question.

"You must! It's what Cinque Terre is known for!"

Really?

The man behind the counter chuckled as he slid four espressos across to the Americans.

"There are trails that connect all five villages," one of the women continued.

"I thought you could only go by train."

They shook their heads adamantly, nearly jumping over one another to correct me.

"No!"

"The trails are wonderful, and a few of them are really simple, just leisure walks along the coast."

"You can take a boat between the villages too, like water taxis."

Huh, crazy. Clearly, you were supposed to research a place before hopping on a plane, but things were working out for me. It was only my first morning and I was already learning.

"What'll you have?" the man behind the counter asked, bringing my attention back to breakfast. *The most important subject of all.*

I ordered tea and an almond croissant, and the Americans suggested I join them outside. I didn't hesitate. Sure, they were older than my gran, but they seemed to know what they were doing. I could gobble up my flaky croissant and learn more about where I planned on spending my summer.

We picked a spot out front on the small patio and they unloaded all these brilliant maps, flopping them on the table and pointing out which trails were best and which ones were better left for the real sporty types.

I was fit, but I didn't really fancy a trek to Everest or anything. They suggested I start with a simple route and then they slid the maps toward me.

"Keep them. We have extra."

I thanked them loads and stuffed the maps into my purse. They were standing, ready to set off for their hike, when I caught sight of a man in a ball cap walking up the main path toward the train station.

Gianluca.

He was alone, keeping his head down as he walked. My heart sped up, watching him approach. A part of me had assumed I'd never see him again, and now here he was, less than a day later!

He took long, confident strides up the road, keeping his hands stuffed in his pockets. I couldn't see his face with his head down like that, and I willed him to glance up and see me so I wouldn't have to call his name. What would I call him anyway? Luca was what his friends called him, and after our short meeting—where I'd acted like a nutter on her deathbed—I had no misconceptions that we were at that level.

I opened my mouth, prepared to call out to him, to say something, *anything*, when a man farther up on the road caught his attention first.

"*Buongiorno* Luca!"

He whipped his head up and broke out into a devastating smile, all even white teeth and deep dimples. My heart sputtered to a stop. God, he was romantic looking, the sort of man who breathes passion into life without even trying.

"Good looking, huh?"

One of the American women nudged me with her elbow and nodded to Gianluca.

I nodded, trying to ignore how shaky I felt.

"He's the kind of handsome you don't see all that often," her friend chimed in. "You're safer staying away from Italian men like that, Georgie."

Maybe she was right.

Maybe I should have kept my distance.

But I didn't.

Chapter Four

Georgie

THE NEXT MORNING, I woke up to the sound of the heavy church bells. They clanged merrily in the square as I lazed about in bed, in no hurry to leave my warm cocoon. I'd left the shutters open through the night and the sea air swelled into my room, fluttering the thin cream drape up and away from the window. I'd only been there for a day and a half and I'd already learned that the scents of Vernazza changed based on the hour. In the early morning, when the restaurants were closed, the air was fresh, crisp. By the afternoon, as the sun blazed overhead, rich Italian aromas wafted up from the restaurants, luring me down to their doorsteps.

I rolled onto my side, stared out at the mountains past my window, and thought back on my first full day in Vernazza. I'd mostly kept to myself, dipping in and out of shops, sampling two gelatarias, and eating lunch outside a small pizza shop, inhaling two slices like a greedy chipmunk. I'd hoped to run into Gianluca again, but by late morning the square was crowded with tourists. The chances of finding anyone in particular were slim to none.

In the afternoon, I'd propped the wicker chair in my room right in front of the open window and sat down to read. My paperback mostly went untouched as I people-watched through the window. I had a perfect vantage point. My window faced the square and if I dipped my head out just a bit, I could watch the kids splashing in the water.

In the late afternoon, I'd watched a group of older Italian men convene in a corner of the square under crisp, white umbrellas. They pulled out a few decks of cards, and for the next two hours, their conversations and card-playing drifted up to my window like a soft hum.

It was all so different than England. The smallness of it, the lack of pretension. I wanted more.

I flung off my sheets, showered, and hurried to get dressed in jean shorts and a white tank top. I took a few extra minutes to apply a thin layer of makeup, just in case I ran into Gianluca outside The Blue Marlin. This time, I would call out to him and strike up a witty conversation. I'd thank him for helping me and I'd offer up a drink or dinner as repayment.

I was positively humming with the idea of seeing him as I locked up and skipped down the stairs of the hotel.

The front desk was empty and I nearly breezed past it before I heard my name behind me. I spun around and saw Chiara pop out of a broom cupboard in the back of the building.

"You're in a hurry," she said with a little smile.

I laughed. "Oh, yeah, just off to have breakfast."

She smiled and drummed her fingers on the doorframe, clearly wanting to chat. I tilted my head. "How are you?"

Her smile widened at my question. "I'm good. Just…wishing I didn't have to work today."

Her English was easy to understand, though she spoke slowly, thinking over each word before she spoke.

"It's supposed to be a beautiful day," she continued.

I nodded. "I might test the water, try to tan my pale English arse a bit."

She giggled and stepped closer, rounding behind the front desk and propping her elbows up on top of it. "I mean to ask you…" She glanced out the door and then back to me, working up the courage to continue. "The first day, you were with the two guys…"

"Massimo and Gianluca?"

Her eyes lit up. "Yes! I was wondering, um, how you became to know them?"

"How I met them?" I asked, making sure I'd understood her.

She nodded.

I explained to her how they'd helped me when I'd passed out in the square, how they'd carried me into the abandoned bed and breakfast across the square and then suggested I get a room here.

"I didn't know them or anything, but they were very nice to help me out."

"And Gianluca? He helped too?"

I frowned, a bit confused. "Yes. Why?"

She smiled. "Many girls in the village…*lo amano*."

The way she spoke about him, the slight glow on her cheeks proved that Chiara was likely one of these girls.

"*Love*," she continued, as if I hadn't understood her point already.

"Does he date any of them?" I asked before I could stop myself.

She shook her head vehemently. "He's, umm..." Her cheeks went red as cherries. "He sometimes goes just for one night or so. Nothing serious."

Interesting.

Footsteps sounded on the stairs behind us and Chiara straightened up to greet the guests trickling down. I offered her a wave and promised to chat soon, enticed by the possibility of her continuing to spill info about Gianluca.

Like the day before, the square was quiet in the early morning hours. Shutters were locked tight, restaurants were closed, umbrellas and chairs were stacked out of the way. I scratched the sleepy cat on the boat cover again (lazy bugger) and reminded myself to bring him back a bit of meat from my breakfast.

Small trucks and carts were driving up and down the road for their early morning deliveries and midway to The Blue Marlin, I glimpsed the beginnings of an open-air market. Trucks and stalls, small tables, and umbrellas were popping up. None of them were ready for customers yet, but I surveyed their goods as I passed. A few of them were selling fresh produce from around the region, fruits and vegetables in every color. There was salami and cheese, pesto and olive oil, lemons the size of my head! A woman at a flower stand rearranged buckets of fresh blooms and I longed to buy some, but I had nothing to store them in back in my small room.

Vendors smiled and nodded at me as I strolled by, and I promised to return after breakfast. I could watch them setting up from my perch on the patio at The Blue Marlin. My American friends weren't there, so I ate alone, treating myself to eggs and bacon and a second cup of milky tea. I told myself I wasn't in a rush to leave; I was enjoying the morning, but really I was lingering there, hoping to catch another glimpse of Gianluca.

He was nowhere to be found, but in the middle of my breakfast I'd locked onto a woman across the street. She stood out among the crowd of vendors with her long blonde hair and pale skin. Bright red lipstick stained her lips and her forehead was covered by a bit of fringe. She was wearing this amazing blue dress, all tight up top and flowing around her legs. Gold bangles clinked on her wrists as she worked to unload racks of clothes. She wasn't the only vendor selling clothing, but hers were the most stylish. She had loose linen shirts and bright sundresses. I already had my eye on a few of them when she stood back, wiped her brow, and turned her sights on The Blue Marlin.

I tried not to stare too much as she breezed past me, but I caught a quick flash of her perfume; it was a floral scent I recognized from a shop back home in London. When she emerged a second later with a to-go cup in her hand, she paused at the table in front of me and popped off the black plastic lid.

I watched her tear open a packet of sugar and dump it in, and then I leaned forward, knowing in that moment that I had to make this girl my friend.

"I really like the clothes you're selling."

She glanced over with a prepared smile, but it faded as her eyes fell on me.

"*You.*"

I leaned back in my chair, caught off guard. *Do I know her?*

She realized her mistake a moment too late and then laughed.

"Sorry, you don't know me, but aren't you the girl who passed out in the square the other day?"

I inwardly groaned. How many people had witnessed

my embarrassing moment? I'd hoped it'd been contained to Massimo and Gianluca, but if this girl knew about it, there was no telling how many others had seen it as well.

"Yes. I'm the utterly naff girl who can't ride trains without getting sick. I guess it's my superpower."

She grinned. "Don't worry about it. I only know about it because my boyfriend was one of the guys who helped you. He told me about it afterward, and—"

"*Who?!*" I croaked. "Who is your boyfriend?"

She beamed. "Massimo. He's brilliant isn't he?"

I hadn't known relief could feel so bloody good. "Yes. Absolutely brilliant. And handsome too," I added with a big smile.

She was clearly smitten, completely lighting up when she mentioned him. She was quite beautiful up close, with round eyes and a small nose. Her skin was a million shades lighter than mine, but it worked on her. She pulled off the ethereal fairy look quite nicely.

"How long have you been dating then?" I asked, hoping to prolong our conversation for a few minutes. Traveling alone can be...*well*, lonely.

"Oh, nearly three years," she replied in an accent that wasn't a far cry from mine. "We got together just after I arrived."

"Really?"

"Yeah, I'd only planned on staying on in Italy for a week or so, but he convinced me to stay."

"Sounds so romantic."

A few people were starting to wander around the open-air market, passing stalls and glancing over the vegetables and flowers. She glanced over, and I knew she needed to get back to her shop before more people arrived.

"I know you've got to get back to your stall, but could

you tell Massimo thank you for me? I didn't really get the chance when they dropped me off at my room."

She glanced back at me and tilted her head as if studying me for a moment. "How about you come to dinner with us tonight instead? You can thank them yourself."

"Them?" I asked, playing dumb. Really, I just needed her to say his name.

"Massimo and Luca. It's been ages since we all sat down for a proper meal and it'd be fun to get more time to talk." She was glancing back and forth between her stall and me then, needing to rush off. "Eight o'clock down at Taverna Del Capitano. Say yes!"

I laughed. "Yes. Okay!"

"Brilliant." She grinned and reached her hand out as if to shake on it. "I'm Katerina by the way."

"Georgie."

Our hands hung together in the air for another moment and then she let go to rush off, throwing a farewell over her shoulder.

"Welcome to Vernazza, Georgie! I'll see you tonight!"

Chapter Five

Gianluca

MY VILLA IN Vernazza sat up on a terraced hill overlooking the square. It was private and secluded, surrounded on three sides by grape vineyards and gardens. Everything was overgrown, greedy for sun and water, soaking it up until most of my house itself was covered in bougainvillea vines. They sprouted up bright purple in late spring and I didn't have the heart to cut them back. Eventually, the plants would completely overtake the crumbling villa, but I'd do something about it then. Maybe.

A single rocky road led from the square up to my villa. It was half a mile long and though a few houses sat at the base of the trail, most of it belonged to me. When it was level, I could use my motorbike; when it wasn't, like now, I had to walk. During the last storm, the ground had soaked through and started to erode the stone wall built to prop up the hillside along the path. It was a long section of trail that I was responsible for maintaining and I'd been putting it off for the last few months. The job would be tedious to say the least.

All the walls around Vernazza were built using dry-stone masonry. Centuries ago, they'd skipped mortar and concrete, opting to lay the walls by skill alone. Over the last few weeks, I'd started to pick apart the wall, pulling off stones that had shifted or fallen. Once I got it down to its bones, I could build back up from there.

Now, I was working on it with the late afternoon sun on my back and the wind ruffling my hair beneath my cap. I lugged a heavy stone from the wall and dropped it into a small wheelbarrow resting beside my feet. Then, another. My muscles were tired. I'd been going at it for most of the day, but it needed to get done and I had no plans of hiring someone else to do it.

A small green lizard scurried across the top of the wall, trying to hurry away from me. I bent down for my water, giving him the time he needed, just as Massimo's voice carried up the trail. He was cursing in Italian, specifically cursing *me*, wishing I'd fall into the depths of hell for forcing him to make the trek up to my house.

I smiled and moved a few more stones before he finished his ascent.

"*Merda*," he groaned, breathing hard and propping himself up against the stone wall.

"There's water inside if you need it," I said, continuing my work.

He propped his hands on his hips and glared at me, but that wasn't new. Massimo was always going on about something. It was easier if I pretended I didn't notice until he'd calmed down.

"Do you have a phone in that house of yours?"

I glanced back at the two-story villa my grandmother

44

had left me when she'd passed. It'd been ancient and crumbling when I'd found it, but I'd done a good job of restoring it over the years.

"Last time I checked."

"I phoned you half a dozen times."

I shrugged. "I've been out here, fixing the wall."

He shifted in front of me, stopping me from grabbing another rock. "Forget about the wall! We have plans."

I arched a brow and shifted around him, starting on a new section. "Plans?"

"Dinner plans."

I held in my reaction. He and Katerina were good mates, but lousy dinner partners. Even years after getting on, they couldn't make it through a meal without hanging on each other, sipping from each other's wine glasses and sharing meals. Given the choice, I'd have rather gone hungry.

"You go on ahead, I've got to—"

"No, mate, you haven't let me explain. It's not just me and Kat. We've got another person coming."

I was still working then, removing stones from the wall. "Who?"

He'd gone suspiciously quiet then, so I dropped the stone I was holding into the wheelbarrow, tugged off my gloves, and turned to watch as he let out a big grin.

"Georgie."

He seemed to think the name would hold weight with me, but my mind came up utterly blank.

"Who?" I asked, frowning.

He threw his hands in the air. "Oh, bloody hell. *The damsel in the dress!* She's the girl you carried into Nonna's bed and breakfast."

I nodded, not bothering to correct his idiom. "Right.

45

You go on then. I need to keep working."

Massimo was an easygoing bloke, but every once in a while, I pushed him too far. This was one of those times. He ripped my gloves from my hands and tossed them over the side of the hill, down into the trees along the edge of the cliff so that I couldn't go after them unless I had a death wish.

"You're coming! You can't continue living the life of an *eremita!* A recluse!"

We had a standoff then. I stayed silent, a bit cross about my gloves, and he fisted his hands and puffed up his chest as if warning me away from a fight. It was laughable, really.

"It's been five years next week, and it's time to move on, mate." His voice didn't cool then. He was past the point of handling me with kid gloves. "Go shower and change. I'll wait for you and we'll go together."

I relented, not because Massimo was right, but because I was hungry—starved, actually. I needed food and I would go down and eat; it didn't much matter who I did it with.

I left the barrow full of stones and turned back for my house. Massimo let out an audible sigh, glad to have won the battle.

"You owe me a new pair of gloves by the way," I said, tossing the words over my shoulder. His colorful curse words were cut off when I slammed the door of the villa behind me.

Chapter Six

Georgie

I MET KATERINA at Taverna Del Capitano at 8:00 PM. The restaurant was at the far end of the square, close to the water and the massive breaker. Like the other restaurants in Vernazza, most of the seating was outside. They'd clustered a group of small tables beneath colorful umbrellas and by the time we arrived, most of the seats had been filled with people sipping wine and enjoying a leisurely dinner.

I worried for a fleeting moment that we wouldn't get a table, but a waitress directed Katerina and me to the best table in the bunch with a wink. Apparently, Katerina had some connections.

"There's really no point in eating here if you aren't getting that view."

She pointed out to the water and I nodded. It was true. Anything would taste good with that backdrop.

"Here, sit," she said, pulling out a chair on the side of

the table that faced the water.

"You're sure they won't mind if we take the good seats?" I asked, hesitating over the chair.

She sat down beside me and waved her hand. "Massimo has lived here his entire life. It's nothing to him."

I couldn't believe it. Sure, the sights around London hardly inspired feelings of awe in me anymore, but this was different. Vernazza was paradise on Earth.

Katerina was still wearing her blue dress and gold bangles, and when she complimented my dinner outfit, I knew I'd done well. I'd picked a little red dress that was more silk than anything else. It showed a bit of skin, so I'd brought along a little jacket for when the sun started to drop.

As it was, the sun hung low in the sky, right over the distant village of Monterosso al Mare and the mountains surrounding it. We had a perfect view of it all from our seats and for a moment I sat there, struck silent by its beauty.

It was the golden hour, that perfect time of day when everything gets painted in a light pink hue. Even Katerina seemed to glow with it, and I told her so.

"It's lovely, isn't it?" she said, turning to face me. "It's like that on you too."

She was right. I glanced down to my bare arms and could see the effects of the sunset on my skin.

"No wonder you've stayed on so long. The light in London isn't like this."

"That's where you're from then? London?"

The waitress returned with a bottle of white wine and poured a glass for each of us. Katerina told her to leave the bottle and I smiled, confident that I'd get on well with her.

"I grew up on my family's estate, but I moved to

London when I was eighteen."

Her brows perked up. "An *estate?*"

"Oh…it's just a little—"

"Sorry! Sorry!" Massimo's voice boomed behind us. "I know we're late, but we'll make up for it with more wine."

He reached down to kiss Katerina's cheek and then bent over her to kiss me hello as well. Gianluca was behind him and though I'd braced myself for a welcome kiss from him, he did little more than nod at us before he pulled back the chair across from me.

For once, he wasn't wearing a cap, and I nearly blacked out from the sheer beauty of him. He had deliciously wavy brown hair, thick and unruly. It should have been a crime to ever cover it with a cap, but I resisted the urge to tell him so.

The table suddenly felt claustrophobic, too small for Gianluca's tall frame. He adjusted in his seat, brushing his jean-clad leg against me, and I folded up my legs beneath my chair, trying to give him more room.

"Sorry." I cleared my throat, suddenly confused at how to act in the presence of a man like him.

"Luca, you remember Georgie?" Katerina said, touching my shoulder.

He glanced up to me as if only then realizing I was there.

"Feeling better?" he asked.

My face heated from the attention. Two words and it felt like he'd just seduced me.

"Yes. Thank you."

"You look loads better than you did the other day," Massimo chimed in with a big grin.

"*Massimo*," admonished Katerina, kicking him under the table.

"I didn't mean it like tha—" protested Massimo, laughing.

"Don't worry, Katerina, he's right—I was more than a bit peaky that day," I said.

"Well let's toast to a new day," Katerina said, beaming at me. She reached forward to pour them wine. "And to new friendships!"

"Yes," I agreed, unsure if everyone at the table was excited by the prospect. Gianluca seemed tense, unsure of himself at the table.

The next time the waitress came round, he asked for a beer and I decided to go for it.

"Not a wine person, Gianluca?"

He shrugged and glanced off over my shoulder. "Tonight calls for beer."

I couldn't decide if the words were meant as a dig or not, but either way, he didn't make a point to continue the conversation.

Katerina leaned forward, salvaging the moment. "Right, well Georgie was just telling me about her childhood. Apparently she grew up on an estate in England!"

Massimo waggled his brows. "What, are you royalty or something?"

My throat tightened up. "Or *something*," I emphasized. "It's no big deal."

"Wait, so are you titled?"

Technically, I was a lady by birth, but I'd die before telling them that. I decided to sidestep the question. "My father was a duke, and now my brother has the title."

"What's your last name?" Massimo asked.

"Archibald."

"Shut up!" Katerina said, dropping her wine glass on the table and turning to me with her full attention. "I knew I'd seen you on the telly back home in England! You're Freddie Archibald's sister?"

I gulped down another sip of wine, bored with this conversation. I'd had it countless times over my life.

"It's no big deal, really. I went to snooty private schools and had to put up with real arsehole girls my whole life. I'd have much rather grown up in Vernazza," I said, smiling at Massimo.

He shook his head. "It's not fun when you're a teenager and there's no decent night life. Now I've come to appreciate it, but I used to want to leave as soon as I was old enough."

"But you stayed?" I asked, curious about his decision.

He nodded and turned to Gianluca. "I changed my mind when Luca moved back a few years ago. I decided the grass was probably no greener anywhere else."

As if sensing that he was about to be the subject of the conversation, Gianluca held up his hand for the waitress and requested another beer.

It went on like that all through dinner. Massimo, Katerina, and I would carry the conversation and Gianluca would sit quietly, sipping his beer or eating his food as if we weren't there. He wasn't exactly brooding, just quiet and far more comfortable with the attention away from him.

It was just my luck. The person I wanted to get to know the most was the least forthcoming with information. Still, any chance I got, I stole glances at him and tried to pick apart the details that lured me closer. More than anything else, he had a warmth to him. His days were spent outside and it showed. His skin had a rich tan and he carried a comforting scent I associated with childhood: warm summer days and salty sea air. His hands were big, rough,

51

and calloused. His forearms, the bit that showed beneath his rolled shirt sleeves, were coiled with tight muscles.

He picked up his beer and brought it to his lips, the only part of him that could have been called soft. They were full and bowed in the center. When he dropped it back to the table, his eyes flicked up to me and I turned away quickly, aware I'd been staring for too long.

"So what brings you to Italy then, Georgie?" Massimo asked. "Vacation?"

Maybe if I hadn't been on my third glass of wine, I'd have nodded and replied with some response about wanting to experience summer in the Italian Riveria, but Gianluca was finally looking up at me, waiting for my answer, and I didn't want to lie to him.

"I'm here to find a husband."

Katerina nearly spit out her sip of wine. "You're what?"

I laughed, but Gianluca didn't. A quick glance back at him proved that he'd narrowed his eyes on me, curious and maybe even a bit annoyed by my answer.

"I mean, there's a bit more to it than that, but that's basically the gist of it."

"You're going to have to explain," Katerina said, filling up my wine glass. I didn't protest. The sauvignon blanc was chilled and delicious, the best I'd ever had.

"Okay," I relented, staring down at the stem of my wine glass as I spun it between my fingers. "Well, for the last few years, my mum has done her best to set me up with every terrible bloke in the northern hemisphere. She thinks it's crazy that I'm still single at twenty-six and I'd had enough of her matchmaking—"

"*So you up and fled the country?* Why couldn't you just tell her you weren't interested in being set up anymore?" Katerina asked.

"It's not that simple. My mum is very persistent..." I decided to leave out the details of our family's tragic few years, skipping over all the reasons it was so hard to say no to her. "And I knew it made her happy, so I just sort of went along with it."

"So why here, why now?"

Gianluca had finally spoken again, *directly to me*, and I tried my best not to make a show of how excited it made me. I turned to him with a shrug.

"Well she won't rest until I'm married off, so I had to get away, and to be honest, it's not like I wanted to go on living life alone either. I figured if I got out of London, I could test things on my own. Go on dates *I've* set up, that sort of thing."

"And you like Italian men?" Katerina asked, nudging my shoulder suggestively.

"I've hardly gotten a chance to get to know him— *them.*"

I blushed and stared down at my wine glass.

The conversation felt so personal, like I was practically throwing myself on Gianluca or something. I was ready to shift things back onto someone else, but Katerina spoke up first.

"Have you got a list of requirements, then? A type?"

I frowned, confused.

"It just seems like you would. You're gorgeous and single, which tells me you're probably quite picky."

I couldn't force my blush to recede. "I mean...there are a few things—"

She clapped. "I knew it! Tell us then, from the beginning."

"It's not much, really. He has to be intelligent and handsome..."

"Boooo," Katerina moaned. "Tell us the real stuff. He obviously has to be smart and handsome. What are you really going after?"

I grinned, giddy from the wine. "Fine, okay. *Preferably* he would like to read. He'd have a well-worn edition of *Great Expectations* or *A Tale of Two Cities*—y'know, proper literature."

Katerina nodded with a big cheesy grin, encouraging me.

"He'd be tall, but not gargantuan, you know? Um, let's see…he'd like to have a good laugh. He'd like footie, but he wouldn't be obsessed with it or anything. Oh! Most importantly, he'd be open and ready for love, without a ton of baggage—"

Massimo tossed his napkin on the table and leaned back. "That rules out Luca."

Katerina laughed, but I didn't.

What did he mean?

Gianluca was peeling the label off his beer bottle, seemingly unaware of the conversation going on around him, but then he glanced up and locked eyes with me. It only took a moment for me to see that he hadn't just been ignoring us, he'd been in another world altogether.

He fidgeted, aware of everyone's eyes on him, and then dropped his beer and stood.

"This has been fun, but I ought to get back before the sun drops too much lower."

He reached into his back pocket for his wallet, tossed a few bills onto the table, and offered us a curt nod.

"I'll see you around," he said to Massimo and Katerina before turning to me. "Gigi, nice to see you."

What the—

My mouth dropped, but he'd already turned and moved

past the table before I could shout after him that he'd gotten my name wrong. We'd sat across from each other for the last two hours and he couldn't even remember my name.

Katerina reached her hand out to touch my arm. "Please don't take it personally. He doesn't mean to be rude."

Massimo nodded. "He's been like that ever since Allie."

Chapter Seven

Gianluca

I MET ALLIE at university the spring before we graduated. I was already set up to take a job in finance in London and she was going to teach. We should never have crossed paths, but we did. We *crashed* into each other's lives. I was riding my bike on campus, racing to meet my mates at a pub a few blocks away. Allie was heading in the opposite direction. I skipped a traffic light and collided into her. She went flying and landed with a thud on a spotty patch of grass a few feet away. Her pink bike was nearly bent in two.

I opened my mouth, prepared to defend myself, but she was laughing, lying flat on the grass with a giant grin on her face.

"Oh god, are you okay?" I asked, rushing forward to help her up.

She didn't move right away, not really concerned with me.

"Why are you laughing?"

She tried her best to quell her laughter, but it was no use. For a minute, I thought she might be insane, but finally she pressed her hand to her mouth and glanced up to me. "I have absolute shite luck. My parents bought me that bike as a graduation gift, just this morning."

I groaned. "And now I've gone and ruined it."

Good going, Luca.

She sat up and shook the hair out of her face. For the first time, I got a good look at her. She was lovely. Blonde and sweet.

"It's okay, really." She turned to assess the damage and her smile faded. I didn't want it to fade. "I'll tell them a car smashed it. They'll moan about it but—"

"No," I said, shaking my head adamantly. "I'll repair it."

Her brows rose. "You know how to mend bikes?"

"Yes," I lied.

She grinned. "Brilliant. It's the least you can do considering it was *you* who crashed into *me*."

She was teasing and I liked it.

I didn't end up meeting my mates at the pub. No man on Earth would have gone to meet his mates after meeting a girl like Allie. I rolled our bikes back to her flat and she invited me to come in with a promise of "lukewarm beer, crisps, and a well-stocked first aid kit."

We got married a year later, ignoring our parents' warnings about how young we were. Allie and I knew what we were doing. *There's no sense in waiting,* Allie would say.

She moved to London with me and looked for a teaching job. My entry position at the firm kept me busy, but Allie and I made the most of the time we had together.

We loved being outside, riding bikes, and hiking. On the weekends, we'd pack the car and go on adventures. We talked about getting a dog and raising kids in the city. We strolled hand in hand through Hyde Park, feeding the ducks in front of Kensington Palace.

We'd been married for four years when she started falling behind on hikes, blaming it on a sore knee. I encouraged her to see a physio about it, but she put it off for a few months, icing and laying off of it when she could.

Finally, I set up an appointment for her, after a canceled backpacking trip with friends. The first doctor she spoke to chalked up her injury to hiking, and suggested more ice, rest, and naproxen.

Six months later, Allie fractured her tibia on a simple hike we'd breezed through dozens of times. At the hospital, the MRI revealed an osteosarcoma tumor.

I went through a period of denial. We both did. We consulted multiple doctors, assuring each other it was a simple mistake, a bad radiologist, an off day. How could something like this come out of nowhere?

"I guess I really do have shite luck," Allie said to me after the third doctor confirmed her prognosis.

Just like the first day we met, I took her hand and promised her I'd fix it.

"You know how to mend cancer?"

"Yes," I lied.

Allie was 24. She was tall and slender. She liked to wear bright dresses that wrapped tight around her middle and cut off high on her thighs. She always knew the right thing to say and she was an ace in group settings. She loved bringing people together and she had a real knack for it. She put me at ease, she was comforting and kindhearted. She was my wife and she had cancer and I couldn't do anything to fix it.

Seemingly overnight, our vernacular turned clinical: osteosarcoma, metastases, clinical trials, treatment plans, survival rates. Allie's life hung in the balance of cold statistics, and we clung to that limbo. When her oncologist told us to not lose hope, explaining that there are better survival rates for young women, I had to bite my tongue.

What about survival rates for someone's wife?

What about survival rates for the future mother of my children?

What about survival rates for the person I can't live without?

What are those survival rates?

They scheduled surgery to remove the tumor on her knee, but further scans showed metastases in her lungs, stage III. They started Allie on aggressive chemotherapy while she was still recovering from the tumor removal. Those weeks were utter crap. Her hair fell out. The radiation did a number on her body. If she wasn't sleeping, she was throwing up. If she wasn't throwing up, she was crying and asking me why this was happening to her.

Toward the end of chemotherapy, things started to look better. Allie was handling treatments well. She was up and walking around, going through physio for her knee.

We started to talk about our life post cancer. P.C. How we would live, where we would visit, how big our family should be.

"P.C. I'm going to hike every single day," she said over lunch in the hospital one day.

"P.C. we are going to make love every single day."

"*Luca,*" she hissed, blushing.

I couldn't recall the last time we'd slept together. It'd been months. She'd grown shy in the bedroom, less confident now that radiation had added pounds onto her once slender body. She hardly ever let me see her without a scarf on, and when I insisted that the baldness, the pounds, the patchy radiated skin didn't matter to me, that I'd love her forever, she'd smile and press a kiss to my cheek, promising intimacy soon.

I reached across the table and gripped her hand. "I love you, you know that?"

Her thumb brushed across my knuckles. "I know."

Two months later, during a follow-up CT scan, they found the worst case scenario: the tumors had spread to Allie's hips, and just like that, we added another term to our vernacular: life expectancy.

One year.

Allie could expect to wake up 365 more times.

There was never any question of where Allie would spend her final days. Growing up, I'd spent my summers in Vernazza, visiting my grandmother and my cousin, Massimo. Allie had never been, but I'd told her about it. My grandmother's crumbling villa had been passed down to me after her death and that afternoon, after the final CT scan, Allie dragged a suitcase out of our guest room, declaring that she was foregoing further treatment and would like to spend the last year of her life in Vernazza. She wanted every last sunset to be in the golden light.

Chapter Eight

Georgie

GIANLUCA WAS A widower. Katerina and Massimo had walked me through a short version of his story after dinner. I'd sat in silence and listened, but really, I was being selfish. *Incredibly selfish.* Because deep down, in the center of my soul, I was thinking of how it was such a bloody shame. I was in Vernazza to have a laugh, meet a few blokes, and loll about on the beach. I wanted to have a proper holiday fling with lots of sex and maybe some flippant promises of love. I was in no way looking to mend a broken heart. It wasn't fair, really. Gianluca was the nicest-looking man I'd seen in the last decade and he was unavailable, moping about for a wife he'd lost five years earlier.

I know it seems so callous to think of his situation as anything but heartbreaking. It wasn't that I didn't feel for him or that I didn't understand everything he'd suffered through with Allie. God, untimely death is the saddest thing of all time. Unfortunately, I'd experienced it firsthand. I'd lost my father when I was a young girl and my eldest brother a few years later. Heart failure and a car crash. Both sudden. Both devastating. Two deaths in a family of five had nearly crippled us. My mother fell into life as a widow. My brother, Fred, took over the family title and all the responsibilities that came with running the estate, and I settled into the only role I knew: the court jester, the clown, the only bit of light in our family during those tough few years. I was there through my mother's heartache; I'd endured the dates and the silly setups because it took my mother's mind off the real troubles of her life to see me get tarted up for an evening out. I'd joked and I'd forced her smiles through all the hard times because she needed to be reminded that life marches on even when we desperately wish it wouldn't.

A few years back, my brother had met Andie, the love of his life. They had three children now and my mother doted on them whenever she got the chance. With so many good things going for our family, I finally felt as though I could pack away my jester hat. They didn't need me anymore, which was why I didn't feel bad up and leaving London for an adventure of my own.

And then as fate would have it, upon my first day in Vernazza...*WHAM*. I met Gianluca. The widower.

See?

What tragic luck.

• • •

The next morning, I lazed in bed, thinking over the story of Allie. It should have made it easy to subdue my silly crush on Gianluca. Normal women would run for the hills, but it only intrigued me more. I'd never had a man love me like that. In some grim way, the depth of his despair over losing another woman became an advertisement for the quality of his love. I felt guilty for thinking that, but not guilty enough to stop.

Oh god, I needed to get out of my head and definitely stop thinking about Gianluca. After all, the bloke thought I was named Gigi! *Ha.* I'd file the papers to change my name before correcting him.

I pushed off my covers and decided on a whim that I'd head to Monterosso al Mare for the day. The sun was already high in the sky, warming everything it touched. I strung on a red bikini and tossed my beach supplies into a straw bag: sun cream, my floppy hat, and my worn paperback. I tugged on a loose cover-up and slipped into sandals before locking up my room and flying down the stairs.

Chiara wasn't manning the desk, so I headed out to the station. I hadn't been back on a train since the first day I arrived. Monterosso al Mare was the northernmost village in Cinque Terre and only one stop over, so fortunately, the five-minute journey didn't cause my small breakfast to make an encore appearance.

I stepped off the platform and followed the string of tourists heading toward the sea. Unlike Vernazza, Monterosso had a proper beach that stretched on for a few miles. It was early, but the beach was starting to fill fast. I paid to reserve an umbrella and chair in the first row and plopped myself there, lathering on sun cream as I watched a group of children run into the surf, squealing as waves crashed against their legs and running back onto the pebbled beach as fast as possible.

I let my cream soak in and then I stood and slipped off my sandals, walking with careful steps toward the water. The soft sand turned to pebbles once I approached the water's edge, and though none of them were sharp enough to cut me, it hurt to put too much pressure on them at once. I eased into the surf, hissing as the cold water lapped up over my legs and thighs. With a final resolute breath, I pinched my nose and dove under the water.

My brother had taught me proper swimming technique when I was young, and I thanked him for it as I kicked farther from shore. The Ligurian sea was pure bliss: cold turquoise water beneath sunny skies. I flipped onto my back, closed my eyes, and let the waves drift me where they wished. After a few minutes, I'd flop back over and swim closer to the buoys, repeating the process until my fingers were pruned and my cheeks were warm from the sun.

When I swam back to shore, my things were right where I'd left them beneath the umbrella. I sprayed a bit of after-sun on my hair, lathered up more cream, and set off toward Monterosso for a snack. It wasn't quite lunchtime, but my small breakfast had burned quickly in my swim. Like Vernazza, Monterosso had a few small shops wedged between restaurants and hotels. I begrudgingly walked past the gelateria and instead went into a small grocer.

"*Le fragole sono succose,*" said the girl behind the counter, pointing to the small basket of strawberries I'd nabbed as soon as I'd walked in. "Juicy."

She hadn't been kidding. I carried the strawberries back to my beach chair and ate them leaning over the sand. I'd never tasted fruit so fresh in my life. It wasn't like the produce I could pick up in the shops around London. The strawberries were soft and tender, so full of flavor I couldn't help but moan with pleasure every time I bit into one. Had anyone been sitting near me, they'd have assumed I had a bit of a berry fetish, and well, maybe I did. I didn't stop until I'd eaten every last one, and then, full of sugary sweetness, I waded back into the sea, using the cold water to wash the juice off my chin and fingers.

By the time I rode the train back to Vernazza, I was sated. Even with the sun cream on, I had a nice tan going on my arms and legs. My hair was wavy and wild, and my skin was still sticky from the sea and sand and strawberries. (I'd caved and gone back for a second basket.)

I took my time strolling down the main road, popping into one of the fancier shops to pick up some olive oil to send home to my mum and Freddie. I picked up some lemon candies for Andie and wrote a note to slip into the post—something that would put my brother's mind at ease about my stay in Italy.

Dear Freddie,

I know you think I'm silly running off like I did, but I swear I know what I'm doing. Mum had gone completely mental with the matchmaking and I needed to put some boundaries between us—rather large boundaries, it seems, like the Alps and the English Channel.

I'm sure she's furious, and knowing her, she's probably reading this over your shoulder—HELLO MOTHER. I'll have you know that Italy is fantastic, and the men here are just as gorgeous as I'd hoped they would be! I know you'll worry less if you think I'm in the company of a good man, so I'll have you know that I've gone on a date with a lovely man called Gianluca and of course, I will send word as soon as he commits to spending his life with me. Please prepare my dowry. Ha. (Fred, that joke was for you. I'm

67

sure Mum is glowering at this point...)

Anyway, give those little nieces and nephew a massive kiss for me.

All my love,

Georgie

With a smile at my white lie there at the end, I sealed up the package and slipped it in with the outgoing post back at the hotel. I took the stairs slowly, exhausted after hours of swimming. I had plans to take a long, steamy shower and then read by the window as the sun set, but just as I rounded the top of the stairs, I spotted a little yellow note pasted to my hotel room door.

It was from Katerina, asking me if I fancied going on a double-date that evening. There were hardly any details about it, just the name of the restaurant and the time they'd be there. I had half a mind to crumple up the note and pretend I hadn't seen it, but there was a small, *minuscule* chance they were setting me up with Gianluca, and so for that reason, I went.

• • •

Everyone was already seated by the time I arrived at Belforte. The restaurant was a bit nicer than the place we'd eaten the night before and I was glad I'd slipped on a pair of flats instead of flip-flops. Katerina saw me approach and her face split in two with an infectious grin. She and Massimo stood, and then my date stood as well.

I felt my smile falter as his features came into view. It wasn't Gianluca. It was a very handsome man, but my appreciation for his features felt forced after realizing I'd wanted him to be someone else.

"Georgie! This is our friend Paolo!"

The man rushed forward to kiss me on either cheek and I was engulfed in a sweet smelling cologne. I was stiff at first, a bit awkward as we went through introductions and protocol. He held out my chair for me as Katerina explained how everyone knew each other.

"Paolo helps Massimo up at the farm, although I think they actually just drink and take naps up there all day."

I nodded and slid my gaze over, trying to get a good look at him.

He had rich black hair, quite a few shades darker than Gianluca's, and striking pale green eyes. The combination held my attention so well I didn't hear him ask me a question until he'd repeated it a second time.

"You're traveling in Italy?"

His English was strained and unpracticed, but it only added to his appeal.

"Yes," I grinned. "Only for the last week or so. I was in Rome until I came here."

"Did you like it?"

I caught a twinkle in his eye that told me he didn't want the standard response. "Quite crowded, isn't it?"

He grinned, wide. "Did you see the Colosseum, then? The Pantheon?"

"Well I saw the *outside* of the Colosseum, but not much else. The queue went on for nearly two hours it seemed."

He nodded in agreement. "Cinque Terre…*è meglio*, no?"

I looked to Katerina for help, but Massimo chimed in first. "Better here?"

I laughed and nodded. "It's amazing. I actually went over to Monterosso today, down to the beach."

Katerina moaned. "I wish you'd asked me to come along! It's been months since I've managed to get over there."

I kicked myself for not thinking of the idea myself. I would have enjoyed a bit of company. "I didn't know if you'd be working at the market or not."

"No, no." She shook her head. "Most days, I keep a clothing shop just along the main road off the square. It's only open in the late morning and early afternoon, when the tourists are really out and about."

I grinned. "Perfect, then I'll come by the shop before you close up to have a look around and then we'll go swimming."

She nodded, excited. "Tomorrow?"

Paolo laughed and turned to Massimo, rattling off fast Italian.

Massimo turned to me with a cheeky smile. "He says he's supposed to be the one asking you on a second date, not Katerina."

I blushed and adjusted the napkin on my lap. That's right. There I was on a double date and I'd been more interested in chatting with Katerina than I was in getting to know Paolo. After that, I made a real effort with him, turning my body toward him so he'd have my full attention.

He told me about his work up at Massimo's farm, how they were currently harvesting the summer produce.

"Big, ripe zucchinis and fat lemons. We grow them there and then bring them down for Massimo to use in his restaurant."

"You should bring some for Georgie!" Katerina chimed in.

"Oh, no. It's all right. I've only got the small room and there's no kitchen or anything. I'd just let them go to waste."

Paolo's smile fell as if I'd turned him down instead of the vegetables. I laid on the sweetness, assuring him I'd take a lemon or two, but it didn't really help.

After that, the four of us sat in silence, waiting for the food. Paolo had ordered us the fish of the day and when they brought it out from the kitchen, it was presented in a massive tin pan, a few inches deep in sea salt.

The waiter turned it down for us to see, we clapped and smiled, and then he set about cleaning it and serving it up on plates for us.

"It's lovely," I said, leaning into Paolo. "Thank you."

And then Paolo took a big bite of fish and chewed…with his mouth open.

I understand that for some people, it wouldn't mean much, but for me, it was a deal breaker. His gnashing teeth gave me flashbacks to my blind date with Chompers, and I knew whatever chemistry we might've had was extinguished. I didn't know where mums had gone wrong teaching table manners to their sons, but I wasn't having it.

Katerina nudged me beneath the table to get my attention and when I glanced over, she tilted her head, trying to get a read on the situation.

"Good?" she mouthed.

I knew she wasn't talking about the fish.

"Mmhmm," I said, but I shook my head *no*, gently enough so the boys couldn't see.

After dinner, Katerina insisted on walking me home, telling the boys we had things to discuss. I hugged Paolo and thanked him for dinner. Though I'd tried to split our bill down the middle, he'd insisted on paying, which I thought was very kind.

"You'll come up to the farm?" he asked, hopeful.

I let my mouth hang open for a moment, trying to work out a proper response, and then I caved and nodded, adding an indecipherable hum on top. He grinned and Katerina looped her arm through mine, tugging me away from the restaurant.

We hurried back to my hotel and I insisted she come up and see my room.

"It's very messy," I warned as I turned the old key and pushed the door open.

"If you've got wine, I won't mind the mess."

I grinned and presented the bottle of Sciacchetrà I'd picked up on a whim at the shops that afternoon. I'd nearly stuffed it in the package for Freddie and Andie (lord knows they needed it with those nieces and nephew of mine running them ragged) but I'd held on to it instead.

Katerina clapped with excitement.

"I don't have any glasses though."

The hotel wasn't like the proper ones I was used to staying in. There were no mini bars or room service.

She shrugged. "We'll share."

And with that, she popped the top and took a long swig, handing me the bottle after her. It was my first time trying Sciacchetrà, but the woman at the shop had *raved* about it. Apparently it's made from Vermintino grapes and has a sweet, honey-ish flavor—perfect for sitting at my window with Katerina and taking in the last few minutes of the sunset.

"Pass it, you hog."

I took another quick sip and she laughed as I handed it back over.

I hadn't known Katerina long, but there was a level of comfort between us that usually took years to develop. I glanced over to her, admiring the way she'd wrapped up

72

her long blonde hair into a knot on top of her head. Her dress was just as stylish as the one she'd worn the day before, and I guessed she'd been quite popular in school. She gave off that sort of vibe, but without the snarky attitude.

"So Paolo didn't sweep you off your feet?" she asked, handing me the bottle.

I took a long swig, wiped the drop slipping down my chin, and shook my head. "No."

"Shame."

"Shame," I agreed.

"You fancy Gianluca, don't you?"

I blushed, a fierce red shade I prayed she couldn't see. "What? Why would you say that?"

Had I been that transparent at dinner the night before? I'd stared at him a few times, but I hadn't realized I'd made a show of it or anything.

She sighed, this sad, hopeless sound that nearly broke my heart.

"Because women always do," explained Katerina. "They think they'll swoop in and coax him out of his shell. They want to heal him like a bird with a broken wing, but it's actually easier with birds, because they want to fly so badly. Gianluca—well, for the past five years, he's made it clear he doesn't want to be healed. He wants to stay on the ground."

"Where it's safe," I muttered.

After that, we passed the bottle in silence until it was empty.

Chapter Nine

Gianluca

"YOU KNOW, MOST people shower before they eat in my restaurant."

I glanced up from my plate of seafood pasta to find Massimo grinning at me from across the bar.

"I came from the farm. I was helping Paolo with the harvest."

"Hopefully the produce was less ripe than you are. You're scaring away my customers."

I turned round to find every table was full. I turned back to him with an arched brow and he chuckled before walking away.

I was sweaty, but nothing more than normal. The arsehole could have thanked me for helping him get out of a bind after one of his employees had called in sick, but Massimo wasn't the appreciative type.

"More wine?"

I glanced at my untouched glass and then up to the new

waitress Massimo had hired last month. I couldn't remember her name.

"I'm good, thanks."

"You do smell," she spoke in Italian with a flirtatious smile. When I didn't reply, she went on. "But I think it smells good. *Manly.* If anything, you're attracting more customers."

I wasn't good at this.

Banter.

Flirting.

I'd had sex since Allie's death. People were always curious about that. Massimo nearly chewed my head off about the risk of "losing it" if I didn't "use it", and well, I had, though not nearly enough, and never with a woman I felt anything for. I'd take the train into the La Spezia with him or Paolo, or another hand from the farm. We'd go to one of the usual spots and sometimes the night ended with sex, and sometimes I rode the train back home with Massimo, him going on about how I'd lost the magic touch.

I hated it.

When I married Allie, I thought I'd moved past the dating part of my life. I still knew all the things I was supposed to do, supposed to say, but it felt forced and unnatural, like I was in a bad dream.

"What are your plans for tonight?" she asked, eyeing me as she wiped down the bar with a rag.

Truthfully, I needed to continue working on the wall outside my house, and I needed to clear away a bit of the foliage that had grown nearly out of control. I could hardly see my front door past the bougainvillea. I could spend the rest of the day working on chores, but she didn't want to know that.

"Work," I replied with a committed tone. There was no

room for change and when she caught on to my meaning, her smile faded a little.

"Well, if you ever want to go for a drink, let me know."

With that, she pushed off the bar and past the door into the restaurant's kitchen.

I finished the last of my pasta, threw a few euro onto the bar, and waved to Massimo on my way out of the restaurant. The waitress was pretty, but I preferred to meet women in La Spezia. The short train ride put enough distance between me and them that I didn't feel so guilty about it in the morning.

It was dusk, and I breathed in the fresh air as I made my way back home. Massimo's restaurant was in the section of Vernazza most tourists never ventured into. It was past the train station, up at the top of the hill. There was no view of the sea, but the food was better than anything you could find down below. Most of the time tourists didn't realize that. They'd accept the frozen fish and stale bread if it meant they could look at the sunset.

I walked past the train station, nodding at the locals I passed along the way. The Blue Marlin had transitioned into a bar now that dinner service was ending, and there were people spilling out onto the patios, enjoying the weather and ice-cold beer.

The road was dense with tourists, and I weaved my way through them, catching bits of laughter and conversation. A small boy ran across my path, nearly colliding into me on his way to get to a shop window. He'd spotted a row of cakes and pastries and made a break for them, ignoring his mother's calls. She ran after him, throwing me an apology over her shoulder, but I didn't mind. For someone who preferred to be alone, Vernazza was the ideal setting. For fleeting moments, I could participate in strangers' lives and enjoy the moments without getting overly invested.

To get back to my villa, I had to walk straight through the main square, curve around the church, and start the steep climb up the hill. There was a faster way through the back alleys, but I liked the view along the cliffs.

I turned past the church and caught sight of a woman sitting on the breaker. It was a common place to sit and watch the sunset, but most of the time, tourists stayed to the concrete section, the dry, safe area with an even path and built-in benches.

The other half of the breaker was made up of hundreds of granite boulders, tossed down one on top of each other so that the surface was rocky and uneven. They were there to break the waves before they reached the concrete landing, but the woman sitting there was perched right on the edge, at the mercy of the sea. I stayed there, watching her and waiting for one of the waves to crash up and carry her away, but they never quite reached her, and she didn't seem preoccupied with the idea of getting wet. She was licking her gelato, turning the cone round and round to keep it from dripping down onto her hand. Her legs kicked against the granite boulders and for those first few seconds, she seemed almost childlike to me—until I realized who she was.

I didn't know her name. She'd told me and I'd forgotten, and now I regretted not committing it to memory. She was the woman who'd passed out in the square, the brunette Katerina had invited to dinner.

I wasn't so shocked to see her sitting precariously on the boulders as I was by the unnerving notion that I should join her. I didn't like the idea of her sitting there alone.

It was stupid. I knew I wouldn't do it. I hardly knew her, and though she was beautiful, I had no business befriending her. She'd be moving on to the next village in Cinque Terre soon and I'd go back to my villa, back to the memories of Allie.

Chapter Ten

Georgie

PERHAPS I'VE GONE *full lesbian.*

I hadn't previously considered it, but it was starting to look like a viable option. Rather than admitting I was hung up on one unattainable guy, I needed to start considering the possibility that my brain was just trying to persuade me that *all* men were undesirable. I mean, in the two weeks since I'd arrived, I'd gone on *three* blind dates with truly lovely Italian men, and I'd left each one of them without so much as a kiss. I should have let them cart me off to their apartments and have their wicked way with me. I'd have had at least three proper (read: not self-induced) orgasms, and maybe I could have been on my way to planning an Italian marriage. Hear that? Gothic church bells ringing.

Instead, I'd found some arbitrary fault with each of them (as I did with every man) and I'd latched onto it. Ridiculous. *Would it really be so bad to marry a man with a few flaws?* God knows I had some—too many, really. My brother Freddie had told me on the phone just yesterday that I was flighty and irresponsible. A bit selfish too, he'd added when I'd told him I hadn't been paying attention and to please repeat the last ten minutes of his ramblings.

"You can't just move to Italy to escape your problems and assume they'll work themselves out. Eternal optimism will only carry you so far. I worry, Georgie."

"Well, you shouldn't. I know exactly what I am doing."

I didn't.

Of course I had no bloody clue what I was doing. I'd spent the last two weeks in Vernazza and I was in no rush to leave. I'd asked Chiara about an extended-stay rate at the hotel and she'd promised to ask her mom about it. I knew it was a bit insane, but even if I didn't know what I was doing, I knew it felt a lot better to be going through a quarter-life crisis in a place like Vernazza. I felt like I belonged. I went to The Blue Marlin every morning for breakfast, and Antonio greeted me with a familiar smile and asked if I wanted tea or coffee. Sometimes I'd order a fluffy croissant, or if I was getting a late start, I'd tuck into some eggs and bacon while I people-watched on the patio.

After that, I'd pop round to Katerina's shop to see if she needed any help with stocking or folding new clothes. Even though there were quite a few clothing shops in Vernazza, I thought hers was the most chic. She didn't bother with silly t-shirts or baseball caps. She sold frocks and linen trousers, shirts and handmade leather sandals she sourced from a man in Corniglia, the village just south of Vernazza.

If her shop was closed, I'd take a train to a neighboring village in Cinque Terre and spend the day exploring. But my favorite pastime by far was just sitting out on the boulders with gelato and eating it slowly beneath the giant red sun.

In those two weeks, I kept careful watch for Gianluca. Sometimes I'd catch sight of a man with his build or hair coloring and try to convince myself I'd seen him, but I never really did. I even made a point to walk by the shuttered bed and breakfast to check for any activity, but Massimo and Gianluca kept it locked. In the two weeks I'd been in Vernazza, no one had entered the building. Shame, really. It was in such a brilliant location, right across the square from my hotel, which meant it had a view of the sea rather than the terraced hills. They were mad men to let it sit there, empty.

• • •

"Georgie, put the box down. You don't need another pair."

I was helping Katerina in her shop. She'd tasked me with unpacking leather sandals and I'd set aside a strappy pair that happened to be in my size.

"But I don't have this style yet."

"You've bought four pairs already. No one needs that many leather sandals."

She was wrong. I did. I tucked the box behind the counter for safekeeping and got back to work unloading and displaying the shoes the way she liked.

"I can't keep having you work here for free."

I shrugged. "Are you saying I'm hired?"

"I can't afford to pay you."

I shrugged again. "Wow. Fired on my first day."

She laughed. "How about I repay you with a lovely meal instead?"

I turned over my shoulder to watch her going at it with a mannequin, trying to stuff it into a thin, fabulous sundress.

"WAIT," I said, pushing to my feet. "I need that dress. Don't bother finishing what you're doing."

She groaned. "I've been at it for ten minutes already!"

I didn't let her argue. I pulled the dress out of her hands and laid it on top of my pair of leather sandals.

"Now what were you going on about? A meal?"

"I want to cook something at my flat. It's not a posh place or anything, but it'd fit the four of us."

"*Four?*"

I dreaded the idea of another blind date.

"You, me, Massimo, and Gianluca."

I turned round before she could see my smile.

"Sound good? I've already asked the boys if they're free."

"And are they?" I croaked.

"Yes. Massimo said they'll be round at eight, so wear that sundress you just stole from me and be there at seven to help me cook."

I laughed. "I thought this was a thank-you meal?"

"No. The dress is your thank you. I need help cooking."

I grinned. "Deal."

• • •

I knocked on Katerina's door at 6:55 PM and she opened it with a big, exhausted sigh.

"I'm so glad you're here!"

She stepped back and waved me in hurriedly, telling me to stow my things in her room to the left. Her apartment was small and ancient, but she'd made it into a lovely space. She'd hung art all over the walls, not just in the normal spots. Paintings and drawings and art prints covered nearly an entire wall in the living room.

She noticed me inspecting them. "At the market, artists come and sell their paintings and things. I can't bear to see the good ones go unsold."

"It's beautiful, really."

And I meant it. I'd never seen a space filled with such care and love. She had fresh hydrangeas on the coffee table and books stacked to the ceiling in the corners, no shelves in sight. Whatever she'd started to prepare in the small kitchen smelled absolutely divine, fresh garlic and onion, I thought.

"You didn't wear the sundress," she frowned, taking in my t-shirt and shorts.

I patted my bag. "I didn't want to spoil it while we cooked. I'll change before the boys get here."

She grinned. "Perfect! You're on salad duty."

After I'd stowed my things, she gave me the grand tour of her kitchen. It was tiny, hardly enough space for one person to cook, let alone two. The appliances had probably been around during World War II, but she'd done up the place as best she could. Her cabinets had a fresh coat of white paint and she had pretty wine bottles on display on the bar between the living room and kitchen.

"I love it in here, Kat."

"Me too. You should have seen it when I first moved in though. The place was full of rotted wood and there were leaks everywhere."

"You fixed it up yourself?"

She laughed. "God no. I hung up the decor and painted the cabinets, but Luca did all the construction. Replaced all the leaky pipes and things. Boring stuff, but he's brilliant at it."

I tucked away that bit of information, careful not to

seem too interested by it. Ever since Katerina had informed me that I was the latest in a line of women who'd gone gaga for Gianluca, I tried my hardest to train my features into neutral expressions. I didn't want her to think I was pining for him or anything. Truthfully, I just wanted another chance to be around him. Even with his sullen demeanor, he was the most interesting man I'd ever come across, and despite the fact that he'd been nearly mute in our few encounters, I knew he had more to say. It was in his eyes. They were a deep chocolate brown and they seemed to carry the weight of his unspoken words.

I took all my salad ingredients to the dining table so I could chop things out of Katerina's way.

"Everything you've got there was picked from Massimo's farm! He dropped it off this morning."

I cut up big, ripe bell peppers and stole a slice or two when Katerina was too busy to notice. She was sautéing the onions and garlic, making a delicious-smelling sauce for the chicken. After I'd finished chopping and preparing the salad, I poured us big glasses of wine and set up a little radio she kept in the corner beside the book stacks. She had it programmed to a popular station and we went to work, drinking and prepping with Italian pop songs on in the background.

I set the table and lit a few candles in the middle. I cut up large pieces of crusty bread and arranged them on a little plate with a pat of butter. Katerina pulled the chicken out of the oven, covered it to keep it warm, and then we hurried to change before the boys arrived. They were due any minute and I had an anxious feeling in the pit of my stomach, a swirl of butterflies at the idea of seeing Gianluca again. I prayed he wouldn't cancel last minute.

"Oh god," she groaned. "I sort of hate you for looking

that good."

I laughed and twirled around in my new blue dress. "It's not me, it's the dress."

The light, silky material spun around my legs.

She shook her head. "It's lovely, but you're wrong. Your hair has gone a bit lighter from the sun and your arms are a lovely brown now. You're tan and toned from all the swimming you've been doing. You're in full Italian mode and you're practically glowing from it."

A knock sounded from the front door before I could let her compliments sink in.

She clapped excitedly. "They're here!"

I followed her out into the living room as she rushed to the door. Massimo was standing on the other side with a bottle of wine in his hands. Gianluca stood behind him, a little taller, with his hands tucked into his pockets. His medium-length brown hair was styled away from his face, wavy and blissfully thick. He'd dressed up in a pair of dark jeans and a white button-down. The color complimented his tan skin and I was struck again by how excruciatingly beautiful he was. He stepped past the door, saw me standing near the coffee table, and offered up a small, easy smile. My heart nearly broke from the sight of it.

Katerina kissed Massimo and accepted the bottle of wine from his hands. Then, she popped up onto her tiptoes and planted two kisses on Gianluca's cheeks. I wrung out my hands as Massimo stepped forward to greet me, planting two kisses on my cheeks and then turning to compliment the table arrangement.

"You've cooked my favorite sauce, haven't you?" he asked, turning to Katerina with a giant, cheesy grin.

She smiled coyly and I turned back to Gianluca, aware that he had ducked past the door and we still hadn't really said a proper greeting. I turned to face him and he stepped forward. My heart shot up into my throat as he bent to kiss me. To him, it was all very polite and customary, but I nearly fainted from the feel of his lips on my cheeks. God, it was an intimate greeting, wasn't it? I could have turned my face an inch to the left and *oops,* his mouth would have been on mine.

"You look lovely," he said, admiring my dress with a quick gaze down my body before turning his attention to Katerina.

I swallowed past the lump in my throat and turned to cover my blushing cheeks. "Thanks."

Lord it was annoying how much I clammed up when he was around. I'd never gone this mental over a man before.

"I'll pour some wine," I said, my voice a bit peaky. I turned quickly and set out doing tasks that kept me flitting around the apartment. I brought Massimo and Gianluca full glasses of red wine then tossed the dressing into the salad. I set everything out onto the table and relit a candle that had blown out. Katerina laughed and asked if I was all right when I'd set out cutting up even more bread. She put her hand over mine to stop me from slicing. "I think we've got enough bread to feed the village. C'mon, let's sit."

Gianluca pulled my chair out for me and I squeaked out a quiet thank you.

Katerina poured the sauce over the chicken and set it down on the table. We had loads of food and more wine than we knew what to do with. I gulped down another long sip and draped my napkin over my lap, aware of how close Gianluca was sitting to my left. Katerina's table was small and we were sort of crammed together over the food and candles. It was heaven, all of it. She'd left her windows open, so a soft breeze swelled in every now and then, spreading goosebumps over my bare arms.

Gianluca noticed. I saw him glance over and furrow his brow. I thought for a second he'd say something or offer to shut the windows, but he swallowed and turned his attention back to his chicken. Massimo broke the silence.

"Georgie, what are we going to do once you've left Vernazza? Katerina says you've been helping in the shop a lot lately."

She moaned. "Don't even bring it up. I don't want to think about it."

I laughed. "I actually think I might stay on a bit longer. I asked Chiara about a prolonged stay at the hotel."

Massimo's brows arched. "Really? That's great!"

"What will you do?" Gianluca asked. "If you stay?"

"It's not like she needs a job or anything, Luca," Katerina chimed in, hinting at the posh life I'd left behind in England.

"I think I'd like one, though," I admitted. "I've loved exploring and relaxing, but I can't just loll about all day, every day."

Katerina frowned. "I really don't think I could hire you on right now. This is my busy season, but I have to save up everything I earn for when things slow down in the winter."

I shook my head. "Don't worry, Kat, I know you can't hire me on. I have a different idea."

"What is it? Have you been offered a job somewhere else?"

"If it's at one of the restaurants in the square, I wouldn't bother," Massimo added. "You can come work for me and I'll give you real hours. Whatever you need."

I reached for my wine, took another gulp, and turned my attention to Gianluca.

"Actually...I was thinking I could purchase the bed and

breakfast and fix it up."

Chapter Eleven

Georgie

THE THREE OF them stared at me as if I'd gone mad.

"What do you mean you want to *buy it?*" Katerina asked.

Gianluca cut her off. "It's not for sale."

Massimo leaned forward and propped his hand on Gianluca's shoulder. "Let's hear her out. For the right price, anything is possible…"

"No. Absolutely not."

"You haven't even heard what she has to say yet!" Katerina said, defusing the intense stare-down developing across the table.

"It doesn't matter."

Massimo grunted. "It might matter. We aren't all living like *you*, Luca."

Gianluca shot him a sharp glare. "You have more than you need with the farm and restaurant. That inn belonged to Nonna and it's been in the family for centuries. We aren't going to sell it to the first tourist who throws us an offer."

"So to honor our heritage, we let it rot instead?" blustered Massimo.

Once the dust had settled on his words, three sets of eyes turned to me expectantly.

"If you aren't prepared to sell it outright, I have a compromise I think we can all support."

Katerina and Massimo whipped their attention to Gianluca. He didn't make a move to reply right away; I could tell he wanted to put an end to the entire conversation, but eventually, he nodded, giving me the okay to proceed.

"Right, well like Massimo mentioned, it's a shame that such a beautiful place has fallen into a state of disrepair. I haven't seen anyone in or out of the building since the day I arrived. It's got such a lovely spot in the square and I know the views would draw people in. So, I'd like to help restore the place to its former beauty and reopen it for business."

Gianluca assessed me as I spoke, suspicious of my intentions.

"What would you get out of it?"

I smiled. "Well, for starters, I'd get the satisfaction of seeing the place up and running again. Second, I could finance the renovation in exchange for a small stake." He opened his mouth to protest, but I continued on. "So there's no risk for either of you. When it's ready to open, you'd have an employee with a vested interest in its success!"

He reached for his glass of wine and downed the rest of it.

Massimo laughed. "How long have you been thinking of this?"

"Oh, not long. An hour, maybe two."

Gianluca laughed then, this rich, deep chuckle that

swelled a sense of pride inside me. I liked the sound; I wanted him to laugh more, even if it was at my expense.

"You've dreamt this up over the course of an *hour* or two?" he demanded. "And you expect me to hand over the keys to my family's business?"

I rolled my eyes. "That seems a bit dramatic. As of right now, I'd say you're doing more harm to the family business by letting it completely go to waste. All I'm asking is for you to let me into an empty building, as a partner, to see what we can make of it."

"The answer is no. Drop it."

Massimo held up his hands. "Now, now. Let's pour some more wine and talk this over."

Gianluca stood from the table so fast he nearly toppled it over. "This is insane. We don't even know this...this *girl!*"

Those words. That was the moment I knew I wouldn't back down. That exact moment when he pointed to me over the table and couldn't even remember my name. That's when I knew I wouldn't give up until he gave me what I wanted.

"Katerina, thanks for dinner," he said, already en route to the door. "Gigi—"

"MY NAME ISN'T GIGI, YOU INSUFFERABLE GIT."

My shouting stopped him dead in his tracks. He turned over his shoulder, narrowed his dark eyes on me, and for the first time, it felt like he really saw me.

"It's Georgie," I said, more calm now that I'd gulped in a few breaths of air. "My name is Georgie."

He narrowed his eyes on me for only a moment and then pulled open the front door with enough force to rattle its hinges. He disappeared into the night, the door slammed closed behind him, and the three of us sat in silence for a few seconds, trying to make sense of what had just transpired.

I cringed, thinking of how much Katerina and Massimo must hate me now that I'd antagonized Gianluca like that. I started to think up some way to apologize for my outburst, but then Massimo started clapping and laughing. It was a small, quiet chuckle at first, but then it grew and picked up steam. Katerina joined in, and then I was helpless to the sound of it.

"You called him a git," Massimo laughed, wiping tears from his eyes.

"Right, well, the man deserved it."

He held up his hands. "I won't argue that. It's high time someone knocked some sense into the bloke. I've tried to do it for the last five years and I've never been able to get a rise like that out of him."

I moaned. "Lovely."

Katerina leaned over to rub my shoulder. "No, no. Don't let it get to you." She waved her hand over the table, where most of our food had gone untouched. "We've prepared all this food and we aren't going to let it go to waste. Massimo, you can tuck into Gianluca's portion if you'd like, and Georgie, eat up. That sauce takes hours to make and it's Massimo's favorite. I absolutely refuse to let this night be ruined by that arsehole."

"Aw, c'mon Katerina. You know he means well. Honestly, I'm happy to see any kind of emotion out of him! Anything is better than that mopey stare of his."

She waved her hand, not wanting to hear it. For the next few minutes, we ate in silence, too scared to speak and upset her more. Her sauce *was* delicious, full of butter and garlic. It complimented the chicken perfectly and I'd nearly cleaned my plate before she spoke up again.

"For the record, I think making over the bed and breakfast is a brilliant idea."

Chapter twelve

Gianluca

WHEN ALLIE AND I moved to Vernazza in the last year of her life, I tried to convince her to help me fix up the bed and breakfast. Nonna would have rolled in her grave if she'd known how far we'd let the building fall into decay. She'd put so much pride and joy into the business when she was alive, but with Massimo running the farm and restaurant and me living in England with Allie, there was no one to help with upkeep. We'd closed it, locked the shutters, and mostly forgotten about it until Allie and I moved back.

I'd taken her down to the building the first week we'd moved to Vernazza. I'd covered her eyes up and told her to not to peek.

"What's going on? Where are you taking me?" she laughed, giddy with excitement.

I liked the sound. It'd been months since I'd heard happiness in her voice.

I positioned her in front of the building and pulled my hands away from her eyes with a dramatic flourish.

She blinked her eyes open and inspected the wooden sign hanging halfway off the front of the building.

"Bed and breakfast?" she read, confused.

I grinned. "It belonged to my grandmother. She left it to me and Massimo and I want us to fix it up."

Her smile fell, just a bit. "Fix it up? What for?"

Her meaning hung thick in the air.

If I'm going to die, what's the point?

I didn't argue and we never went back.

Now, the subject of fixing up the bed and breakfast had been brought back up, and I was humming with anger at *Georgie*. Lord knows I wouldn't forget her name now. Not ever. She was a spoiled brat on holiday from England, used to getting her way. She assumed she could just snap her fingers, take my nonna's bed and breakfast from us, and I wouldn't put up a fight? Like hell.

The fact that Massimo hadn't been on my side of things was even more infuriating. He didn't know Georgie any more than I did. His farm and restaurant were doing well. He didn't need the money, which meant he had other motives. Nonna would have been so disappointed.

I took the long way back to the villa after I'd stormed out of dinner. I was in no rush to get back to its deafening quiet, so I wove through the back alleys of Vernazza, listening to the sounds of life. There were two ways to live in the village: down in the center where everyone was nearly piled up on top of one another, or out in the hills with a bit more privacy. My villa was perched on the edge of a cliff, looking out over the ocean, and while the view was worth the trek, it was a lonely existence up there.

I was still worked up by the time I made it home, unable

to quell the surge of adrenaline that would make it impossible to sleep. I wound through the ivy in the dark and felt for the shed tucked behind the villa. I pulled open the heavy wooden door and fumbled around inside until my hand hit my work lamp. Its stand was lying beside it and I yanked both out of the shed and carried them to the front of the house.

Once the light was plugged in, I had enough light to work on my wall. I yanked off the button-down shirt I'd worn for dinner and wiped my brow, intent on working until I was too tired to stand. I pushed the wheelbarrow out from the shed and tore at the stones on the wall, tossing aside one after another. They clanged against the metal, and I focused on the sharp sound until I'd settled into an easy rhythm.

I wouldn't entertain the idea of selling the bed and breakfast to Georgie. She could butter Massimo up all she wanted, but I saw through her façade. Her family had money, and she'd lived a cushy fairytale life. She could buy any bed and breakfast in any village on any continent. But she would leave mine alone.

• • •

The next morning, I woke up to loud banging on the villa's front door. I was an early riser by habit, but I'd stayed up late into the night working on the wall, and I wasn't quite prepared to leave my bed as the banging continued. *Bloody hell. It'll be Massimo*, I thought, *come round to rage at me for storming out of Katerina's*. I padded down the stairs, prepared to tell him to sod off and crawl back in bed, but then I caught a hint of woman's voice instead.

"Hellooo! I know you're in there!"

BANG. BANG. BANG.

"Please come open the door or your coffee will get cold!"

I yanked the door open, vaguely acknowledged the fact that Georgie was standing there, and then tried to close the door in her face.

"I don't want coffee."

She pushed the small paper cup against my chest and I had to reach for it before it spilled. I was still shirtless, and I didn't feel like having third degree burns on my chest.

"Bloody hell. Are you mental?"

She grinned. "Never been confirmed one way or the other. Regardless, I've come to have a chat."

She propped her hands on her hips, all proud and confident, and I registered then that she wasn't dressed like normal. She had on denim overalls, a tight white t-shirt, and a red bandanna tied round her head. She looked like she was about to work construction and the idea of it nearly made me laugh, but then I remembered how annoyed I was.

"You're probably wondering why I've come round looking like a construction worker." She waved her hand down her front. "Well, we have a big job ahead of us and it'll be best if we get started right away."

She didn't take a breath. She pushed through the front door of my house and made her way inside.

"I know you're not keen on the idea of selling me the bed and breakfast, and I completely understand. But, I'm not asking for a majority stake or anything, just enough so my brother can be proud that I've done something with my life. Did I tell you I have a brother? Fred? He's this real superstar, actually, an Olympic swimmer for Great Britain, and he's quite annoying to have in the family. My mom's

100

always going on about how much he's been able to accomplish and then she'll say how I haven't even snared a husband yet. It's like I'm the black sheep, only that's ludicrous, because I happen to think I'm the only normal one in that lot."

I held up my hand to stop her, but she just rambled on, oblivious to the fact that I was waving for her to leave my house.

"That building is so lovely and it's not right to leave it empty like that. It's *cruel*, really. I'm not a designer or anything, but I think I have a good eye for color and furniture. I grew up living on a bloody estate, so goodness knows I've seen enough posh homes. I'm not saying the bed and breakfast should be that extravagant per se, but I know how we can make it welcoming and warm. We'll need lots of color—that's where I'll come in, of course. I'll do all the superficial interior stuff, and you, you'll be in charge of construction. I think you can manage all right; you have the build for it."

She patted my naked chest, as if kicking the tires on a car she was test driving.

"You're quite muscly, you know, and that's a weighty compliment. I've been around Olympic athletes and you wouldn't stand out too far from that crowd."

I snapped at her to be quiet. Her mouth dropped open and I swore she nearly thought of continuing on again, but I stepped forward and covered her mouth with my hand to ensure she'd shut up.

"You're barking mad and I want you out of my house. *Now*."

Her eyebrows knitted together in confusion and I realized I was still rather close to her, covering her lips with my hand. I could feel her breath hit my palm and I whipped back, putting a bit of distance between us.

"You won't help me fix it up?"

"No."

"Why?"

"I don't owe you any explanations. I just need you to leave."

I walked back to my front door, yanked it all the way open, and waved for her to get out.

She crossed her arms, narrowed her eyes, and kept her footing, right in the center of my living room.

"You think you're the only person to experience loss, Gianluca? You think you get to mope around here forever?"

I saw red. Georgie didn't get to talk about loss. She didn't get to judge me or the way I chose to deal with mourning. This girl who lived life with a silver spoon in her mouth, this girl who floated around on clouds—she had no clue what she was talking about.

"You don't know anything about me," I replied with a tone that would have warned most people away.

Georgie seemed to dig her heels in deeper.

"Nor *you* about *me*. If you had ever cared to ask me about myself, I'd have told you that in the span of a few years, I lost my father and my oldest brother. One day they were there with me, alive and well. The next? *Poof*. Gone.

"So you see, I'm no stranger to death and dying either, but I've moved on with my life, and *you*...you're just like that dreary bed and breakfast. You've let yourself fall into ruin. Katerina says it's been five years. *Five years* and you act as if you lost her just yesterday!"

I was shaking then, shocked at how far Georgie was willing to push the subject. Normal people would have backed off. They'd have faltered, realizing how many lines

102

they'd crossed. They would have apologized and left.

Not Georgie.

"You can sit up here in your villa and mope around for eternity for all I care, but don't you feel like even Allie herself would have wanted you to be happy someday?! You're this lovely man with real potential! I see it, but it's under all these layers you've built up around yourself. *Why can't you move on?*"

"It's none of your business!"

"I'm *making* it my business! What are you trying to prove, anyway? That you're the most miserable sod on Earth?"

"*That's enough—*"

"Well congratulations, YOU'VE DONE IT!"

"GET OUT!"

I reached out and yanked her by her bicep, dragging her out of my house. She was nearly tripping over herself and I knew I was hurting her, but I couldn't see past my anger. She'd pushed too far, too fast.

I tossed her out the front door and slammed it closed behind her, squeezing my eyes closed and leaning back against the door jamb. I felt bad about kicking her out like that, but she deserved it. Who did she think she was? Storming into my house? My grief? I didn't need a pompous English girl lecturing me on the ways of life.

I leaned back against the door, trying to calm the burning anger welling up inside of me. Eventually, the adrenaline started to fade, and by then, I'd assumed Georgie was long gone, crying her way down the hill and prepping her speech for Katerina (*The miserable arse tossed me out of his house!*), but then I heard a soft voice just on the other side of the wood.

"Good progress. We'll start tomorrow, then?"

103

Chapter Thirteen

Gianluca

I WAS UP early the next morning, seemingly the only person alive in Vernazza. I eased down the trail and followed the path around the ancient church in the square. The bell inside its tower would start chiming soon, but for now, it sat quiet, allowing everyone another hour of sleep. The plan was to take the train into La Spezia. I made the trek about once a month, picking up supplies that the small shops in Vernazza didn't keep in stock. I needed a new shovel for my work on the wall, but then I spotted Georgie in the square.

I shouldn't have been surprised to see her, but I was. I'd assumed after the day before, she'd take the hint and back off, but she was there, wearing jeans and a white t-shirt, flitting around the outside of the bed and breakfast. The front door was locked so there was no way for her to get inside, but she didn't let that stop her. She had a clipboard in one hand and she was jotting down notes as quickly as her pen could go, measuring windows and doorways and front steps. I hadn't a clue what she was doing and I had no intention of interrupting her until I saw the sign pasted to the front door.

OPEN SOON. UNDER NEW MANAGEMENT.

Bloody hell.

"Morning!" she called when she spotted me approaching from the side of the square.

I grunted in response and headed straight for the door so I could tear down the sign.

"Hey! What'd you do that for?"

I crumbled it up in my hands and leveled her with a steely glare, but it had little effect on her.

She shrugged and glanced away, the early morning light playing up her delicate features. "Fine, if you don't want the sign, we won't have it then. I thought the customers would like to know they wouldn't be dealing with *you* every day, scaring them and all."

I didn't let her see my amusement at that.

"This is better though," she said, turning back to me with another wide grin. "Element of surprise and all that. They won't know we're redoing the place and then WHAM, we'll open and have the best bed and breakfast in all of Vernazza!"

I turned away with a yawn and headed up the long road toward the train station. Unfazed, she followed along, chattering about her inane plans for the next month. God, she was exhausting. The persistent positivity, the sheer stubbornness. If the woman put her mind to it, I bet she could make herself the prime minister of England in two weeks flat.

Normal women would have been standoffish, or at least a bit cross. Not Georgie. She was a moving locomotive; I

106

could either get out of her way or let her roll right over me.

I still wasn't quite sure which option would hurt less when I rang up Massimo a few days later and asked about getting some building supplies from the farm.

"You're going to do it then? Fix it up?"

"Only because I want to, and I think Nonna would want to see it open."

There was quite a long pause after that.

"What?" I asked, annoyed that he wasn't getting on with it.

"Nothing," Massimo said. "Just shocked is all. I mean, I don't buy your reasoning. You're totally doing it because you've always struggled to tell a beautiful girl no—but it doesn't matter. You could be fixing it up for Morgan Freeman for all I care."

I ignored his suggestion. "I'll be round in the morning to pick up those supplies. Just have them ready for me."

Chapter Fourteen

Georgie

I WASN'T AN oblivious girl going through life unaware of how people felt about me. I knew Gianluca wanted me to bugger off, and I knew I was making him uncomfortable talking about Allie. I knew, I just didn't care. I wanted to shake him silly, to shout at him, *WAKE UP. THIS IS YOUR LIFE AND YOU'RE WASTING THE BEST BITS OF IT.*

The bed and breakfast was the only way I knew how to do that. Sure, I wanted to have a hand in fixing it up and I knew I'd have fun decorating it and getting it back in good shape, but more than that, I suspected it'd be good for Gianluca to have a project.

When he'd shouted at me in his house (right before he'd dragged me out and locked the door), it wasn't out of rage, it was out of fear. It clouded his eyes and made him address some issues he'd kept buried. From experience, I knew it was loads easier to crumble under the weight of grief than it was to stand up with it on your back, but every day you carry it forward you get stronger and stronger, and eventually it doesn't feel as heavy as it once did.

He needed to take that first step.

I showed up at the bed and breakfast the next day, and the day after, and the day after that. It was nearly a week since he'd tossed me out of his house, and my small hope that he would come to his senses was beginning to dwindle. I sat out on the stoop with two espressos and a couple of pastries in a brown paper sack and waited for Gianluca. I watched the old man across the square sweep out his doorway and I fed a bit of crumbs to one of the boat cats. It meowed and twisted itself round my legs, doing quite a good job of coaxing a bit more croissant out of me.

"Okay, that's it, you greedy cow," I insisted, showing it my empty hands. "You've stolen even more than you did yesterday. Soon you'll just have to flop around like a chunky sea lion."

"You shouldn't feed them. They're all fat enough as is."

My head shot up at the sound of Gianluca's voice. I couldn't believe it at first. He'd just arrived in the square, dressed in jeans and a worn pale blue shirt. He had a tool belt wrapped round his middle and a big trolley loaded up with supplies resting beside him.

"His diet starts *tomorrow*," I explained.

He nodded and wheeled the trolley closer. There was lumber and paint and brushes and giant saws loading it down.

"Have you decided you'll help me then? Or is this a cruel joke?"

He shook his head as he stepped past me, yanking a set of keys out of his back pocket. I glanced up at him, nearly swooning at how beautiful he looked with his work clothes on. He'd taken the time to shave and his smooth jaw was

110

enough to do any girl's head in.

He unlocked the door and pushed it open. Fresh air rushed into the abandoned building and I stood, wiping my hands on my jeans and following him through the door. It was just like I'd remembered, dusty and dark inside, nearly haunted-looking with all the windows shuttered closed. Right past the front door there was a small desk covered with a dirty cream linen. Beyond that, I knew there was a bedroom, where they'd carried me nearly four weeks ago.

Gianluca tossed his keys on the top of the desk and turned to me.

"Listen, I don't know what plans you've got in that head of yours, but I'm not selling this place to a stranger."

"Understood."

"Then why are you so keen on helping me fix it up?"

"Because when we finish, you'll give me the job as manager."

"Have you ever managed anything?"

"On paper? No, but I have *managed* to get this whole project started, haven't I?"

He dragged a hand across his forehead, most likely ready to toss me out again, but I spoke up first.

"Look, you'll fix the building, all the electrical and plumbing, the real boring stuff, and I'll spruce up the interior, paint and all that, make sure people actually enjoy their stay here. I've already picked up enough Italian to know how to say *Do you need more shampoo?* and *Thank you, I do look lovely today don't I?*"

He sighed. "Let's say we do get this place to a point where it could be opened, and let's say I needed someone to manage it. I couldn't pay you much," he said, dropping his hand and turning to fully face me.

I grinned. "I don't need much."

"It's not glamorous work. Renovating an old place takes longer than you'd think. Once we get going, we'll probably find quite a bit of damage in here."

"I'm not a quitter, if that's what you're getting at."

"Oh, *believe me*, no one would ever suspect you of quitting."

I smiled and reached out my hand for him to shake. He glanced down at it for a few seconds, seemingly working out the arrangement in his head.

"Partners," I said.

He accepted my hand and I nearly shivered from the warmth of his large grip.

• • •

The bed and breakfast consisted of three floors, each a little more worn down than the last. Gianluca look me on a tour, leading me through the first common room with the check-in desk, living room, and dining room. There was a kitchen tucked in the back across the hallway from a bedroom and bathroom. Gianluca informed me that was where the manager usually stayed when the place was operating.

On the second story, there were two more bedrooms and a bathroom, and then one large penthouse and bathroom on the top level. In all, the place was small, but it needed a lot of work.

That first day, we began by clearing things out. We couldn't even really assess the damage until the place was empty, and though I'd assumed it would be a fairly simple task—throw out the bits of trash until the place was clean—we'd been at it for three days and were still no closer to being finished. Gianluca's grandmother had collected quite a lot of stuff over the years. Furniture aside, there were enough trinkets, books, and knickknacks to fill a normal house three times over.

And of course, Gianluca didn't trust me to toss things out on my own. I had to show him every single item I picked up so he could decide if it was trash or not.

"We ought to save that."

"But it's just an empty peanut tin."

"Nonna loved peanuts."

"Right." I rattled the empty tin as if to prove to him how silly he was being. "But we should toss it. It's useless."

"She might have liked it."

"It's rubbish, Gianluca."

He yanked it out of my hand and dropped it in the "save" pile.

"*Bloody hell.*"

It continued on like that for the first week. No real conversation, no fun banter or silly joking. We worked tirelessly in awkward silence. I'd pick up something that ought to be tossed, and Gianluca would insist that it had some sort of value. The bloke was a full-on hoarder. It got to be so bad that I would sneak stuff into the trash when he turned his back. I appreciated the value of family heirlooms and sentimental keepsakes, but he was being mental.

"What will you do with the top half of that music box?"

"Keep an eye out for the other part and glue them back together."

"'Course. Seems logical that Nonna would break a *treasured* box in half then hide the pieces…"

"You know, I can do this myself if you're bored."

"No! No. It's fine. I can tell you've got a real vision for that pile of lemon candy wrappers you've got going over there."

Conversation—or lack thereof—aside, Gianluca seemed to also have a distaste for breaks. Each day, we skipped right over lunch. I'd ask him if he was hungry, and he'd insist he'd rather just keep working. I'd try to hang on as long as I could, but by 1:30 PM I usually caved and went out into the square to find a quick bite by myself. The first few days, I brought a treat back for him: pizza fresh from the oven, fresh strawberries, chocolate gelato—but after each thing had gone untouched, I stopped bothering.

On Friday, I spent a good deal of the day working up the courage to ask him to have dinner with me. I'd prepared a speech and planned it down to every word.

"You'll pass out if you don't eat something soon. Come on, come have a bite to eat with me."

I thought I sounded very cool and casual, like I didn't *really* care if he continued his hunger strike, but he shook his head without even looking up.

"I'll get something on my way back home later."

Right. Wonderful.

In the week we'd spent together, I'd wrestled a handful of words out of him and little else. We were no closer to becoming friends and though I tried to ignore it, with him there, the bed and breakfast had taken on a sort of gloomy energy.

I was moping in my room on Friday night, nursing my bruised ego, when Katerina turned up with some fresh cheese, crusty bread, and more Sciacchetrà.

"You're a heavenly angel...*of booze!*" I said, ripping the bottle out of her hand so I could get to work uncorking it.

"I figured after the week you've had, you might need some wine."

"Please say you've crushed up some drugs and slipped

114

them in here as well?"

She barked out a laugh. "Was it that bad?"

"Nearly intolerable," I said, pulling the door open wide so she could come in. "Gianluca is definitely a gloomy sod. There's no going around it. Drink from the bottle okay?"

"It's a tradition." She grinned.

We set up shop on my bed, unfolding the brown butcher paper from around the cheese and then using it as a makeshift table. We ripped off big chunks of bread and guzzled wine, all while I delighted her with stories of Gianluca from the last five days.

"Why wouldn't he just keep one or two of the wrappers?"

"I know. I'm not making this up."

"Maybe he'll toss them out later? You know, once you've gone?"

"Fat chance. I'm actually forming a backup plan of turning the place into the *Museo di Nonna* in case the B&B doesn't work out."

"So then do you think you'll start actually repairing and painting stuff next week?"

I laughed. "We spent all week clearing out ONE room, Katerina! ONE! We won't be doing any actual work for months—YEARS if Gianluca has it his way."

She wiped a hand down her face. "Wow."

"I know I'm supposed to be gentle with him because of what he's gone through and everything, but something about him makes me want to push back harder, to really trip him out of whatever funk he's in."

"I think that funk is called 'mourning'."

I cringed. "Okay, right, but if five years of everyone bubble-wrapping Gianluca hasn't helped, maybe it's time for some tough love?"

115

She glanced past my bedroom window, out toward the square, and for a while we didn't speak.

The shutters were open to let in the sea breeze. The scent of Italian cuisine spilled out from the restaurants below, and the chatter and clinking dishes served as a welcome backdrop to our silence.

"I understand I hardly know him," I finally continued, "and I never saw him with Allie, but it doesn't take a rocket scientist to realize that he really loved her. I have no clue what's going on with him, and if he really is truly depressed, I know it's naïve to think I can just shake him out of it. Do you think I should back off? Give him some space?"

"Absolutely not," she replied quickly, turning back to face me. "For years Massimo and I have been too scared to rock the boat. Sometimes Massimo will get the courage to push him a bit, but not really, never to a point where they'd have a real go at it. But you…" She smiled. "You're just what we've been waiting for. Don't give up."

Chapter Fifteen

Georgie

MONDAY MORNING, I arrived at the bed and breakfast even more prepared than I'd been the week before. I had a list of talking points going in my head, simple things that would keep the conversation flowing all day. I brought another sack of pastries and two cups of tea from The Blue Marlin.

Gianluca was already there when I arrived, hard at work clearing out the first-floor bedroom. He hardly glanced up when I popped my head in and said hello.

"I've brought you some tea."

"No need," he replied, shaking out another black bin bag and getting to work tossing out things from the wardrobe in the corner.

"How about a pastry? They put out these fresh croissants right when I got there and I brought some for us."

"Thanks. I'll take it home."

It wasn't just what he said, it was the *way* he said it. To him, I was the most annoying git on the planet.

"All right then!" I said, my voice a tad too shrill. "I'll be clearing out the front room if you need me."

That finally got his attention. "No, no. I don't want you clearing things when I'm not there."

I tried hard to keep the lid on it then. It was his family's building and I had to respect that.

"Oookay, well you just tell me what you want me to do."

He put me to work holding the bin bag while he continued to clear out the wardrobe. It was the closest we'd ever been. He was wearing a white t-shirt, tight around his muscular arms and then a bit looser around his slim waist. He was in good shape for someone who lived nowhere near a gym. I figured his muscles were built from manual labor, which for some reason seemed even more attractive to me. He caught me staring a few times, but I always pasted on a big smile and acted as though I was doing nothing wrong.

I even tried to strike up a conversation a few times.

"Do you enjoy reading, Gianluca?"

"Yes."

"What sorts of books?"

"Fiction. Will you try to hold the bag open wider so I can stuff this in there?"

Two more days passed like this and then finally, on Thursday I couldn't take it.

"Put the bag down, Gianluca. We're going to dinner."

He protested, of course. Well, first he turned his back to ignore me, so I had to sort of cut across to stand in front of him and repeat myself twice, and *then* when he couldn't pretend like he hadn't heard me anymore, he protested.

"I haven't got the time."

"Oh, busy night planned at the villa? Going to read

some fiction?"

He eyes cut to me, and I leveled a stare at him and didn't budge. Not an inch. God, it was difficult. My spine nearly buckled under the sheer amount of disdain he focused on me. I fought against my better judgement and arched a brow as if to say, *Your powers don't work on me.*

"There's a place just outside. I'm sure they'll give us a table and we can eat really quickly. I won't even chew and you don't have to bother talking. These last few days with you have shown me how adept I am at one-sided conversation."

He dropped the bin bag he'd been holding and clapped the dirt off his hands.

"Fine. We'll go up to Massimo's restaurant."

I didn't quite believe it. I mean, my mouth was hanging open. I had an argument prepared on my tongue, but he'd agreed.

Holy hell!

I grinned, quite pleased with myself for talking him into a meal with me.

He told me to give him a few minutes to finish up and I promised I'd meet him outside. I stopped in the bathroom on my way to the front door to fix my hair and make sure my boobs were settled correctly in my bra. It wasn't a date, *exactly.* I mean Gianluca had literally shouted *This isn't a date!* through the bathroom door enough times that it was now burned in my brain, but I still wanted to look nice if I had to sit across a table from the man.

I'd picked a light sundress that morning and was glad for it as we walked outside. Gianluca locked up. The sun was still high in the sky, burning bright orange. The cool breeze felt good on my bare arms and legs after being stuck in the musty building all day. I twisted my hair into a bun at the base of my neck and smiled over at Gianluca as we set off along the main road. He didn't notice. People waved at him as we passed and he was always polite, but distant. I got the feeling they would have enjoyed a long conversation with him, but he kept us moving along.

"I figured you must be hungry," he said, holding the door open for me once we arrived at Massimo's restaurant.

"Oh! Well, thank you. I am pretty starved after all the work we've done today."

He grunted in response and I knew he wanted to mention that I hadn't done much, but that's because it took nearly half my energy just to stand in a room with him, enduring the weight of his grumpiness. It was doing a number on my knees.

A waiter directed us to a small table in the corner, set up right near the kitchen. Massimo came out to greet us, a bit shocked to see us sitting there at first, but he played it off.

"Only the best *vino* for my two favorite customers," he joked right before flitting off and returning with a dusty bottle of red wine. It looked ancient and the moment it hit my lips, I had to stop myself from guzzling down the entire glass in one go.

"It's so good," I moaned, sipping slowly and watching to see if Gianluca was enjoying it as well.

He hesitated for one long, excruciating moment before offering a reply.

"It's from his family's vineyard, up near the farm."

My brows nearly hit my hairline. "Are you serious? They produce wine there too?"

"It's common here in Vernazza. Most families own a piece of the terraced hills. They build their homes in the center and then they grow grapes and olives, whatever they want, really. Massimo has a massive plot of land so he grows all sorts of things."

I could tell my eyes were wide with wonder, because Gianluca was watching me with a curious little expression—not really the way a woman hopes to be looked at by an attractive man. It was more like he was looking at an alien from another planet.

"It's just so different than London. Sure, we have an estate with gardens, but it's all flowers for show, no food. It's all very…two dimensional."

He nodded, understanding what I meant. "It's different here."

Either they'd laced the wine, or we were having a normal conversation wherein I said words, Gianluca seemed to hear them, and then responded in kind. It was a bloody miracle. Gianluca didn't do small talk and the fact that he was even sitting there with me at a restaurant was an unbelievable amount of progress. I wanted to see how far I could push it before he closed up again and told me to bugger off.

"How is it different?" I asked, keeping my gaze on my wine glass. I felt like I'd been tossed into the bear cage at the zoo and any sudden movement might spook the beast.

He sipped his wine and stared off over my shoulder. "Everyone is growing and producing, fishing or harvesting things so that if they wanted to, they'd never have to leave. Have you been shopping in the local markets?"

"Yes, but my hotel room doesn't have a kitchen or anything, so I've been sticking to fruit."

"Shame. You really ought to try the vegetables they sell at the market on Tuesday mornings."

"I've seen that market! Katerina sells her clothes there too, right?"

A waiter dropped off a fresh loaf of focaccia bread and

then dropped down some oil and vinegar. Gianluca mixed them up on a small plate and we got to work tearing off pieces of warm goodness to dip into the mixture.

"Yeah. Katerina has sold there for a few years now. I try to stop in every now and then to buy produce, but I don't get down there as often as I should."

"If I lived in your villa, I'd hardly go down into the square either."

He offered up a half smile. (*I think I peed a little.*)

"It is a nice place to live."

"More than nice, Gianluca! It's massive, right up at the top of the hill. I swear it's the best piece of property in the whole village."

"It's been in my family for ages. When my nonna passed away, she gave Massimo the farm and land, and I got the villa."

"So that's why you moved back to Vernazza?"

Katerina had told me Gianluca had grown up in London, which was why he had a bit of an English accent.

His half smile flattened then, hardly at all, but I noticed. "No."

There was a long silence after that and it didn't take a genius to realize I'd completely ruined the meal with my line of questioning. Whatever progress I'd made with him was wiped clean. Back to level one. Eventually, Massimo turned up to take our order with another bottle of wine for us. He wouldn't hear of me eating anything but the seafood pasta. According to him, it was a life-changing meal.

"Make it two," Gianluca said, handing off his menu.

When he left, I took another sip of wine and decided to try to repair the damage I'd caused. "Listen, I know it's normal to keep private things private, but I've never quite operated like that. I could see that you became sad when I asked about why you moved to Vernazza. To be very blunt, I can guess it had something to do with Allie, and it just won't work if you keep closing yourself off like that."

"What won't work? What are you trying to get at?"

His brows were furrowed in an accusatory way, like he assumed I thought this was a date or something. Believe me, *no one* would get that idea. It was more of a public execution by this point. Death by disdain.

"Well, it seems we'll be fixing up this bed and breakfast for a while, and after that, I plan on staying and working as the manager. I know if you had it your way, I'd come to work with my mouth taped shut and never even *look* at you, but I don't operate like that. I'd rather we become friends, and friends don't tiptoe around touchy subjects."

He looked away then, out past the door of the restaurant. I leaned back in my chair and sipped my wine, more than happy to give him the time he needed.

Eventually, he turned back to me, rolling the stem of the wine glass between his fingers.

"I moved back to Vernazza with Allie when her cancer was deemed terminal."

There was no lead-in, no argument about becoming friends.

I nodded, trying to keep my emotions from my face. Gianluca didn't want my pity. "Right."

He glanced away again, tugged a hand through his adorably tousled hair, and then turned back to me with a bit more determination behind his eyes. "I've gone on so long without talking about her in normal conversation. Most people are desperate to bring up any other subject, and I'm happy to oblige them."

"Well, maybe it's time for a change then, huh?"

Massimo swooped back over with two heaping platefuls

of seafood pasta. There were prawns and shrimp and clams all floating in creamy sauce over hand-rolled penne pasta. I took a hesitant bite, never one to go for shrimpy-looking food, but then I swear I did a little dance in my chair because of how good it tasted.

"I think I've died and gone to heaven," I said, using a bit of the focaccia bread to sop up the sauce.

Gianluca glanced up, presumably because he was hoping I had actually died. Then he just shook his head and went back to eating.

Joke's on you, pal. Bread only makes me stronger.

Chapter Sixteen

Gianluca

I KNEW GEORGIE had a plan worked out in that stubborn head of hers. She showed up every morning at the bed and breakfast with an unwavering smile and a level of optimism that grated on my nerves. Each day there was a new pre-planned topic.

"Tell me about fishing!"

"Have you hiked between the villages much?"

"What's this tool called?"

I wanted to find her insufferable, and I *had* in the beginning. She forced conversations that were uncomfortable, and she teased me about my hoarding habits. I thought it would make my life easier to keep her at arm's length, to maintain a safe distance. There was no need for small talk. We could work twice as fast without it.

We were working on clearing out one of the bedrooms one day. I was working in the closet, tossing things into a bin bag when I heard Georgie laughing. I turned around and she was rolling on the ground, having finally cracked, I thought. Good, better if she's away in a loony bin; I'd finish the renovations quicker.

"What is it?"

"It's...I..."

She couldn't even speak through the laughter, but she managed to hold up her hand. There was a worn photograph clutched between her fingers, and even from across the room, I knew what it was. I'd assumed I'd burned every image from that day years ago, but apparently Nonna had held on to a copy for herself.

"You were a *very* pretty little girl, Gianluca!" she said, wiping at her eyes.

I pushed to my feet and went over to snatch the photo out of her hands. Sure enough, a seven-year-old version of myself stared back at me, covered in makeup and wearing a dress. I'd lost a bet to Massimo and as retribution, I'd had to go around the village dressed up like that all day.

"Laugh all you want. I was probably prettier than you were."

That only made her laugh harder. Her cheeks were flushed and her eyes were pinched closed. She held her hand up to shield her smile, telling me she'd get ahold of herself in just a second.

I tried to fight the infectious sound of her laughter, to turn the spotlight on her and save a bit of my dignity.

"You'll get laugh lines if you keep that up."

She ignored me. "You were dressed like a GIRL. A tiny little girl with a bow and everything."

"Yeah, I can see them there, by your eyes."

"I think I even had that same dress!" she said through tears of laughter.

Eventually, the sound of her laughter was too hard to

fend off. A chuckle sort of erupted out of me like a knee-jerk reaction, and it made her eyes go round as saucers.

"Holy shit! Did you just laugh? Or is that just some strange new sound you make when you're brooding?"

I turned then, trying to put more distance between us. I went back to work, shoving things into the bin bag with a tad too much force. She stayed on the ground.

"I can't get up. Every time I blink, I see the picture. I'm afraid you've scarred me for life."

"Shame you'll have to lie there forever. I'll build a door for the cats so you'll have some company."

Her laughter filled the room, chipping away at my grumpy façade. She was experiencing that kind of laughter that hurts after a while, and even when we tried to go back to work, every time we'd meet each other's eyes, she'd start the whole process over again.

"Stop! Stop," she insisted with a light groan, pressing her hand to her stomach. "My stomach can't take it."

"You were the one looking at me," I pointed out.

"Right, well. You just stay on that side of the room facing away from me and I'll work over here."

I shook my head, working at wiping the hidden smile off my face.

• • •

"Why do you insist on wearing those overalls?"

She looked like an overgrown toddler in them.

She grinned and patted her hips. "They've got loads of pockets. I stuff candy in them in the morning."

I didn't reply, which I knew infuriated her.

"Do you want to know why I stuff candy in my pockets

in the mornings?"

"You fancy a bit of diabetes?"

"It's a reward system. Every time I get you to talk, I reward myself with a piece of chocolate."

• • •

"You're doing it again," I said.

"What?" she asked.

"Singing."

• • •

"GIANLUCA!"

I jerked up and slammed my head against the bottom of the sink.

"*Fuck.*"

"HURRYYY! HURRY!"

I pressed the heel of my hand to my head as I ran up the stairs to find Georgie cowering in the corner of the back bedroom, pointing to the opposite wall with a shaky finger.

"What? Jesus, what's wrong?"

"There's a tarantula over there! A massive one!"

I shuffled around a few boxes in the opposite corner, trying to find the so-called tarantula. Georgie hovered behind my back, pointing me in the right direction.

"Try that one," she whispered as if the spider was keyed into the sound of her voice.

I flipped it over and the spider scurried out.

It was a tiny thing, no bigger than a coin.

Georgie jumped a mile in the air and ran from the room. I caught the spider and released it outside. When I returned,

Georgie was walking back up the stairs with a pair of gloves that reached her elbows and the protective glasses I used when I was woodworking.

"You didn't kill it, did you?"

She seemed concerned, but with the glasses covering most of her face, I couldn't be sure.

"No, but that thing looked like it could scale walls. I'd lock my windows tonight if I were you."

• • •

"Pizza?" she asked near the end of one workday.

"I'll eat later."

She let out an exasperated sigh, heavy enough to ensure I heard it across the room. "I know if I bring back hot, cheesy pizza, you're going to silently plead with me to give you a piece."

"I've never done that."

She snorted. "Yesterday you practically salivated on my sandwich."

"That was drool from boredom. You were taking so long to eat it."

• • •

"What were you like as a child?"

I was down below the sink on my back, trying to repair a minor leak in the first-floor bathroom. At some point, Georgie had walked in to watch me.

"Shy. Stop hovering over me and go work."

She grinned, reached into her overalls for a piece of chocolate, and unwrapped it as she walked away.

Chapter Seventeen

Georgie

AFTER THE FIRST time we ate together at Massimo's restaurant, my relationship with Gianluca changed. We're talking *miniscule* amounts of change here, not even discernable to the naked eye, but change nonetheless. We continued working together clearing out the bed and breakfast. He always arrived before me, chipping away at the work so that by the time I arrived, he already had a task lined up for me. It was an unspoken agreement that I would stop off at The Blue Marlin and get us breakfast and tea, sometimes an espresso if I was really dragging. When Antonio found out I was working with Gianluca he stopped accepting my money, but I always left a fat tip.

When I arrived with our breakfast, Gianluca would take a break and we'd sit somewhere: on the floor of an empty bedroom, on top of dusty countertops in the bathrooms, on stacks of wood in the front foyer. At first, he'd pick a spot across the room from me, but over the last few weeks, I'd been able to coax him closer with flaky croissants. Just like the boat cats.

We'd talk about the progress we hoped to make that day. Well, I did most of the talking. I loved to tell him about the decor I envisioned for the rooms. Sometimes he'd humor me and offer up a hum, a grunt, a nod. It was all very caveman-esque, and without a translation guide, I was left in the dark. In general, I could guess he didn't much care what sort of bedding I wanted to buy for the guests.

We worked hard after breakfast, sometimes in the same room, sometimes on opposite sides of the building. I'd borrowed Katerina's spare stereo so I could play music in the background. We had to switch off on that too. Gianluca, as expected, quickly grew sick of my pop music, but I swore I saw him singing along to it one day. He denied it adamantly.

For lunch, I'd gently suggest (read: force) him to take another break and we'd head out into the square. There were so many restaurants and shops, but I liked having a light lunch and usually talked him into some sort of salad or veggies. He always snuck in a slice of pizza, though I had no clue where he put it. He was in such good shape; I figured he was the type who could eat whatever he wanted, especially while he was working like he did.

At the end of the fourth week, I realized we'd started sticking together for dinner as well, but every couple of days, I'd beg off with plans to meet Katerina.

"Haven't you just seen her yesterday?" he protested one day.

"Not since Saturday."

He frowned. "I was planning on taking you back to Massimo's restaurant. I'm craving seafood pasta."

"So go up and have some then."

"It's okay. I'll wait and we'll go tomorrow."

It took more than a month of us working together before I realized that Gianluca and I had eased into a friendship that suited us. He might have labeled his growing affinity toward me as a symptom of Stockholm syndrome, but I think a part of him (a part hidden deep down inside, probably near his bowels) had become genuinely accustomed to my company—which was good, because I wasn't going anywhere.

I loved Vernazza, and though I'd originally envisioned traveling all over Italy, I knew I wouldn't leave this corner any time soon. I was beginning to sink my roots in, and I felt comfortable. In my free time, I walked through all five villages, hiking from one to another when I felt up to the challenge. I swam in the ocean in the evenings and on the weekends. I did long laps back and forth along the shore and I could see a real change in my body because of it. My arms and legs were toned and my skin was golden. Every day, my hair had a few more sun streaks, and it was growing long.

Massimo, Katerina, and Gianluca were still my only true friends, but I stopped and chatted with Chiara whenever she was working in the hotel, and most of the locals nodded and smiled when I walked along the main road. They knew Gianluca and I were fixing up the bed and breakfast, and I think they were starting to see me as a worthy visitor, if not yet one of their own. I really felt it too, this sort of confidence in my place there. I wasn't one of the silly tourists stumbling out of the train station in the late morning, with their rigid visors and their chunky cameras hanging round their necks. I truly belonged. I knew the best spot to watch the sunset was right at the edge of the breaker, on the granite boulders, and I knew the best restaurant—Massimo's—wasn't in the main square, but up past the train station, in a part of Vernazza most visitors never even ventured.

Katerina was always quick to remind me to keep an eye out for good-looking blokes around the village, but it wasn't the most important thing on my agenda or anything. More accurately, it was just this constant longing in the back of my mind. It'd been ages since I'd had sex or even had a decent make-out session with a man, and I was starting to go a bit stir crazy.

One morning, I arrived with breakfast and called out to Gianluca to come down and eat, but he didn't answer. I dropped my things on the counter and took the stairs two at a time, following the sound of a hammer up to the top floor. I rounded the top of the stairs and froze, staring. I'd seen Gianluca shirtless in his villa, but that was during our war of words. Now in the context of our temporary peace, watching him tug the front of his shirt up to wipe his brow nearly made me trip over myself. My brain played the images in slow motion as if to safeguard my heart from bursting at the sight of his hard body in real time. He was facing me, wearing these low-slung jeans. His Calvin Klein underwear peeked out from the top, and from there it was nothing but tight, golden abs leading up to his toned chest.

I wanted to throw up. Cry. Stomp my feet.

He dropped his shirt, caught sight of me, and let loose a devastating smile.

"Morning G."

He'd taken to calling me G, which in that moment, nearly made me cry from the unfairness of it all.

"Here, you go," I croaked, dropping his coffee onto the floor and sort of toeing it toward him so I wouldn't have to step closer. He could definitely see how severely I was blushing. Most blokes would have smirked and spouted off something crap like, *Enjoying the view?,* but Gianluca wasn't like that. He was quietly confident, the kind of man who knew he was handsome, but didn't make a real show of it. His chocolate-brown hair was wavy and tousled because that's how it dried on its own. I knew because I'd asked him about it once. He didn't know what pomade was, and said he hadn't owned a bottle of gel since he'd quit his job in finance, which made me smile.

"Have you brought any of the croissants? Or did you end up eating both again, like yesterday?"

He was teasing me then with that smile of his, and it was the same teasing and the same smile I'd endured the day before, but for some reason that day my knees were weak and I was scared my voice would break if I tried to speak.

I nodded dumbly and turned on my heel, aware for the first time in months that I was maybe, possibly, *most likely* getting myself into real trouble. I gripped the railing on the stairs, annoyed with my shaking hands. Gianluca followed after me—for his croissant, of course—and I tried to push myself back into my comfort zone, back to the early days when we would just work together in silence.

"Are you all right? You look as if you've seen a ghost. Did that spider come back?"

"I'm fine," I squeaked, tearing open the brown paper sack and pushing it in his direction.

"None for you? I normally have to pry the bag from your fingers."

"No. Not hungry."

I'd been starved up until a few minutes ago.

Instead of accepting my answers and tucking into breakfast, Gianluca circled the front counter and came to stand in front of me.

"I don't buy it. You're never this quiet."

"You've only known me for a few weeks, remember?"

He narrowed his dark eyes, studying me.

"I've known you for nearly three months, but it only took a few days to learn that words are not something you lack."

"Yes, well, maybe I'm feeling a bit off today. Lay off, will you?"

He smiled. "What was it you said to me in Massimo's restaurant? That most people keep private things private, but you don't operate like that. Wasn't that it?"

I pinched my eyes closed, annoyed with him for having listened to me.

"C'mon, just get on with it so I can go back to eating my croissant."

"Okay fine, let's lay it out."

There were a hundred warning bells ringing in my head, but words spilled out of my mouth anyway.

"You know how I first came to Vernazza because I wanted to get out of London and meet new people, maybe find a nice Italian man, all that?"

He nodded.

"Well, I've been traveling for over three months and have yet to go on a date with a single decent bloke. And before you say anything, the blind dates Katerina and Massimo force me into don't count."

His eyes narrowed gently.

"At this point it's not even the relationships I'm missing. It's that I'm a bit..."

"Lonely?"

Sure, if lonely was a euphemism for desperate, horny, *burning up inside*.

"Yes, sort of."

He chewed a bite of croissant, mulling over my dilemma before turning back to me. "And you've worked out this list of all the things you want in a man, right? He's got to read and all? Specifically Dickens, if I remember?"

I blanched. "I didn't think you were listening to that conversation."

He rubbed the back of his neck and shrugged. "It's better, really, that you've got this list, because I nearly suggested that you and I—"

A little squeal escaped my mouth, like I'd swallowed a mouse and it desperately wanted out. I masked it with a loud, aggressive coughing fit and only stopped when I was sure he hadn't noticed my slip.

"We *what?*" I stammered.

He shook his head. "It's just that we really happen to get along—though I didn't think we would at first—and any guy would crawl on his hands and knees to spend this much time with a woman like you..."

Oh my god. Have I died?

"But, you've got this list a mile long of what you want in a boyfriend, and frankly I don't meet many of the requirements—I mean, I didn't make it even halfway into *Great Expectations*—and that's good, really. I don't quite feel ready for any sort of relationship right now. It's good to know that you and I can be friends without the other stuff getting in the way."

Our conversation was giving me emotional whiplash. One minute I was soaring on the back of a miraculous unicorn, so prepared to say, *YES! YES! TAKE ME TO BED, YOU LOVELY MAN!* and then in an instant, he'd slapped me across the face and stabbed my unicorn, reminding me that regardless of the feelings I'd developed while working on the B&B, he and I were a million miles away from having any kind of romantic relationship.

I recovered quite quickly though, so fast in fact that I was pleased with myself for how cool and calm I could be under such extreme circumstances. "Yes. I couldn't agree more."

He smiled, looking very relieved to find I wasn't pining for him. *Miserable arse.*

"I have an idea though," he continued. "You hate going on these double dates with Katerina and Massimo, but you're spending the rest of your husband-hunting time cooped up with me."

"So what are you saying?" I asked.

"What if we plan a beach trip instead? I can invite a few people and Massimo knows a ton of lads. You'll have all the men to choose from, with none of the pressure of a formal date."

I groaned. "I don't want everyone knowing what's going on though. I swear Katerina's already told half the village I'm trying to find a *lover*."

He grinned at my use of the word lover, but then quickly tried to hide it. "No, no. It'll just be a natural day at the beach with a few of our friends. If you happen to meet someone to smash, that's great."

"Thank you for the delicate phrasing, Gianluca."

"That's what you need isn't it? A proper lay?"

"I'll have you know that I have no problem in the bedding department. Males are practically clawing at each other to get to me."

"Those are just the boat cats trying to nick a bit more croissant from you."

"Could we please end this conversation?"

He leaned over the counter so I was forced to meet his

eyes. "It'll be fun, and if you don't meet any decent men, you can just hang out at the beach with me."

My stomach dipped.

"What a miserable afternoon that would be."

He grinned. I reluctantly agreed and we got to work planning it all out right then. We decided it would be best to cut off work early that Friday and go as soon as Katerina could close up shop.

He relayed the information to Massimo and I told Katerina. Everyone was excited about it, but the sad thing was, the closer it got to Friday, the more I hoped he and Massimo wouldn't find any decent men to invite. Why? Because if there weren't any good guys at the beach, that would mean I could stick close to Gianluca.

The moment I had that thought was the exact moment I became the most pathetic sap in the whole of Italy.

How do you say loser in Italian? Georgie bloody Archibald.

MY CRUSH ON Gianluca reminded me of the sort I used to have in grade school. It was a quiet, volatile sort of infatuation, the kind rooted mostly in fantasy and lifelike dreams. I'd wake up in my hotel room in a cold sweat and press my hand to the back of my mouth or adjust my twisted pajama bottoms and admonish myself. It was 2:14 AM. 3:37 AM. 1:03 AM. Gianluca wasn't in love with me, just like he hadn't been in love with me the night before. Sure, in my dream he'd just stripped me down to nothing and bent me like a pretzel, but in real life, he still hated me. Also, in real life, I was nowhere *near* flexible enough for that.

I knew my crush could have been chalked up to lust or it could have meant a whole lot more, but so much of it took place in my head that I couldn't be sure what was real and what was fiction. To me, Gianluca was the sun. My days revolved around him, but when I took a step back, it

141

felt so silly, like I was lusting after one of my brother's older friends. That had happened a few times growing up, and it had always ended the same. They'd laugh and nudge my shoulder or, god forbid, pat my head and tell me they thought I was a sweet girl, that one day, when I grew up, I'd find someone better suited for me.

I dreaded the moment Gianluca would pat my head with a sad little smile. *"How could you have been so silly as to have fallen in love with me? I told you I was unavailable. I told you I wasn't ready for a relationship, and even if I was ready, I wouldn't fall in love with you, Georgie. Come on, of course it couldn't be you."*

My brain could be quite cruel about it, so I tried not to mull over my silly crush too often. Besides, it was just that: *a crush*. Easy to tuck away and think about when I was back in my hotel room, reading by my window and staring up at his villa shining in the moonlight. I meant what I'd told him about it being the best piece of property in Vernazza. It sat up on top of the hill overlooking the square, close enough that I could see its tan paint and dark green shutters but far enough away that he could have a bit of peace and quiet. It was best for the tourists to keep him up there, as well—less chance of his grumpy energy spoiling their suppers.

There was only ever one light on at night: a hazy yellow glow from the top right window—his bedroom, I assumed.

I never talked about my feelings for Gianluca with Katerina, not after that night she'd informed me that every girl with a pulse had fancied him at one point or another. Even still, she was suspicious of me, especially when I informed her that Gianluca and I were planning the beach trip.

"You and *Gianluca?*"

I shrugged. "Yeah, it's no big deal."

"You guys have been spending a ton of time together, more than me and Massimo even."

"Which is why we want to go to the beach. We'll probably kill each other if we stay cooped up in that bed and breakfast for much longer."

"And you don't think it's weird that the first friend Luca has made in years happens to be a beautiful girl?"

I looked away. "No more weird than you and me becoming friends."

She barked out a laugh like I was being utterly ridiculous. "Let's just say I don't look like Gianluca when I take my shirt off."

I ignored her, but she continued.

"Will you be inviting boys?"

"He said he would invite some mates for me to get to know."

"And will he be inviting other girls? For himself?"

I bristled at the thought.

He never talked of bringing girls home, though I knew he wasn't the type to brag about that sort of thing. Still, that night I kept a ridiculously vigilant watch on his property, just in case. It wasn't until we met the group at the train station on Friday afternoon that Katerina's terrible prediction came true: I had my first glimpse of Gianluca with other girls. And it was all my fault.

Katerina and I walked up the stairs to the train station to meet the group and I was taken aback when I saw the rest of the group standing there on the landing. There was Massimo and Paolo standing with a guy they introduced as Matteo. He was one of Massimo's friends from La Spezia and he'd taken the train into the village to spend the day with us. I offered up a hello and tried to give him a bit of attention, but I was focused on the other half of the group, the side that included Gianluca and other girls.

I'd invited Chiara early on, anxious to spend some time with her outside the hotel's front lobby. Now, I wasn't sure it had been the best idea, especially since she'd taken the liberty of inviting a friend: a tall, lean Italian girl with enough confidence to outshine everyone within a hundred-mile radius.

She had amazing black hair, curled and full of body as she tossed her head back and laughed at something Gianluca said. The bloke was a lot of things, but he wasn't really a laugh. She was overdoing it.

Chiara turned to wave at me and it caught Gianluca's attention.

He turned over his shoulder, caught sight of me, and grinned. My heart did this little sputter thing and I thought for a second it'd stopped altogether.

"I was worried you were going to bail on us," he said, breaking off from the girls to come say hello. I'd been with him just that morning, but then I'd gone around to Katerina's shop so I could help her pick out a bikini.

I tilted my head toward Katerina. "Blame her. There was this lady in the shop who was lingering for ages as we tried to close up."

"She didn't even buy anything in the end! God, I hate customers like that."

Massimo tossed an arm around her and tugged her into his side. "Just call me next time. I'll buy any dress in the place if it means you can close up and come to the beach."

"Okay, but you have to wear it," she laughed.

Chiara and her friend came over to join the group and they introduced themselves to everyone. Her friend was called Adrianna and when she turned to smile at me, I realized I'd been giving her too much credit. She was pretty, of course she was, but the things I found exotic and exciting about her were the same things that made me exotic and exciting to Italian men. Everyone had something to offer and when I reached out to shake her hand, I did so with a genuine smile on my face. The day I got intimidated by another woman would be the day I was no longer Georgie Archibald.

She fired off something in Italian that I didn't understand. Gianluca leaned over to tell me she was joking about the train taking forever. I smiled up at him and then the crackly speakers announced a warning to stand back from the tracks.

"Everyone got their beach supplies?" I asked, adjusting the thin sarong over my shoulder.

Gianluca tapped my bulging straw bag. "It looks like you've got enough for an army," he teased.

"I like to be prepared."

"Is there extra sun cream in there for me?"

"I told you I didn't have much! You can't steal it all."

He grinned. "I'll bring you more tomorrow."

Katerina cut in after clearing her throat. "You two working on the weekends now?"

"Georgie insists on it."

Adrianna smirked. "I can think of something much better to do on Saturday mornings."

Gianluca leaned in close to my ear and whispered, "She's talking about sex…"

I narrowed my eyes. "Yeah, I got that, you fool."

He grinned wider and by then the queue for the train had gone down enough that we could hop on. I slid into a seat beside Katerina.

"Have you been keeping something from me?"

I leaned down in my bag for my sunglasses. "What do you mean?"

"It's just the way you two are acting. The flirting, it almost seems like…"

"We're friends?" I cut her off with a laugh. "I promise it's nothing. I mean, he was the one to suggest this trip so I could meet a few of Massimo's mates."

"So then why aren't you talking to Paolo and Matteo?"

"I will! We've only just gotten on the train. Once we get to the beach, I'll make a real effort to get to know them."

Her narrowed gaze told me she didn't believe what I was saying, but I shrugged off her concern and turned toward the window. The sea whipped past as we cut in and out of the cliffs. Waves crashed against the rocky shore, promising relief from the stuffy train car.

A part of me knew Katerina was right. I needed to give Paolo and Matteo a chance. I hadn't even really paid attention to Matteo when he'd first introduced himself on the platform. I decided to rectify that, and as we each finished renting our chairs and umbrellas on Monterosso's beach, I made sure to place my things right beside Matteo's. He smiled over at me before he reached up to tug off his shirt. He had an intricate, colorful tattoo that wrapped around his right shoulder. His light brown hair fell over his forehead and his accent was thick and charming as he asked if I'd been to Monterosso before.

"A ton. I come over to swim a few times a week."

"It shows," he said, dragging his gaze down my body. I still had my sarong covering my bikini, but I might as well have been naked from the way he took me in. It was a bit much, but at least it was good to know all my swimming hadn't been in vain.

"G, we're doing a run for drinks. You coming?"

Gianluca, Katerina, and Massimo were standing near the sidewalk, waiting for me to join them. The old seaside village of Monterosso stretched out behind them, flat and just as colorful as Vernazza.

"Uh...no." Matteo grinned wider as I continued, "You guys go on ahead."

I didn't wait to see Gianluca's reaction, instead turning back to the shore and smiling when Chiara dropped her things in the vacant chair beside mine. Paolo and Adrianna plopped down on the other side of her and we had a good group going, chatting and laughing as we lathered on sun cream beneath our umbrellas.

"You hardly even need it," Adrianna said, twisting in the sand and tipping her head toward the sun.

"I assure you, my pale English arse needs to be dipped in it."

Chiara laughed. "You're so tan now. *Sunkissed.* Not like when you first got here."

Exactly, and it would all go away if I burned myself to crisp. "Do my back, will you?"

Matteo nearly cut in then. I could see him out of the periphery of my eye, salivating at the idea of lathering me up.

Chiara grinned suggestively. "I think he can do it for you."

Oh bloody thanks, Chiara.

Matteo didn't even wait for my approval. He stepped forward and yanked the tube out of my hand, squeezing a bit of cream on his hand and dipping down beneath my umbrella. I nearly jumped out of skin when his hand hit my lower back, mostly because the cream was freezing cold against my skin.

He laughed. "Are you okay?"

"Yes, yes. Get on with it then," I teased.

In truth, it'd been ages since I'd had a man touch my bare skin. I forgot how nice it felt. I let my head fall forward as he brushed it up between my shoulder blades and was really getting into it when a giant ice chest slammed down into the sand an inch in front of my feet.

"Hey!"

I whipped my head up and glared at Gianluca, who was standing on the other side of the cooler with his hands propped on his hips. His head was tilted to the side and he had this funny little expression on his face.

"You almost done?" he asked. "I'm ready to swim."

"We've got enough wine and beer for days!" Katerina sang, twirling through the group with a bottle of wine in each of her hands. She looked like a goddess in her white cover-up. "Here, everyone drink up before we head into the ocean."

Oh god, I'd skipped lunch because we'd had such a late breakfast, and I knew dipping into wine this early in the day was a recipe for disaster, but then Katerina popped the cork and handed me a plastic cup nearly filled to the brim. The white wine smelled delicious and it was still chilled from the refrigerator in the shop. I took a tentative sip and nearly moaned with how good it tasted, so crisp and light.

Katerina clinked her plastic cup with mine. "Cheers!"

"Cheers!"

I tipped back the rest of my cup, too anxious to get in the water to bother with ladylike sips. I'd hardly finished when Gianluca peeled off his t-shirt and dropped it on my lap.

I stared down at it. "What? Haven't you got a chair of your own to clutter up?"

"Why bother? We can share. Now come on and show

me if all your swimming has paid off."

At some point Matteo had finished putting sun cream on my back, but I hadn't noticed. Gianluca had arrived and everyone else had sort of faded into the background. He turned and headed for the ocean and my gaze followed after him on its own accord. I'd caught glimpses of his abs when he'd wipe his brow during work, but this was different. This was Gianluca shirtless in black swim trunks. This was Gianluca with his tall frame and strong, muscular back. This was Gianluca turning to look over his shoulder and waving at me to join him in the water with a perfect dimpled smile. *Bloody hell.* He was so gorgeous I wanted to scream, and I wasn't the only one. Chiara and Adrianna were watching him with stars in their eyes as well, and then they turned to one another and then to me and we all sort of let out this exasperated laugh. At least I wasn't alone in my longing. As long as Gianluca had his shirt off, we would all suffer.

Chapter Nineteen

Georgie

THAT DAY ON the beach was a dream, a day that comes around once or twice in a lifetime. The group got along so well. Once it was clear that I wasn't really interested in Paolo or Matteo, they turned their sights on Chiara and Adrianna, and I was free to just hang out and enjoy the day.

We started in the water, swimming until our feet couldn't touch and then going a bit farther. I didn't get out until my fingers were pruned and my arms were sore. I headed back to shore and tugged my chair out from the beneath the umbrella so I could tip my head back, close my eyes, and enjoy the sunshine on my skin. It was so warm and lovely. I dug my toes into the sand and kept my eyes closed as long as I could, trying to soak the rays into my soul.

"Here, you little beach goddess."

Katerina held out another cup of wine for me and I didn't even pretend to resist this time. She pulled her chair out beside mine and we sat there, watching the boys in the water and enjoying the view in silence until we'd sipped the last few drops of wine.

"It's brilliant, isn't it? Life here?"

I nodded, staring out into the distance. Monterosso beach felt like a secluded gem. On one side, clear blue water extended to the horizon with Vernazza shining in the distance, and on the other side, high rocks plunged into the sea, seemingly separating Monterosso from the rest of the world. "It's not even fair."

She hummed. "Shame you didn't get on with Matteo. I really thought you'd appreciate his tattoos."

I grinned. "I did. Who doesn't love a man with tattoos?"

"Gianluca doesn't have any."

"How would you know? He might be hiding a little heart, inked right on his bum."

She laughed and I stood, reaching for her cup so I could refill them again. I'd assumed they'd gone overboard with the drinks, but we made clean work of the cooler, sipping on wine and beer like it was water. The boys went out for another drink run, and I turned over in my chair, laying out on my stomach as exhaustion settled into my bones.

I'd nearly nodded off by the time the boys returned, proud of themselves for gathering up supplies for a beach picnic. We pushed all the chairs together underneath the umbrellas and tucked into caprese salad, pizza slices, and even more wine. It was all magic: our day at the beach with the sun and the wine and the pizza so full of flavor it ruined all other pizza for me from that day on.

I stood and stretched, prepared to slip back into the water to work off my lunch, but then Paolo brought out a soccer ball from his bag and we started to kick it around on the sand, trying our best to create a little game of four on four. My sister-in-law was ace at soccer, and had played professionally most of her adult life. She'd taught me a few things, enough that I could just barely keep up with Massimo and Gianluca.

"Brilliant, Georgie!" Gianluca complimented when I managed to slip a ball past Paolo into our makeshift goals.

I accepted his high-five and smiled, proud of myself.

"You only managed that goal because you're wearing a bikini!" Paolo moaned. "It's not fair really. All the men are distracted."

Katerina laughed. "Whatever! You guys have your shirts off and you don't see us losing our minds over it."

Speak for yourself, Katerina.

"Gianluca, would you mind helping me?" Chiara asked, tugging on his arm to get him to show her how to kick the ball properly. It was a clever ploy to get his attention, pretending to be crap in soccer, but the more she kicked it around, the more I realized she wasn't putting on an act at all. Bit clumsy, that one.

I wanted to ask Gianluca to come swim again, but he had agreed to help her, walking off from the group so they could kick it back and forth between one another. My stomach twisted with jealousy and when she grabbed his arm and tossed her head back to laugh, I immediately regretted asking her along. I forced myself to turn away and head back into the water, but it was impossible to miss her chasing after him. From then on, Chiara hung on his every word. In the morning, she'd been paying attention to Paolo, but I suppose she'd seen an opening for Gianluca and jumped on it.

I was in a sour mood after that, and forced myself to start to collect the trash from our late lunch as a way to distract myself. Gianluca came over to help me. Chiara

153

followed.

"Oh, Georgie, you should go out and swim while you can. I can help clean up," Chiara said, nearly ripping the pizza box out of my hands.

I wasn't going to fight over who was going to clean up stale pepperonis, so I stepped back and let them have their moment together.

After that, they were nearly inseparable. When Gianluca swam out into the sea, Chiara followed all the way to the buoys. They bobbed along together out in the distance, swimming in place, probably getting on like two peas in a pod. I hoped a massive sea turtle would swim up and eat her whole.

"You okay?" Katerina asked as I took a long swig of wine directly from the bottle.

"*Perfetto!*" I replied with an edgy tone. "Let's go get some gelato."

I needed some time away from the group and Katerina was never one to turn down dessert in the middle of the day (*i.e. my favorite kind of person*).

Katerina pointed back to the sea as we walked away from the group. "Italians have a saying for times like this: *c'e maretta.*"

"And what does it mean?"

"Choppy sea. It's used when there is obvious tension between two people, and a storm could come at any time," she intoned with a devious smile.

I rolled my eyes at her. "Well I'm sorry to disappoint you, but the sea looks quite calm today."

"So you don't want to talk about it then?"

"About what?"

"The fact that Chiara seems to be Gianluca's shadow."

"I'd rather swallow my tongue."

154

She laughed. "Good, because that's boring and we have much better things to talk about."

"Like what?"

"Like whether or not we can find wine-flavored gelato."

• • •

By the time we made it back to the beach, I was as drunk as a clam. *Or was it happy as a clam?* Let's just say I was an inebriated mollusk having a good time. Katerina and I never found wine-flavored gelato, but we found more wine and the best chocolate gelato I'd ever had. I ordered three scoops in a waffle cone and lapped it up as quickly as I could, but it was no use. I'd ordered too much and most of it was melting down the sides. Katerina refused to help me eat it, instead standing a few feet away, pretending she didn't know me.

After I'd only managed to eat a quarter of it, I tossed it in a roadside bin and tried to clean my hands. It was really no use. Katerina wrapped her arm around mine and tugged me back toward the beach. I protested, calling for another bottle of wine, though I couldn't even remember how many glasses I'd had by that point.

We went back to the beach stickier and tipsier than when we'd left. As soon as our feet hit the sand, Massimo swept Katerina up and kissed her, complaining that we'd been gone too long. She squealed and batted his chest, swearing she'd shout if he didn't let her down. I gagged and complained that my gelato was nearly coming up just from watching the two of them.

"I swear, I can feel it in my throat."

"Oh Georgie! You just want in on the action, don't

you?" Katerina tried to turn it on me, to pull me into their hug, but I ran away before they could chase me down, now *actually* feeling my gelato coming up from the exertion.

I tried hard not to find Gianluca as we approached the group, but he was sitting in the chair *I'd* rented.

He glanced up as I approached, squinting his eyes to see me as I stood in the sun.

"Did you manage to get any of the gelato in your mouth?"

I frowned. "What do you mean?"

He pointed at my chest and I glanced down to see melted gelato on my chest and down the front of my white bikini top.

Chiara, who'd taken the chair beside Gianluca, laughed and handed me her water bottle. "Here, you want to wash it off?"

I brushed it away. "No thanks. I'm good."

It felt good to turn her down, like I was taking the world's smallest stand or something. Really, I was just ensuring that my bikini became permanently ruined. She and Gianluca exchanged an *isn't she a sad sap* glance and my blood boiled. Were they a full-on couple now? With their own little love language? Pathetic.

"We're all ready to head back," Adrianna said with a long moan. "We were just waiting for you two."

"What? Already? It's not even late."

Paolo moaned. "The sun is nearly set! We've been here all evening."

Crap. Had Katerina and I been gone that long? It had seemed as if we'd only sat at the beachside bar for a few minutes.

The group wouldn't listen to my protests. They packed their beach bags and headed back to the train. I tried to get

Gianluca's attention, but he wouldn't look at me. Chiara stuck close to him and I couldn't hear what they were talking about, which was probably for the best. Gianluca had been with women since his wife's death and though he swore he wasn't ready for a relationship, he seemed plenty capable of bedding Chiara. Utter bullshit if you ask me. I'd put the group together. I'd thought to bring Chiara along and had I known she *really* fancied Gianluca so much, I would never have thought of doing it.

Katerina sat by Massimo on the train ride back and Chiara stole the seat beside Gianluca, which left me sitting by Adrianna the bore. She plopped down in the seat and pulled out after-sun cream for her skin.

"Want some? Smells like vanilla."

"Nope."

Rule number one in any war: don't accept face cream from the enemy camp.

Gianluca and Chiara were seated in the row behind me, speaking Italian so fluidly it nearly made me cry. It was a travesty that Gianluca ever spoke anything *but* Italian. In English, his words were sharp and confident, but in Italian they were absolutely seductive. I adjusted the towel around my middle (my sarong had seemed much too complicated to put back on) and tried hard to block out the sounds of love spewing around me.

Chiara giggled and Adrianna sensed my unease.

"She really loves him, you know," she whispered so they couldn't hear.

I nodded, not keen on continuing the conversation.

"They've known each other *forever*. He used to summer here and they had a fling once when they were teenagers."

The longer she spoke, the tighter my stomach twisted. I let my head fall against the train's window and squeezed my eyes shut. Would it have been too much to ask for the train to derail and kill everyone on board but me and Gianluca?

He was supposed to go for me. If he ever wanted to date someone or bed someone, it was meant to be *me*, not Chiara. It just wasn't fair that the first amazing man I'd met in years didn't fancy me back. *Of course he doesn't, Georgie, you have gelato down your front and enough alcohol in your system to bring down a horse.*

I spent the remainder of the train ride dissecting what Chiara had that I didn't. She was Italian. She had lovely brown skin, quite a few shades darker than mine. Her black hair was long and silky. She wasn't supermodel gorgeous or anything, but she was pretty and quite kind. You know who else can be kind? Kidnappers who tell you they've got puppies and candy inside their windowless van. He really ought to be careful with her.

I groaned and my breath fogged up the glass. Gianluca was perfect though, beyond. Utterly annoyingly beautiful and smart and thoughtful. The man could have picked anyone (me!) and he'd gone for her! A colossal mistake if you ask me. *I should tell him what a mistake he's making,* I thought. *There aren't any puppies in that van, Gianluca, and if there are, they probably have rabies.*

"We're here," Adrianna said, bumping my shoulder and interrupting my emotional nosedive.

"Oh."

I stood, adjusting my towel and beach bag, and chanced a quick glance back at Gianluca. He was talking to Massimo with his back turned to me, but Chiara saw me looking. There was recognition in her eyes and I whipped back around, trailing after Adrianna off the train.

What a mess. The day had started out so brilliantly. I

was knackered from swimming and sunning and I knew I'd turned another shade darker. I'd had some of the best food in Italy and my muscles were sore from all my laps in the sea. But somewhere along the way, Gianluca had pulled away, distancing himself from me so he could make a real play for Chiara. God, he'd just gone on and on about how he wasn't ready for a relationship, and now he was flirting with her like that?!

My brain hurt from trying to think past my tipsy haze.

"That was wonderful," Katerina sang as our group stumbled out onto the platform. "We'll have to do it again before the summer's finished."

"Absolutely!" Chiara clapped.

"Count me in," Paolo said, tossing his soccer ball from one hand to another.

I stood off the side, wanting to get on with it. I only had a short walk back to my hotel room and I was sick of being around Gianluca and Chiara. If he was going to invite her back to his villa, I'd rather not be around for it.

"All right, well night everyone," I said, tipping an imaginary hat and turning on my heel. Katerina called after me, telling me to phone her as soon as I arrived home, but I didn't respond. She'd understand when I explained it to her in the morning.

My sandals slapped against the stairs on my way down from the train platform and when my feet hit the main road in Vernazza, I breathed a sigh of relief. It wasn't just Gianluca I was pining for, it was Italy. Even if he went off with Chiara, I still had this place with its golden light and its painted buildings and its overflowing abundance of sea and sky. I strolled down the road toward my hotel, slightly aware of my tipsy state. I wouldn't have walked around in London alone like this, but Vernazza was different.

Besides, my walk wasn't long and the sun hadn't completely set. Tourists were still out in hordes, buying up gelato and wine and finishing their dinners at a snail's pace. I was halfway home when a hand wrapped around my forearm and pulled back.

"Wait up, will you?"

Gianluca's voice sliced through the sounds of Vernazza and then the feel of his hand wrapped around my forearm sank in; he'd come after me.

"I've been calling your name."

"I didn't hear."

He grinned. "Which is why I had to plow through a family of five back there just to get to you."

He wasn't kidding. Just over his shoulder, two parents were glowering at us and brushing dirt off their son's shorts.

"Wait, did you really trample a child to catch me? That's so sweet—unless, wait have you really hurt him?"

He waved away my concern. "He came out of nowhere, really. He'll be okay."

I started laughing then, *really* laughing, and all the pent up rage from the last few hours just sort of faded away. Gianluca wasn't going home with Chiara.

"All right, well you've caught up to me. Now what?"

"I didn't want you walking home alone. It would be a shame if my only employee drunkenly drowned in the sea before the place even opens."

"Well I'm nearly halfway home, and I haven't even tripped. I'm not half as drunk as you think I am, although I'm less than a quarter as drunk as I should be."

"Good, then let's stop in here for a drink."

We just happened to be standing in front of a small restaurant close to the main square, and they just happened to have a small table available in a dark corner nearest the kitchen. It was noisy, but we huddled over our bottle of wine and replayed the day, picking our favorite parts and moaning about how annoying it'd been when Massimo and Katerina went into lover-mode.

"I invited the lads for you to get on with and you completely ignored them."

"Did I? I let one of them rub sun cream on my back for Christ's sake."

He laughed. "And then you proceeded to ignore him for the next eight hours."

"Well I must have been focusing on Katerina or something."

He shook his head, trying to hide his smirk. "And nice going inviting Chiara by the way," he said sarcastically. "I tried to pry myself away from her half a dozen times."

"What?! I thought a bigger group would be fun. And it didn't look like you seemed to mind all that much."

"She's been infatuated with me for years, and I haven't had the heart to set her straight. The signals bounce right off of her."

"Poor Gianluca has to deal with girls throwing themselves at his feet."

"Ha ha. You didn't even respond to Matteo half the time. The poor bloke has probably lost all his self-esteem thanks to you."

I moaned and tossed back another sip of wine. "All right, let's toss today in the bin. I swear next time you arrange for me to meet a decent bloke, I'll mount him right then and there in front of everyone."

He looked away and laughed.

We made our way through a shared dinner and another bottle of wine. We people-watched when we were tired of talking and teased each other at will. We were still in the restaurant when the owner wanted to close up shop, and he nearly had to pry us from our seats in the end. He shot me a smile and started rattling off to Gianluca in Italian. I had no clue what they were going on about, but as we strolled down the dark street toward my hotel, Gianluca insisted that it wasn't anything too serious.

"He said you were pretty and asked if he could take you out."

My mouth dropped. "What'd you say?!"

"That he'd have to get in the back of your very long line of suitors."

"Oh god, you didn't. Gianluca, that's embarrassing!"

"It's true isn't it?"

"You and Katerina are absolutely mad. People will think I'm this desperate Englishwoman."

"Well aren't you?"

I nearly smacked him after that, but he wrapped his arm around my shoulder and swore he was only kidding.

"I don't think I like you much anymore," I declared as we approached the outside of my hotel.

"Ah, c'mon. You don't mean that."

I was fumbling with the hotel door, trying to push when it clearly said *pull* just above the handle. He laughed and reached round me, pulling it open with a cheeky little smile.

"Now I positively hate you."

He moved around me and started to lead the way up the stairs.

"Wait. Where are you going?"

"I'm walking you home."

"I'm home."

"Not quite. I'm very thorough."

I laughed and brushed past him, and we started a sort of silly race to see who could get to the top of the stairs first. He reached out and grabbed my arm, yanking me back to try to stop me from getting there first.

It was all a bit ridiculous, fueled by the wine and sun. I wasn't quite drunk, but I was in a carefree little haze.

We continued stumbling up the stairs, making so much noise I knew I'd get a complaint about it in the morning.

"Shhhh, Gianluca!"

He pressed his face against my shoulder, trying to muffle the sound of his laughter. I tried to keep a straight face for the two of us, but it was like trying to stop falling dominoes. Nothing was really funny, but we were laughing anyway, gripping on to one another to keep from tipping over.

"Oh god, we'll have annoyed everyone by now. Hurry, my room is on the next landing."

"I can't believe you left me with Chiara all day," he moaned after me, ignoring my insistence that he lower his voice. Fortunately, Chiara didn't live at the hotel, so there was no danger of her overhearing him. "You could have saved me at some point."

"You two were glued together! Why do you think I left with Katerina? I thought you two were going to shag right there on the beach—y'know, stuff your crevices with sand and all that."

He started laughing again—apparently the idea of shagging Chiara was quite funny—and then I was nearly dragging him up the stairs to my hotel room door.

"Look, I've gotten us home safely," he said with a wide, proud smile once I'd unlocked the door.

Even like this, silly and disheveled, his beauty disarmed me.

"I'm sorry, what exactly was your contribution to the journey? You nearly knocked me down the stairs a dozen times."

He pushed open my door and tugged me in behind him. "No. No. I was *saving* you, keeping you from rolling down."

We were inside my room then. I closed the door and dropped my beach bag. He was still going on about how he'd saved me, laughing once I'd done a proper impression of him and Chiara at the beach, but then he turned the tables on me, teasing me about the gelato I'd spilled down my front. I tried to hit him with my towel to get him to stop, but he reached out and grabbed it from me. We fought for it, but he was stronger. One moment I was tugging it away from him and then he yanked it hard and I went flying to him. Still, I clung on to it. He pried my fingers from the towel one by one as I squealed and tried to keep hold of it.

It was all innocent until the precise moment it wasn't.

Until I realized I was pressed right up against him in nothing but my gelato-stained bikini.

Until I felt his hard chest rising and falling against mine.

Until I stopped trying to fight for the towel and tried to step back, but he was there, wrapping his hand around my waist and keeping me pressed against him. I could smell the sea and sand on him. His skin was warm, another shade darker from our day outside.

I focused on his sharp jaw as I spoke. "You win."

God, I could feel the tension in the air. It nearly sizzled from the way he held me like that, right up against him.

"Georgie," he breathed, right up against my ear.

A delicious shiver shot down my spine, and it was like

he'd put a spell on me. One word and I was under his control.

"Yes?"

"I really want some gelato."

I laughed and tried to shove away from him, but he held me still and bent low, pressing his face into the crook of my neck. "I haven't had any in a very long time."

He was so tall and muscled that I felt puny by comparison. I squeezed my eyes closed, trying to slow my heart. It was pounding so hard I knew he could feel it. How bloody embarrassing that I was on the brink of death from just being *near* him.

"Get some tomorrow, then," I offered, trying to lighten the mood.

"I want it now."

The real pain of the moment was that I couldn't tell if Gianluca was still playing around, teasing me as a friend would tease another friend, or if maybe, *possibly*...he wanted more. He was holding me so tight, I couldn't get a full breath.

"Gianluca?"

"Yes?"

"I can't breathe."

"Me neither," he whispered.

I smiled and tilted my head back, trying to get a good look at him, but it brought my face right up to his. I realized my mistake a second too late. Our lips were only a few inches apart. Gianluca reached up and cradled my head so I couldn't turn away. His fingers wound up into my hair and he tugged my head back even more so he had perfect access to bend down and...*holy.*

I stopped breathing. His mouth hovered over mine and he brushed his lips back and forth, testing the waters. My

165

stomach flipped and I made a little sound, a desperate plea. Then, *finally*...he sealed his mouth to mine.

Our lips melted together as he kissed me. Hard. Aggressive. Impatient. If kisses could kill, ours would have. It drew the life right out me. We were biting and teasing and sucking. Tilting our heads to get better access and still, I wanted more.

He was so sure of himself, holding me against him as he tilted my head back and demanded more, teasing his tongue with mine. We were done being patient. My fingers curled into his shirt and it wasn't enough. He hauled me up against his chest, yanking my hair back to expose my neck. Warmth spread between my legs as he blazed a trail of kisses from my chin to the top of my bikini and it still wasn't enough. We were frenzied. I tore at his shirt until finally he yanked it off. I brushed my palms down his toned chest and pressed up on my tiptoes to reach his mouth again.

We were ablaze, kissing and touching each other until his fingers found the knot behind my neck. My bikini top was hardly keeping us apart, but then it was gone, slipping down to the floor between us. I was naked from the waist up and Gianluca stared unabashedly down at me, his chocolate brown eyes searing across my skin like he'd never seen someone as beautiful as me, like he couldn't get *enough.*

He slid his big, masculine hand from my waist, up over my slender stomach to the underside of my right breast. He caressed my skin, testing his resolve. I squeezed my eyes closed and let my head fall back. Every nerve ending in my body was firing all at once, and then he slid his hand higher and brushed the center of his warm palm over my nipple. I swayed as a million tiny charges detonated all at once, and before I could recover, his mouth dropped to replace his hand. He kissed my breasts, cradling each in his hands. He stroked my nipples with his tongue and covered the aching flesh again and again until I was shaking in his arms, stringing my fingers through his thick hair to keep him there.

It felt like we were starved for each other, like I'd gone years abstaining from men like Gianluca, and now that he was there, holding me, touching me, kissing me passionately, my body didn't know how to respond. I wanted more. My leg wrapped up around him, his fingers dug into my small waist. I wanted him to guide us onto my unmade bed and show me what it would be like to feel the weight of him on top of me, to have him touch between my legs. The experience would surely kill whatever was left of me, yet I made no effort to stop him as he guided me backward.

The bed hit the backs of my thighs and he tipped us, keeping hold of me until my head hit the soft blankets. I was perched right at the end, about to scoot up when he wrapped his hands around my thighs and kept me there, right on the edge of the bed for him. I offered up a hoarse protest, trying to shift higher so he could join me on the bed, but he gave me a devious smirk and bent between my parted thighs.

His deft fingers wrapped around my bikini bottom and pulled it down my thighs, over my knees, and then, as if unwilling to finish the job, he left the material wrapped around one of my ankles, dropping to press his mouth to my hip. He soothed me with his hands, stilling me when I tried to twist out from beneath his hold, to conceal myself.

"*Tesoro*," he murmured. "Open your legs for me."

When he lowered his mouth and I realized he was all

but eye level with the most intimate part of me, I flushed with embarrassment.

"Gianluca…"

He shushed me as his mouth wandered lazily over my skin. His hands worked to part my thighs and then he slid one fingertip down the center of me. My back arched up off the bed and I dropped my hands, trying to anchor myself to reality. He groaned as my fingers dragged through his hair, tugging gently as his fingertip softly stroked up and down.

"So beautiful," he whispered, just before his lips pressed against my vulnerable flesh. At the same time, his finger stroked inside, deeper this time. The rhythm was maddening. I couldn't keep up. His finger stroked me so deftly I was quivering beneath his touch. His tongue lapped me up, and then he slid another finger inside, spreading me tenderly.

There was no reprieve from his tongue, the soft thrusts of his long fingers. He increased the pace and I twisted on the bed, clutching anything my hands could find: the crumpled sheets, the back of his neck, his broad shoulders.

He continued on and on, relentlessly stroking his tongue across my sensitive flesh, coaxing and demanding until I started to shake with pleasure, crying out and arching against his mouth. My fingers dug into his shoulders as I cried and gasped. His tongue and fingers continued on until the last residual wave of pleasure had gone. Even then, he fluttered kisses across my skin, soothed my thighs with his palms, and bathed me in gentle caresses.

There was no concept of time when we were in the dark hotel room. Gianluca slid up onto the bed beside me and twined his fingers through mine, bringing them up over our heads as he kissed me. I wasn't sure how far he would take it, but he drew the line, kissing me senseless without taking it a step further. I tried to reciprocate, to show him the same pleasure he'd shown me.

"There's time," he insisted, kissing my right cheek and then my left, nuzzling his nose against the crook of my neck.

I would have given him everything that night, but he didn't demand it. He kissed me until my lips were sore and my eyes fluttered closed. I was so thrilled to have him there beside me in bed, and yet I was sated enough that when exhaustion hit, I didn't try to fight it. He wrapped his arms around me from behind and scooted close.

"You should sleep."

I shook my head, though sleep was close on the horizon regardless. I didn't want the day to end. I fought hard against it, jerking awake every time I started to drift off. Gianluca kept talking to me, ensuring me that I could fall asleep, that he would stay. He whispered stories about Vernazza's history as a fishing village, how the castle on top of the hill was previously used as a lookout for pirate invasions. He kept switching in and out of Italian and by the time I finally drifted off, his accented words wrapped around me like a warm blanket.

When I woke up the next morning, my bed was empty, but the scent of Gianluca clung heavy in my bed.

Chapter Twenty

Gianluca

I STAYED WITH Georgie until she drifted off and then I lingered there in her bed, watching the rise and fall of her chest. She looked serene laying there, swollen red lips and pink cheeks and chestnut brown hair splayed out in every direction. She was tan from the top of her head down to where the sheet wrapped around her waist, and I wondered if she'd sunned without her top on. Women did it in Vernazza all the time, and I wouldn't put it past Georgie to join them. That kind of exhibitionism took a certain level of confidence, and Georgie wasn't lacking in that department.

I should have left as soon as she fell asleep, but for some reason, I felt compelled to stay. For a few inexplicable hours, I felt more comfortable down there in the village with her than I would have back in my refuge up the mountain. She could have woken up at any time and seen me there, watching over her like I was mad—and maybe I was, a little. My eyes followed the line of her frame slowly, from her chin down across her neck and smooth chest. I tried to memorize the dips and valleys of her body, the curve of her breasts.

She was an agonizing sort of beautiful, the kind that reached out and demanded everyone take notice. When she smiled, the world smiled with her, and more than once, I found myself wishing I was the man she deserved to be with, the one she had come to Italy to find.

I couldn't pretend I wasn't a mess. While I lay there with Georgie in her bed, I didn't watch the rise and fall of her breath because it was beautiful, but for the fact that it was reassuring. Despite their best efforts to pull me out of my desolation, most people in my life had eventually been conditioned to withdraw from me at the first sign of displeasure. They were practical adults who, after touching the hot stove once, learned to avoid it. But it had been different from the start with Georgie—her almost childlike indifference to my feelings and heedless disregard for my aggression had allowed her to come closer than anyone before her, even though I'd only known her for a short time. I didn't know whether or not that was a good thing.

I hovered my hand over her mouth and felt her exhales heat the center of my palm because I had to reassure myself that she was alive and well, young and healthy. The few times it seemed as though she'd stopped breathing, I'd lunged forward and felt for her breath. After the last time, I tugged my hand through my hair, angry with my fear. I stood and tugged on my shirt, felt around in the dark for my shoes, and let myself out of Georgie's hotel room without glancing back at her.

I took the dark path up to my villa and collapsed into my bed when I got there. I wanted to wake up and go back to the way it had been before I'd met Georgie. I wanted to rewind the last few months and erase the feeling of helplessness. I didn't want to fall for Georgie. I wanted to keep her at arm's length, and even though I'd taken every precaution to do that, it was too late. Even before we'd kissed, I'd known. I looked forward to working with her at the bed and breakfast too much. I waited for her to arrive each morning, busying myself with something that looked productive, but really, I counted away the seconds until I would hear the gentle creak of the hinges as she walked through the front door.

Allie's photo stared back at me from behind glass when I woke up the next morning. It had been taken on our wedding day and she was beaming right at the lens, picking up her heavy dress so she could spin around for me. I sat up in bed and dropped my feet to the ground, wiping sleep from my eyes and reaching out to turn the photo down. The metal frame clanked against my wooden night stand and I stood, craving distance.

I'd slept with women since Allie's death. They were one-night stands, meaningless flings I could justify as part of the basic needs of life, but this thing with Georgie already felt a lot like love. I *cared* about her, and because loving someone else, *wanting someone else,* wasn't an essential part of my existence, I began to feel, in a sense, that I was betraying Allie.

There's a difference between losing a loved one and losing a person you're *in love* with. To be in love with someone is to live inside them. Allie's breaths were my own and when she drew her last one, I was the one left gulping for air. I hadn't breathed deeply in five years.

• • •

I dragged my feet, heading to the bed and breakfast later that morning. I ate slowly, standing at my kitchen window and staring out at the sea. I found a few miscellaneous tasks I'd been putting off and told myself I couldn't leave the house until they were done. I took out the trash and put up the clean dishes. I watered the plants outside and took a long shower, standing under the spray until the temperature had long turned cold.

I tugged on an old pair of jeans and a soft t-shirt, punched my feet into work boots, and then finally set out down the path toward Vernazza's square.

Georgie was sitting outside the bed and breakfast, locked out. She was wearing a loose sundress and her hair fell in a relaxed braid down her back, glistening in the early morning light. She didn't notice me approach so for those few moments, I had an unhindered few of her profile as she reached into her brown paper sack and tore off a piece of croissant to feed one of the stray cats in the square.

"There," she said with a timid smile, offering the flaky bread out for the cat. "Now shoo before Gianluca finds out."

It didn't hesitate, accepting her offer and scurrying beneath one of the docked boats to eat in peace.

She clapped the crumbs off her hands and leaned forward, resting her head on her knees. Her timid smile lingered as she stared off into the distance, presumably thinking over our night. I wondered if she regretted it.

I didn't.

I'd wanted to. After all, it would have been so bloody easy if only I regretted it, but there was no question that I wanted Georgie.

"Now you won't be able to get rid of him," I said,

announcing my presence when I was still a few yards away.

She jumped and pressed a hand to her heart.

"Are you mad?! You just scared me half to death."

I smiled. "That's what you get for feeding the cats."

She stood and shook the dirt from her dress. "Oh please. There's global warming and hurricanes and droughts out there—in the grand scheme of things, what's the harm in me feeding some croissant to a chubby little cat?"

"I wonder how he got chubby."

She grinned. "He's got big bones. He's got common ancestors with lions and tigers, y'know."

"Sure it's not from the pastries you feed him every morning and the fish scraps he nicks every evening?"

"Never."

I was smiling then. Sometime between first spotting Georgie on the steps and coming within a few feet of her, the gloom and unease of my morning had lifted.

"It's about time you showed up, by the way. Your tea has gone cold and there was nothing I could do about it."

I accepted the cup she extended toward me and then reached into my pocket for the keys.

"Did you put a little honey in it?"

"More than a *little*. You always moan if I don't put enough in. Just admit you like your tea with loads of honey. Nobody will judge you."

I grinned, unlocked the door, and held it open for her. "I like my tea with loads of honey."

She curtsied as she passed, this little teasing move that made me laugh. "What a big man you are, admitting you've got a sweet tooth."

I tossed the keys onto the counter and tried a sip of the tea. It wasn't yet cold.

She came to stand beside me, dropped the brown paper

bag onto the counter, and tore it open. The smell of baked goods filled the air and we wasted no time tucking into each one, sharing the pastries we both liked.

"Gianluca?"

I tore off a piece of the almond croissant. "Hmm?"

"Should we discuss last night? It's okay if you'd rather not. It's just driving me a little crazy not knowing where we stand." She continued without giving me time to cut in. "And, of course I don't expect us to start going on proper dates or anything. *God*, that'd be so awkward, right? I was just wondering if the whole stripping me down to nothing and uhh...*doing what you did* was something I should expect to happen again or if we're just going to brush it under the rug and pretend like it never happened? I'm prepared to do either. I'm really very good at acting cool in situations like this. I won't make a big deal of it. I've had flings before. Granted, they were a few years back and the blokes weren't as handsome as you. Some of them might've had better personalities, but I never hung around to find out because they were just flings after al—"

"Georgie, you're doing that thing again, where you can't stop talking." Her eyes swept up to mine in shock. "I'm not any more prepared for a relationship than I was yesterday, or the day before." She opened her mouth to cut in, but I shook my head. She needed to listen for a change. "You've seen that I'm a mess, so I'm not going to make false promises to you, but last night was...last night was—"

"Brilliant."

I grinned. "Exactly. And I'm not going to stay away from you unless you want me to."

Her eyes went wide as saucers. "God no. Please don't stay away."

"You're not scared you're wasting your time? You're

beautiful, y'know. If you actually opened yourself up a bit, you could have any guy in Vernazza that fits your list."

She waved away my concern like it meant nothing to her. "I'd rather have this right now. This...no-strings-attached thing. Right? Just fun?"

"Right," I agreed.

We agreed on it, though there was really nothing to agree about except that we didn't want to stay away from each other. After that, we finished our breakfast in silence. She sipped her tea and I sipped mine. I'd feel her gaze on me and look over just as she turned away, back to the plaster wall in front of us. It was surprisingly funny—I'd spent weeks with Georgie and we'd never had a bit of silence between us; she ensured that. Her brain must have been working overtime to get a handle on our situation.

"All right then," she said, finishing off the last bit of croissant and tossing the bag in the bin by the door. "I'll start prepping the third-floor bedroom for paint and you'll be down in the first-floor bathroom, right? Fixing that leaky sink?"

I nodded. "Shouldn't take me long."

She smiled, tipped her head, and took the stairs up to the top floor. The sound of music spilled out after a few moments. I gathered up the tools I'd need for the job and carried them into the bathroom. It was a tight space, so I had to lay my things out in the hallway so I could lay down flat and get up inside the cupboard. I turned the faucet on and off, laid out my tools, and propped my hands on my hips, staring down at the project before me.

I flipped the light switch off and then on again, narrowed my eyes at the sink, and then turned on my heel, heading for the stairs.

I couldn't focus.

177

Not after last night.

I gripped the railing and took the stairs two at a time.

Georgie was already on the second-floor landing, shouting down for me.

"Gianluca! On second thought, the paint could probably wait—"

She didn't get the full sentence out before my lips were on hers. I hauled her body against mine and then turned, pushing her up against the wall of the stairwell. Her hands were in my hair, her hips were in line with mine, her tongue swept into my mouth, and she let out a tiny moan as I forced her legs up around my waist.

"I'm going mental," she said as I strung kisses down the side of her neck, unfastening the first two buttons of her dress.

She had on a lacy bra, so soft beneath the palm of my hand that it was likely driving both of us a little insane.

"Take it off. Please."

I yanked her dress down to her waist and then she tore at my t-shirt.

"This too."

I grinned and reached back to yank it off.

She dragged her palms down the center of my chest, admiring the marks she'd made.

"You're the most beautiful man I've ever seen."

I dropped my head to the crook of her neck and sighed. She smelled like jasmine and it was especially strong right there. I had one hand gripping her thigh, keeping her pinned against the wall, and my other hand found the strap of her bra. I slipped my finger beneath it, dragging the back of my knuckle from the top of her shoulder down past her collarbone. Her sharp intake of breath spurred me on, and I let the strap fall down her arm, revealing another few

178

inches of her supple curves.

She tried to press her chest against mine, to hide herself, but I pushed her shoulder back against the wall, locking my eyes with hers. Every emotion was right there for me to see. She was feeling vulnerable up against that wall, but I wouldn't let her shy away from this.

"Let me touch you," I said, skimming my finger pad across the top of her bra. Her chest quivered when I hit the center of her ribcage and I went back and forth two more times before gently pushing the material down, baring her nipple for me.

I'd seen her the night before. I'd lain there for hours staring at her, but the light was different here and she looked completely new again, so beautiful and smooth. I dropped my mouth and tasted her there, in love with her skin.

She gripped my hair, keeping my mouth on her. Her legs tightened around my waist and she moaned when I closed my teeth, gently biting her.

"Gianluca!"

I smirked and smoothed my palm over her breast, soothing the ache. Her bra fell away after I released the strap on her other shoulder, and then I moved us, carrying her back down to the first-floor landing and kicking the door open to the bedroom. She wrapped her arms around my neck, pressed her chest to mine, and kissed me senseless as I walked us back to the bed. We tumbled down onto the sheets and she laughed, adjusting so she wouldn't fall off the side.

I stood back, staring at her as she lay there topless with her brown wavy hair fanned out around her. Her body was every man's dream, like a petite hourglass. Her breasts filled my hands and her waist curved in, small and slender.

Her hips were enough to drive me wild, but I wanted to see all of her. I tore at the rest of the buttons on her dress and then she kicked it to the ground. She wore lacy blue underwear and the color complimented her tan.

"You look like you've been living on the beach," I said, dragging my hand up the inside of her leg. Her skin was the same everywhere: silky soft and demanding to be touched, caressed, *felt*.

She squirmed beneath me and I held her legs apart gently, pressing a kiss to her knee and then climbing higher, pushing my weight onto her. I knew my jeans scratched against her bare skin. We weren't on an even playing field, me still half-clothed, but I liked the advantage.

I kissed the inside of her knee and then her thigh, skimming my lips higher until her back arched off the bed. I kissed her hip, just over the lace, and then I pressed my mouth to the side of her bellybutton, not wanting to rush. We had this forgotten room with its boarded shutters and the creaky bed all day; we had forever.

But Georgie was squirming and moaning and I knew she needed release as badly as I did. I wanted to feel her come beneath me and I'd grant her that more than once before the morning was through. I skimmed my fingers along the top of her lacy underwear, dipping gently inside and then lower. With the lace there, it felt like we were trying to get away with a secret, me touching the very center of her. I pushed up onto my elbow to get a good look at her; once I saw her eyes pinched closed and her head thrown back, I brushed the heel of my palm across her and she brought her full bottom lip between her teeth, biting down to keep from crying out.

I smirked and repeated the movement, gently…gently

brushing the tip of my middle finger inside her.

Her hand shot up to my bicep, wrapping around and digging into my skin. She wanted me to feel what she was feeling, to return pieces of the sensations I was giving her. I wouldn't let her. I bent down and took her earlobe between my teeth, biting down gently as I slid the rest of my finger inside her. She was tight there and though she was the one moaning and brushing herself up against my palm, *I* was starting to unravel. I knew how good she felt and now, there was no going back. I'd be inside of her if it killed me.

"Gianluca," she begged, bringing me back to Earth.

I'd stilled there for too long, trying to catch hold of the moment, but she was impatient. I looked down and half growled, half moaned at the sight of my hand disappearing beneath her lace. Her legs had spread wide across the cream-colored sheets, no longer from my goading. No, she'd spread her legs herself, giving me all the signal I needed to keep going.

I rubbed circles there, faster and faster until she was breathing heavily and shaking beneath me. I could feel the waves starting to crash within her. They came gently and I circled with a steady rhythm, not so fast that she felt rushed, but enough to keep the sensations growing steadily, until the moment she finally came apart beneath me and I watched her shake and quiver, eyes pinched closed, hands clutching the sheets, head thrown back, and a delicious red flush covering her from chin to navel.

I gave her no time to recover. The last wave was still receding and I covered her with my body, dropping my mouth to hers and gliding my tongue past her lips. We were starved for each other, going at it like the world was ending in minutes, not millennia.

Georgie's porcelain hands found my jeans, and

hesitated there for only a moment before dipping inside and wrapping her hand around me. I tugged on her forearm to pull her back. I wasn't finished with her; I needed days of tasting and touching her before I'd let her make me come.

"Let me."

I stilled.

"Let me, please."

She pressed the words against my neck until there was no hope of resisting.

Her hand brushed up and down, tentative at first, and then she was the one directing the show, pushing my shoulders back so I fell against the bed with her climbing up on top of me. It was a terrible torture, Georgie straddling my hips, topless and playing the seductress.

"You know, men back in London spend hours in the gym every day trying to make their bodies look like yours."

Her small hands were everywhere: on my chest, my shoulders, down my abs, then, unzipping my jeans.

"You just work outside, soaking up the sun here in paradise. And did you know you smell like the sea? This fresh scent that nearly kills me every time I'm near you." She kept talking, but I couldn't process her words. With Georgie's hands on me, she might as well have been speaking Japanese.

"Gianluca—"

I stretched my hands up and cupped her breasts, cradling them in my palms and brushing my thumbs across her beaded nipples.

"Gianluca."

I hummed, finally moving my gaze up to her mouth. She was speaking, but I was staring at her lips. They were so lovely, full and swollen from our morning together.

"You're not listening!"

She brushed my hands away from her chest and I grinned. "I wasn't," I admitted. "Now I am."

"Have you got any condoms here? Maybe up in the top room?"

I nearly choked. "God no. My nonna lived here, Georgie. I doubt there's anything in these bedside drawers except dusty bibles."

She laughed, then looked at me hungrily with a mischievous grin.

"We'll just have to find other ways to occupy ourselves, then," she said, finally working my jeans off. "Maybe you could find one of those bibles and brush me up on the Old Testament?"

"I don't think that will work," I said, playing along with her game.

"And why is that?" she asked, wrapping her hands around me and bending down low with her mouth.

"Because," I rasped. "I have a feeling we're about to break a few commandments…"

She laughed, and then realizing the limitations of our lack of protection, her smile faded.

"There's no rush," I promised her. "Next time we'll come prepared, yes?"

I was already moving my hands back to her hips, gripping her there and rocking her gently back and forth on my lap. The feel of her lace was burning me from the inside out. What need was there for condoms? I meant what I'd said; there was no rush. I wanted to stretch out our time together, to revel in the possibilities. After all, it'd been five years since I'd felt a woman I loved on top of me.

Chapter Twenty-One

Georgie

GIANLUCA AND I were still in bed when Katerina showed up early for our lunch. I'd forgotten all about it (my mind was a bit occupied, *thank you*). After I'd ignored her calls the night before, I'd placated her with promises of a long lunch, but she'd shown up early, shouting my name into the quiet building.

"Oh shit," I hissed, leaping up off the bed and turning in circles for my clothes.

Gianluca propped himself up on his elbows on the bed, watching me flit around the room with an easy, sated smile.

The bastard.

"Get up! Get up!"

"Why?"

He hadn't heard her shouting, but when I explained that I was due to go to lunch with Katerina, he nearly choked.

"Georgie! Are you here?" Katerina shouted again right before I heard her feet hit the stairs.

Good. We had a few moments to gather ourselves before she realized we were together, alone, *naked* in the first-floor bedroom.

"Put some clothes on you, will you?!"

He was bloody distracting lying there in the buff. I'd have stood there, ogling his Adonic body all day if only Katerina hadn't interrupted. Would it have killed her to come round an hour late? Bit rude to show up on time if you ask me.

I hopped into my dress while also trying to hook on the back of my bra. Gianluca helped me, dropping a kiss to my spine, just between my shoulder blades, before turning to find his own clothes. He really would do me in with kisses like that. A girl can only handle so much romance in one day.

"Shit," he hissed. "My shirt is out on the stairs."

I'd forgotten we'd half undressed out there. I hissed at Gianluca to stay put until we were off. He frowned for a minute, I think a bit confused, but there was no time to explain. I winked, pulled open the bedroom door, and shouted up at Katerina.

"Kat! Where are you?!"

She stomped back down the stairs. "Where've you been?"

"Down here. Cleaning and all that."

She arched a brow. "Where's Gianluca? And why are there clothes on the stairs?"

"Oh, those clothes are old, his nonna's or something." I propped my hands on my hips, putting on a brilliant act. "And he's not here because he went off for building supplies. Well anyway, let's head off to lunch. I've worked up a big appetite this morning."

"Oh, has your work been especially hard this morning?"

I choked at her question. "Probably harder than it's been in a *long* time."

• • •

The decision to keep my love life private came naturally. Gianluca and I had no clue what was happening between us, so getting everyone else involved would only make things messier. The sheer volume of advice and warnings and skeptical glares would suck the fun right out of it. It was better this way, perhaps even a little more romantic that our affair was kept secret.

The next few days were an absolute dream. I woke up early and hiked or swam in the sea at Monterosso. Summer would start to fade soon, and I wanted to soak up the sun while I still could. After, I took my time showering and slipping into a loose sundress. I brushed out my long hair, not bothering with a hair dryer. The sea air ensured it dried with a lovely wave to it. I spritzed on a bit of perfume just at the base of my neck. Gianluca loved the smell of jasmine and I loved the feel of his stubble against my skin there. Once I'd finished, I popped round to The Blue Marlin, picked up our tea and pastries, chatted with the locals, and then met Gianluca at the bed and breakfast. Sometimes he was there before me—those were my favorite days. I loved turning the corner into the main square to see him sitting on the front step. Those few seconds when he didn't know I was there, when I could just *look* at him. It was hard to take him in all at once—he was too beautiful, inside and out. He'd sit with his elbows on his knees, seemingly lost in thought. He'd run his hand through his thick hair and stare off in the distance, but as I walked closer, he'd catch me there in the square and flash me a massive smile with his deep dimples. I swooned every time.

Some mornings we'd pretend to get to work, eating quickly and then departing to separate corners of the building. Now that we'd finally finished clearing the place out, restoration was coming along slowly but surely. Gianluca was doing a brilliant job of fixing all the electrical and plumbing issues, and I was working on painting and cleaning, sprucing up every inch of the place and getting everything in order for guests.

Those moments when we pretended to work never lasted long. I'd barely manage to lay blue tape around the trim of one of the walls upstairs and Gianluca would come up behind me, wrap his arms around my middle, and carry me down to the first-floor bedroom like I weighed nothing. I would put up a protest and moan about needing to work, but we both knew it was only an act. That small bedroom was quickly becoming heaven on Earth.

We'd spend hours exploring each other's bodies and slowly building on the day before, though we steered clear of the final act. It was Gianluca's doing. If I'd had it my way we would have christened every room in that bed and breakfast—and I wasn't sure why he insisted on waiting. He avoided the question whenever I asked. The first time we were alone together, we'd been without condoms, but the longer we waited, the more I suspected there was something else at play, almost like Gianluca was holding off on purpose. I hated it. This in between, where I could feel him *against* me but not *inside* me was prolonged torture. He was always the one to pump the brakes. I'd protest with an exasperated laugh, but he never listened. I knew he was as starved for that final act as I was. I mean, I felt him, touched him, *teased* him. The man had the constitution of a monk as far as I was concerned. And I know it sounds greedy. I mean, we were still there, in that bed and breakfast, memorizing every inch of each other's bodies, but it wasn't enough; I'd never wanted anything as much as I wanted to make love with Gianluca.

In the afternoons—after spending the morning in bed fooling around, but not quite doing the actual deed (*groan*)—we'd finally manage to get a bit of work done. Gianluca would take the train into La Spezia for supplies, or I'd pop around shops in Cinque Terre to get necessities for the guest rooms: new pillows, sheets, towels—we needed *everything*. I splurged on a few nice paintings to hang in the rooms and Gianluca balked until he saw them hung with the new light blue paint color.

"Gorgeous, right?"

He looked to me and smiled.

"I'm talking about the *paintings*, Gianluca."

"They're nice too," he replied with a cheeky grin.

After wrapping up our days together, I tried my best to keep my evenings open for Katerina. If I suddenly dropped off the face of the earth, she'd suspect something, so most nights we met up for dinner or drinks. One night, she insisted that Gianluca and Massimo join us. The four us were outside at Belforte, working our way through our second glasses of red wine as we waited for our dessert to arrive. Gianluca sat across from me beside Massimo and though we weren't talking, our legs were twined between the table. We were as close to one another as we could get in such a public setting.

"How are the repairs coming along at the bed and breakfast?" Katerina asked. "I took a peek inside the other day and it looks so close to being finished!"

"It's getting there," I said. "We settled on a name

189

finally: *Il Mare*. Simple. Gianluca says the place should be ready for guests in two weeks. I set up a little website over the weekend so we can start taking reservations."

"She's already got someone booked for a month from now," Gianluca said with a proud smile.

Katerina clapped. "No way! That's awesome, Georgie."

"There will still be work to do," he continued, "but I can do it during the day when the guests are out exploring."

"He wants to fix up that little balcony on the top floor, so the guests can use it."

Her brows perked up. "That'll be brilliant. I reckon they'll have a perfect view of the sea up there."

I know it's silly, but I was thrilled by the idea of Gianluca continuing to work at the bed and breakfast even after it was open for guests. I was eager to move in and start managing the place properly, but I didn't want our days to change. Right now it was easy. We didn't have to make plans or go on dates. I didn't have to linger by my mobile, eagerly awaiting his calls and texts. Every morning, I found him at the bed and breakfast, just like the day before. I didn't know what would happen once he finished up and truthfully, I didn't want to think about it. For the time being, our arrangement was working just fine.

"I've told Georgie she can go ahead and move her things into the first floor."

The plumbing and electrical were finished on the bottom floor. I'd painted the bedroom earlier in the week, trying to stick close to the original sunflower yellow, and I'd left the windows open for a few days to air out the fumes. The only thing left to do was gather my things and move to the opposite corner of the square.

"I'm excited to move out of that tiny hotel room."

Chiara had all but ignored me since our beach trip all

those days ago; it'd been painfully awkward to sidle past her in the mornings.

"That's awesome," Katerina said. "You'll have a real kitchen and living room."

"Well, it's technically for the guests, but I suppose I could hang out there when we haven't got any reservations."

She nodded and reached for her wine glass. "I think this calls for toast. I can't believe you got this moody bloke to fix that place up with you. It was long overdue." I laughed as she continued, "To Georgie!"

"To Georgie!" Massimo added.

I glanced across the table just as Gianluca lifted his glass. To them, he looked the same as always, but I saw the playfulness in his gaze as he lifted his glass for me, that little smirk playing on the edge of his mouth.

"To Georgie..."

"I think we ought to throw a party," Massimo suggested. "To celebrate."

"A party?" I shook my head. "No way! We've just spent weeks fixing the place up. I won't have people trash it just before we open."

Katerina perked up. "How about we do it up at Gianluca's villa! The weather is still perfect and we have to take advantage of it! We could keep everyone outside, and we don't have to invite loads of people, just a few friends. We could have a proper cookout and put on a bit of music. It's so far away from the square that no one would complain."

That actually sounded nice. The three of us turned toward Gianluca, hopeful. He didn't seem too keen on the idea, but I leaned forward and smiled. "C'mon, I think it'll be fun. We deserve to celebrate all of our *hard work*."

With our legs twined beneath the table and memories of our morning still fresh in his mind, I knew he'd caught my double entendre. He nodded and offered up a dimpled smirk aimed right at me.

"All right. Let's do it."

Chapter twenty-two

Gianluca

IN THE WEEKS leading up to the completion of the bed and breakfast, Georgie and I were busier than ever. I helped her move her things into the first-floor bedroom (she had accumulated a significantly greater number of shoes since that first day we carried her bags across the square) and she spent an entire day getting settled in. I was upstairs replacing a patch of crumbling plaster in the bathroom later that evening when she called my name to show me the finished look.

She'd completely transformed the dark, neglected room. The massive window on the right wall was flung open and there were no screens to dampen the moonlight spilling into the room. She'd replaced the old bedding with fluffy white pillows and soft blankets. Furniture was sparse and mismatched; she was using an old wooden stool as a nightstand, but she'd stacked a few paperbacks and set a vase of white hydrangeas on top of it. I'd brought her the flowers from the market that morning.

"It's already loads better than that tiny hotel room. This space feels like my own."

She was standing in the center of the room with a proud smile on her face.

"It's brilliant, right?"

I nodded and stuffed my hands into my pockets so I wouldn't be tempted to step forward and wrap them around her waist.

I wanted Georgie.

Constantly.

Thoughts of her kept me up at night. That body of hers was enough to tempt any man, but I'd pushed off sex, laying down an arbitrary line and telling myself I couldn't cross it. Georgie was more to me than a quick lay.

God, what utter bullshit.

If I was being honest with myself, I was scared shitless. I didn't want to push things too far with her, to get to a point where I felt vulnerable again. I tricked myself into thinking that our mornings spent in her bed were nothing to worry about. If we were just having a bit of fun, fooling around and slacking off on work, there was no need to digest it, to take stock of my growing feelings. I told myself if we weren't actually having sex, I was a safe man.

I was wrong.

• • •

One afternoon, Georgie and I were lying in her bed, taking our time waking up from an afternoon nap. Sunlight streamed in through her window, heating the room enough that climbing out of bed seemed impossible. I was on my back, staring up at the ceiling and drawing slow circles on Georgie's back. It was the first time we'd been in a bed to sleep and it felt strange to have our legs tangled together with our clothes on. It brought up feelings of guilt I tried hard to keep buried. Allie would have understood my need to have sex, but this intimacy, this lying in bed with Georgie just to be close to her was different. It would have broken Allie's heart.

"We *should* get up," I said.

"One more minute," she countered, her breath warm against my neck as she nestled another inch closer.

We'd agreed there would be no strings attached, but that wasn't really how strings worked. It was just a platitude uttered months ago, back when I didn't know what it felt like to lie with Georgie in my arms, to feel her fingers drag through my hair, to feel her soft breath drift across my chest. And her smile—being on the receiving end of one of Georgie's smiles was like feeling the summer sun as it breaks through the clouds.

I pushed the unsettling thoughts from my mind, kissed the top of her head, and sat up. I needed to get out of her bed.

"C'mon, I think we should skip out on work for the rest of the afternoon. I want to take you out on the water."

She blinked the sleep out of her eyes. "On the water? Like a boat?"

I grinned. "Exactly."

That was one of the other great things about being with Georgie in Vernazza: everything was new and exciting for her. There was something about leading her through fresh experiences, even if they had become routine for me, that allowed me to recapture some of the wonder I'd lost over the years.

My old fishing boat was bobbing lazily in the harbor with faded red paint and just room enough for two. Without waiting for instruction, Georgie jumped in, clinging to the low railing to steady herself.

I handed her two fishing poles and then stepped in after her. I kept waiting for her to complain. With her wealth, I was sure she'd been on a few boats in her lifetime, none of which resembled this old clunker.

"How far do we have to go until we can catch fish?"

I smiled. "We could fish here, but I'll take us out a little bit."

I turned on the loud motor and directed us out to sea. Georgie held down her sun hat and laughed as we started battling with the choppy water. I didn't take us out far, hardly a few yards beyond the breakwater. Vernazza sat behind us, the pastel buildings rimming Georgie on either side. She reached into the small bucket for a worm, slipped it onto the end of her hook, and grinned over me.

"I'll bet you didn't think I'd be able to manage that, did you?"

"You're full of surprises."

She spun her pole to the right and cast her line. It was a bit clumsy, but I was impressed she knew how to handle a fishing pole at all. I fixed my line and followed suit. For a while, we sat in silence out on the water, bobbing with the waves and enjoying the sounds of Vernazza in the distance.

A heavy gust of wind whipped up out of nowhere and nearly carried Georgie's hat off before she reached up and grabbed it.

"Sometimes I can't stand how windy it is here."

I shook my head. "Italians love the wind. We can even tell the weather by it."

"Really?"

196

I nodded, though she couldn't see; she was facing the water, checking her line and watching for fish.

"There are the warm winds from the Sahara called *scirocco,* and westerlies from Corcisa called *libeccio*. They pick up moisture from the sea and carry storms into the villages. When we feel those winds coming, we know to close up our windows and stay off the water."

"Hopefully we don't have those today."

I smiled. "We're in luck—we have the wind from the north, *la tramontana*. It affects life in Cinque Terre more than anything. *La tramontana* sweeps cool air down the Alps, across the sky, and clears the clouds and rain away. Kids go out to play and it's good for tourists."

"Well then that's the wind I like. What's it called again?"

"*La tramontana*."

"Right. *Tramontana*."

"Georgie, your line's moving."

"Oh! A fish!"

I laughed and helped her reel it in. It was only a small sea bass, but Georgie held it up, proud of herself.

"We'll cook it up for dinner, right? It will be heavenly with the fresh zucchini Katerina brought me earlier from Massimo's farm."

Her eyes were wide with hope, her cheeks flush and pink from the wind. She was grinning from ear to ear and holding the unlucky fish, waiting for my response.

"We'll need more than that for dinner," I said, pointing to the small creature.

She laughed and leaned forward to press a quick kiss to my mouth. "Well then, I suggest you work on catching one of your own 'cause I'm not sharing."

"OH BLOODY HELL. How much farther have we got?"

Katerina and I were still at the bottom of the hill that lead up to Gianluca's villa. We were lugging a case of wine, some bags from the market, and our clothes for the party. We'd managed to make it round the church just past the square before she threw up her hands and deemed the trek impossible.

"Katerina, we've only got to go up the hill. We can do it."

"We already have our hair done! I don't want to sweat so much my curls fall out."

It was chilly outside with heavy, fat clouds covering the sun.

"I don't think you need to worry about that. Here, give me the wine and you go on. I'll catch up to you."

It was finally the day of the party and I was so excited. Gianluca and I had worked endlessly the last few days to

199

get the bed and breakfast ready, so much so that we'd hardly had time for ourselves. I'd been running into La Spezia for supplies and decorations for the rooms. By the time I would arrive back, Gianluca was usually gone off getting building supplies or smack-dab in the middle of a project he couldn't step away from, like replacing the main light in the first-floor sitting room with a pretty vintage chandelier I'd found at a resale shop in La Spezia. By the time we were finished each day, I'd dismiss dinner in favor of a shower and early bedtime. I was exhausted but determined not to show it. It had been my idea to fix up the place, and I couldn't complain now, not when we were so close.

Our first guest was due to arrive in a two weeks: Taylor Dubrow from Seattle, Washington. We'd emailed over the last few days and she seemed very nice. She was staying on for a while and I'd already thrown together a care package for her filled with Cinque Terre must-haves: lemon candies, olive oil, and hand-rolled pasta. If I could have, I'd have put fresh baked focaccia inside of it as well, but I'd just have to take her to get some once she arrived.

"Looks like the rain isn't going to hold off," Katerina said, a few yards in front of me on the trail. "It'll be storming in no time."

I frowned.

We were due to cook outside and grill up a ton of fish, meat, and veggies. We'd have to cram ourselves into Gianluca's house if it rained and I knew he wouldn't like that. He'd told me as much the day before when I'd listed the people Katerina, Massimo, and I had invited.

"That's too many people."

"It's not even ten!"

"I'd have preferred it to be just you and me."

I'd grinned at that—any girl would—especially since it'd been days since we'd had a chance to be alone together. I swore to him it wouldn't be too many people, but it wasn't true. I'd left off the fact that Massimo had called round to a few pals in La Spezia. Ten people could easily double if they'd all agreed to attend. I grimaced at the thought, took a deep breath, and followed Katerina up the hill. I was determined to make it a fun night no matter what.

Gianluca and Massimo were waiting for us outside his villa, fixing up the grill and starting to heat the coals. They were using the second-floor balcony as a bit of protection from the rain; it was just enough space that Gianluca could still grill outside if it started pouring.

"You should have called for us," he said, rushing forward to relieve me of the wine and grocery bags. "I'd have come down and helped you carry all this."

I grinned. "We are independent ladies with large muscles, thank you very much."

He bent down in greeting and pecked my cheek, nothing too conspicuous since we were in front of Katerina and Massimo. They knew we'd become good friends, but I'd yet to tell Katerina we were fooling around as well. It wasn't like Gianluca had forbidden me from telling other people about us, but when I'd open my mouth to tell her, something would stop me, this little voice in the back of my head telling me to keep the relationship private. Maybe a part of me was a bit ashamed by the setup, but I stowed that thought away and replaced it with more likely ideas. I knew Katerina would pester me to make it official—*why buy the cow when you can get the milk for free* and all that—but truthfully, I didn't mind giving away my milk for free. And, to be perfectly clear, I hadn't yet given away *the whole carton*, but I hoped that would change tonight.

"Gianluca, did you invite Chiara tonight?" Katerina asked, waggling her brows for emphasis.

He frowned. "Why should I?"

I looked at the ground and pretended to be intrigued by a cactus growing up near the barbecue.

"Don't play coy. I just thought you two were really hitting it off when we went to the beach a while back."

"No. We're just friends."

I smiled, but then wiped it away when I remembered Katerina had a perfect line of sight to me.

"Right. Okay."

Massimo laughed. "Don't pester him, Katerina. If he wants to live the life of a celibate monk, we'll let him. Good news is, I invited a few lads Georgie might enjoy chatting with—"

"Oh! You shouldn't have done that. I'm perfectly happy to just hang out with you guys tonight."

Katerina frowned. "What happened to looking for a relationship—a '*proper Italian man*'?"

I croaked out a laugh. "Did I say that? Hmm, well if you'll recall, my whole reason for fleeing London was to escape from matchmaking. There's just too much pressure involved."

Gianluca nodded. "Right, so then we won't concern ourselves with all that. Everyone will be here in a few minutes, so let's worry about all the vegetables that still need to be chopped up."

I grinned, happy for the change in subject. "I'll do it."

If Katerina and Massimo were suspicious of Gianluca and me, they didn't press it. Katerina and I slipped into the kitchen and dropped our things on the broad wooden table. I wasn't ready to change into my party clothes, but I reached into my bag and pulled out my dress so it wouldn't wrinkle. It was fabulous, with little straps over the shoulders and a short skirt. The thin material was light blue, nearly white, and even though it wasn't practical for the cool evening, I knew it would look brilliant with my tan.

Katerina had been inside Gianluca's villa more than I had, so she flitted around the kitchen, pulling out cutting boards and knives for us. I washed all the vegetables in the sink, scrubbing off the rich dirt from Massimo's farm. The zucchini still had the giant yellow flowers on the end. The peppers were massive and misshapen, not like the aesthetically curated ones you get at shops in England.

"Hey! You're supposed to be chopping, not eating."

I winked over at Katerina. "Just doing a quality check."

"Mmhmm," she hummed, stepping over and opening her mouth for me. I slipped her a slice of red pepper and she grinned while she chewed.

"I think we should set these aside and eat them raw. They're so good as they are."

She nodded. "I agree, but we can take everything else out to Gianluca. The grill should be hot by now and there's just enough time to change and fix our makeup before guests start to arrive."

We'd only been inside for a few minutes, but by the time we carried the food out for the boys to grill, the sky had already darkened another shade of navy blue. Swirling clouds gathered over the sea and though the sun wasn't due to set for another few hours, it already looked like night outside.

"I hope everyone still makes it," I said, handing off the bowl of raw vegetables to Gianluca.

A massive gust of wind whipped up around the villa just then, forcing a few strands of my hair across my face.

Gianluca leaned over and pulled them away, grinning down at me.

"Looks like I might get my wish after all."

"What's that?" Katerina asked.

For a moment I'd forgotten we weren't alone.

Gianluca straightened up and took a step back from me. "I told Georgie I would have preferred a smaller party, just the four of us."

"No shock there," she snorted and turned back for the villa. "Come on, Georgie, let's go freshen up."

Gianluca's villa was ancient, and though I could tell he'd worked hard to restore it, there were still features that spoke to its age, such as the worn wooden floors and white plaster walls. Most of the rooms on the first floor were lit naturally by the massive windows. Unlike the windows I had in my hotel and in the bed and breakfast, there was glass in these, allowing for a bit of the dreary light to enter without any of the strong winds.

"Let's flip a light on in here, shall we?"

Katerina reached around for a light switch in the living room and then a soft yellow chandelier illuminated the space. It was beautiful—the entire place was really. The first floor had a massive kitchen that opened out to the living room. A staircase led up to a second story, where I assumed Gianluca had his bedroom, but Katerina and I stayed away from it. I didn't want to invade his space. Gianluca and I were getting closer, but at times he still felt like an absolute stranger to me. In all the weeks we'd been together, he'd never once invited me up to his villa. I knew it was because we had the bed and breakfast. It was just easier to be together there, but still, there were sizeable chunks of Gianluca's life that he kept hidden away. Whether or not it was on purpose, I couldn't tell.

"Georgie?" Katerina called from the doorway of the bathroom down the hall past the stairs. "You coming?"

I'd been standing at the base of the staircase staring up into the darkness above.

"Oh. Yeah, let me grab my stuff."

The ground-floor bathroom was big enough that Katerina and I could both get ready without feeling too cramped. She fixed my hair, untangling it so it fell down my back in loose waves. My dress didn't allow for a bra and most of my back was exposed to the silky strands. I shivered at the sensation and met Katerina's eyes in the mirror.

She grinned. "You look beautiful."

"Thank you."

I stayed in there with her as she fixed her makeup, and then she turned to me. "You hardly ever wear any since you don't need it, but for fun, want to add just a little bit on for the party?"

I stood with my back to the mirror and let her have her way. She promised she wasn't using a heavy hand, and when I spun around, I grinned. She was brilliant with makeup and she'd turned my tan complexion up another notch. My eyelids were covered with shimmery eye shadow. It was subtle, but it made my eyes pop, turning their dull brown color to an alluring caramel.

By the time we'd finished, there were voices out in the courtyard. Paolo and Matteo had arrived with two women I'd never seen before. Their small group gathered around Massimo and Gianluca, the *real* stars of the party, and after we'd said our hellos, Katerina and I flitted around the courtyard ensuring everyone had a drink in hand. I'd just finished handing off a beer to Paolo when Gianluca caught my eye. His brow arched as he scanned down my dress, and I didn't miss the heat in his eyes as he smirked and turned away.

A few more guests arrived, including more beautiful women with dark hair and names I couldn't remember once they'd said them. I laughed, unsurprised that they had all braved the steep ascent in volatile weather for a crack at the elusive Gianluca. Everyone seemed so comfortable with one another, going around and laying on double kisses and big hugs. I felt a little out of place as everyone fell into spoken Italian. Even Katerina knew a bit, loads more than I did at least, and I felt bad having to cut in and ask people to translate all the time. After pretending to get on with a bit of the conversation, I went back into the kitchen to prepare a charcuterie board for everyone to munch on while the meat cooked. I piled cheeses, grapes, almonds, slices of flaky bread, and some olives I'd picked up from the shop next door to Katerina's. Everyone moaned in thanks as I set it on the small antique table in the courtyard.

The group lingered around Gianluca and the cooking meat, and though I wanted to go over and sidle up beside him, I made a point to keep my distance. I didn't want him to think I couldn't fend for myself at a party. I kept myself busy refilling the bread and olives when they were in danger of running low. I was laying out a bit more bread when one of the Italian women came to stand beside me. She was the tallest of the bunch, long limbed and gorgeous. She stood nearly a foot taller than me, and I found myself straightening my shoulders before realizing how silly that was.

"How did you come to know Gianluca?" she asked, sliding her gaze down my dress when she thought I wasn't looking.

"I met him through Katerina."

She nodded, seemingly pleased with the answer.

"Are you a friend of his?" I asked.

"You must not know him very well to think he keeps *friends* besides Massimo and Katerina."

I laughed. "Very true."

I glanced over and watched him take a long sip of his beer and then grin over at Massimo.

"I've only ever been around him a few times and I've never seen him as happy as he is tonight."

It was true; he was getting on well with the group. I glanced back to the woman and smiled, becoming aware for the first time that her English was good, much better than a few of the other guests I'd spoken with that night.

"Your English is fantastic, by the way. Have you taken courses on it?"

She grinned. "My boyfriend is English. I knew two, maybe three words before we met, but I learned for him."

"So romantic."

She shrugged and reached down for a few olives, but I could see the wide smile she was trying to conceal. "It's astonishing, the things we do for love, yes?"

Like completely redoing a bed and breakfast just to spend time with someone?

I sighed and nodded before turning away. I needed more wine and I'd left my glass in the kitchen. I excused myself and promised to find her later.

A bolt of lightning split the horizon as I stepped into Gianluca's house, and the following clap of thunder concealed the sound of him coming up behind me. His hand wrapped around my elbow and he tugged me around the corner into the abandoned hallway.

"This is quite a dress," he said, hauling me up against the wall and pushing his body flush against mine. His hand strung up into my hair and he bent down to press a slow kiss to my lips. "Shame I'll have to ruin it later."

"*Gianluca*," I murmured just before he bent down and pressed another kiss to my lips. One hand kept my face angled to him and the other dragged down my dress, caressing my breast through the thin material. I caught his primal groan as he cradled it, feeling the weight in his hand.

I flushed, aware of everyone outside as he fingered a strap and dragged it down my shoulder. His mouth left mine and then he bent lower, tasting and teasing his way down my chest, dropping even lower until his half-parted lips brushed across my breast. I pressed into him as his tongue dragged across my nipple.

Lust raced down my spine, settling like a warm kiss between my legs. My fingers were in his hair, keeping his mouth on me even as voices spilled into the kitchen. We were so close to being caught and yet I wasn't going to be the one to pull away, to insist that we stop.

I arched into him, quivering in his arms just as the voices grew louder. They were in the kitchen, looking for wine, and I was lost just on the other side of the wall. My eyes flew open and Gianluca stood up, repositioning my strap and pressing one last slow kiss to my lips before pushing off the wall and heading back outside to tend the grill.

I stood there immobile, my rapid pulse pumping as though I'd just run a hundred miles. Then someone rounded the corner—the woman who'd asked me how I knew Gianluca. She smiled as she passed me in the hallway and I could tell by the gleam in her eye that she guessed something had just happened.

"Oh, is that where the bathroom is?" I croaked, pointing

down the hallway. "I was just looking for it."

She narrowed her eyes, not quite believing me. "Yeah. You can go on ahead. I'll wait."

I didn't bother arguing. I scurried down the hallway and locked myself inside. I turned to the mirror and caught sight of my reflection. Gianluca's assault in the hallway was written across my features: wide eyes, flushed cheeks, and red marks marring my tan chest. I leaned down and turned on the faucet, wishing I could splash a bit of cold water on my face without ruining my makeup. Instead, I settled on washing my hands and taking a few deep breaths, trying to calm myself before I returned outside.

Everyone was where I'd left them a few minutes earlier, though a few more party guests had arrived. There was still a crowd of people around Gianluca, mostly women, and I couldn't really blame them. In his dark jeans and black button-down rolled to his elbows, he was a true fantasy. Tall and tan, perfect white smile, and hair thick enough to hold on to when he bent to kiss a path down to—

"Georgie, you good?"

I swallowed and turned my attention back to the group I'd come to stand with: Paolo, Massimo, and Katerina. They were going on about playing another game of footie on the beach, but I couldn't bring myself to contribute. Gianluca was across the courtyard with so much attention pinned to him I doubted he even remembered I existed. He looked statuesque in the deep, contrasting light of the oncoming storm. On one hand, I appreciated my unfettered view of him afar. It was a rare occurrence that he and I were together and not close, but this was getting to be too much. The girls around him were beautiful and speaking Italian so fast I had no chance of picking up the occasional word to clue me in on the subject of the conversation, but their body language translated clearly into *any* language.

Fortunately, a few minutes later, the meat was done and the heavy clouds had settled right over Gianluca's villa. We helped carry platters of meat and fish into his kitchen just before the first fat raindrops started to fall.

"*Al chiuso!* Inside everyone!" Massimo shouted.

It was a frenzy of laughter and shouts as we carried in all the food and drinks from outside. I barely managed to get in before the rain hit, but a few of the other guests weren't so lucky.

"Let's eat," Gianluca said from the kitchen with a proud smile.

I wasn't used to seeing him like this, smiling and happy around so many people. The Gianluca I knew was so used to staying out of the limelight. Now, he was helping divide up the food, making sure everyone got enough to eat. I lingered by the living room window, watching the rain come down in sheets so thick I couldn't see past the edge of the cliff.

"Here."

A plate of food slid into my line of sight and I glanced up to see Gianluca beside me with an amused smile.

"I'm not really hungry."

He eyed the glass of wine in my hand. "You should eat a little anyway. It's good."

I accepted the plate, but didn't take a bite. My stomach was in knots. The party was supposed to be fun, but I hadn't properly thought it through. In the months since we'd started to redo the bed and breakfast, Gianluca and I had lived in our own private world. Selfishly, I realized the only reason our arrangement had been working was because I'd had him all to myself. Now, it felt like I was sharing Gianluca at this party, on top of having to pretend we were just friends—it was throwing me for a loop.

"You've kept your distance tonight."

My gaze swept up to find Gianluca still standing near me. I thought he'd wandered back into the kitchen after handing me my plate. "*Me?*"

"I kept hoping you'd come talk to me while I grilled."

I laughed bitterly. "I'm not one for queues."

He nodded. "I didn't peg you as the jealous type."

"I'm *not*."

In in a matter of seconds, my mood took a nosedive. I was angry with him for teasing me and I was angry with myself for getting worked up about it.

I shoved the plate of food back at him and turned to find Katerina. She was sitting in the kitchen, at the island with Massimo, Matteo, and Paolo. I forced my way into the group and found a seat beside Katerina. She asked if I was okay and I plastered on a fake smile. This was all new territory for me. I was usually the life of the party, the girl always down for a laugh. Now, I was moody and quiet. It was like Gianluca and I had completely switched roles for the night.

Even though I'd put distance between us, I couldn't help stealing quick glances at him. I was still helpless against the pull he had over me. He stayed in the living room for a while, and I couldn't turn over my shoulder to get a look at him, but I heard his voice over everyone else's. Each of his words in Italian spun a thin strand around my neck, all combining to slowly suffocate me. Eventually, he came to join the group at the island, diagonal from where I sat.

One of the Italian girls had found his stereo and put on music. A deck of cards appeared and the alcohol continued to flow. Meanwhile, I sipped my wine, studying Gianluca over the rim of the glass. He didn't seem as pensive as I was, instead appearing rather content with the idea of all these people in his house.

I thought he wanted it to be just the four of us.

Why was he enjoying himself so much?

Then he caught me staring and before I could turn away, he unleashed a seductive smile and tilted his head to the living room where people had started to dance playfully.

He edged around the group and I followed after him, not yet sure if I was ready to let go of my anger, but too curious to turn him down. He reached for my glass and set it down on a side table, taking my hand in his and pulling me close.

There were enough people there that we didn't stand out, but the dancing was different from what we did back in England. There, men sort of flopped around and tried desperately to look like they knew what they were doing. This was different. Gianluca radiated an effortless rhythm. He was so confident that when he pulled me into him, I melted.

"Are you still upset with me?" he asked, ensuring that my hips were aligned with his.

I was burning up, on the edge of giving in when he bent his head and whispered against my ear.

"Don't be, *bella…tesoro…luce dei miei occhi…*"

He was coaxing me out of my sour mood, gently teasing me with Italian pet names. *Lovely, darling…* Before I could ask what the last phrase meant, he pulled back and met my gaze.

"Light of my eyes."

I groaned and rolled my eyes, feigning annoyance. Still, every single ounce of anger I'd held was gone.

"I was never really upset," I started.

He took my hand and spun me around, then pulled me back close, rocking his hips with mine. "No? You've been punishing me for the last hour."

"Maybe you deserved it a little bit."

He laughed and then his gaze dropped to my lips, his smile faded, and I could tell he wanted to kiss me. God, we were on the verge of making a real show of it in front of everyone, but then a clap of thunder sounded again, directly over the villa, and all at once we were plunged into darkness.

"*Merda.*"

Chapter Twenty-Four

Georgie

GIANLUCA ROOTED AROUND the haphazardly organized drawers in his kitchen for candles and we helped spread them around the first floor, but it was hardly enough to illuminate the living room. The rain wasn't supposed to let up until morning and Gianluca refused to send anyone home in the storm. The path down to the square would be muddy and dangerous even for sober people, and most were far from it. It was decided that no one would leave until the morning.

There were a dozen of us sharing four candles that were quickly burning low. Gianluca promised the guest bedroom to Massimo and Katerina, and then Paolo claimed the couch in an office upstairs. Everyone else was relegated to the first floor. Gianluca took a flickering candle and ran around upstairs, collecting pillows and blankets for everyone. I helped him, holding my arms out for him so he could load me down with supplies.

"Should I sleep—"

"You'll stay in my room," he answered before I could even get the question out.

Right. Okay.

In the light of day, everyone in the party would have noticed if I went off with Gianluca, but in this hectic setting, it was all too confusing to keep track of anyone in particular. Most everyone was drunk and getting drunker by the minute. The lights were out and the music was dead, but they were happy to sit in a circle in the dark, chatting and drinking. There were pallets set up on the floor as if meant for a massive orgy, but really it was more of an adult slumber party. Katerina and Massimo quietly stole off to their room upstairs, and Paolo followed suit as the candles dwindled even more, millimeters from going out.

I collected the few dishes I could find and cleaned up the kitchen so we wouldn't wake up to a massive mess. Gianluca was helping me when he suddenly cursed.

Apparently, he'd been showing everyone pictures of the B&B on his cell phone earlier and had left it somewhere outside during the retreat from the storm. The raindrops were still coming down in droves.

"Oh god, it will have been drenched by now."

He told me to stay put, but I could see that he was having trouble finding it in the darkness, so I followed him out. I was completely soaked within seconds. The rain was relentless, pelting my skin like pellets. My shoes stuck in the mud and another clap of thunder forced the hair on the back of my neck to stand.

"Georgie, go back inside!"

I didn't listen; I tilted my head to the sky and let the rain pour down on me. There was no sense in rushing now. My dress was fully saturated and sticking to me like a second skin. I could see the heart of the storm roiling over the ocean, riling the waves and sparking the air with a palpable charge. I shivered and moved toward the door just as Gianluca found the phone under the grill's crumpled canvas cover.

By the time we stepped back inside, two of the four candles had gone out and I had to squint in the darkness to see the kitchen. I slipped out of my shoes, wary of tracking mud through his house. The party in the living room was still going strong despite the circumstances. Matteo was trying to convince the others to play a round of strip poker.

"We won't be able to see anything anyway! I could be naked right now!" he insisted with a laugh.

"Here." Gianluca unloaded my arms of the dishes I'd just gathered from the table. He tossed everything in the sink. I watched him in the dim light, aware that his clothes were just as drenched as mine. His wet shirt clung to his strong shoulders and lean torso. His dark hair stuck to his forehead as he spun from the sink and took my hand.

He led me around the back of the living room couches and up the stairs to the second floor without a word to the group. I was too nervous to care if anyone had seen us disappear. It was pitch black up there and I was freezing cold. Water dripped down my body; I knew I was leaving small puddles on the hard floor. Gianluca didn't seem to care, he just kept pulling me toward the end of the long hallway, toward his room.

He never let go of my hand. He pulled me into the dark room behind him and the smell of freshly laundered linen hit me in a wave. He led us through the dark and I held one hand out in front of me, trying to ensure I didn't walk into a piece of furniture. I should've realized he wouldn't have let me.

He paused and I listened to the sound of him striking a match. Gentle yellow light illuminated the room around us, hardly enough to see, but when he held the small tea candle up between us, I knew it would be enough.

Chapter twenty-five

Georgie

GIANLUCA DROPPED THE candle to the bedside table and then he bent to tug my dress up my thighs. The heavy, wet material dragged across my skin, torturing me.

He was a dark dream, standing there in drenched clothes with his sharp features carved in candlelight. I was always greedy for Gianluca's touch, but that night, the feel of his calloused palms on my thighs only made me more ravenous. It'd been days since I'd felt his hands on me. I'd had to keep my distance from him all night and as a result, I was hungry for him—*starved* really.

One of his hands lingered on my thighs, drawing soft circles higher and higher. The other reached up and dragged across my bottom lip, demanding entrance. He tilted my head back and pressed his thumb past my lips. I closed my mouth, swirling my tongue around his thumb until his hand gripped my thigh so hard I knew I was getting to him. I dragged my teeth along his knuckle and then bit down gently. He smirked and I shivered.

My senses were heightened, anxious about the unknown objects that lurked in the dark. I'd never seen Gianluca's room in the light of day and now, lit only by fire and lightning, it was too dark to see anything beyond him. I trembled as he pulled his thumb out of my mouth and finished pulling my sopping dress off overhead.

Chilled air hit my skin and goosebumps bloomed as I stood there in nothing but my panties, wet from the rain.

His eyes dragged down my full breasts and tight stomach. I nearly closed the gap between us, but there was power in seduction, in loving my body enough to confidently show it off. His hands hit my waist and I let out a sigh. I'd wanted him to touch me higher, to palm my breasts and tease them in his palm, but he ignored them— *on purpose*.

He was on a different mission, slowly dropping to his knees before me.

"What—"

His hands gripped the back of my knees and I let my mouth hang open, my question forgotten. He blew warm air against the inside of my thigh and then pressed his lips there, repeating the gesture up the inside of my legs, higher and higher until I could reach down and grip his hair without much effort at all. At some point I'd squeezed my eyes closed, but I forced them open and looked down the slope of my body to where he knelt before me. The candle hardly reached him at that angle; I couldn't see anything beyond my fingers strung through this thick strands. In the shadows, I had no way to prepare myself for the path he traced with his mouth. He moved up, kissing right below my navel, at the top of my wet panties. Then he slowly made his way down to one thigh, and then the other, tightening his circle with each round.

His mouth hit the groove of my inner thigh and then with one hand, he spread my legs apart another few inches, just enough space for him to lean up and press a kiss to the outside of my underwear. I was so thankful for the darkness; I didn't want him to see how easily he'd stolen my composure.

I kept waiting for him to drag my panties down to the floor, but he used the silky material to his advantage, exhaling a warmth breath there and pushing the soft, wet material against me. My head fell back with the weight of his seduction. I'd barely processed another kiss when his finger hooked into my panties and he brushed them aside, baring me to him. There was no buffer, no way to steel myself against his kisses. His lips pressed against me and then his tongue dragged back and forth so…utterly…slowly. He used the tip to swirl soft circles, dragging me down, down, down, and then he backed off, lapping me up and down. The rhythm was deliberate and maddening. He swirled his tongue until I felt the waves of my orgasm start to crest, and then he squeezed the back of my thigh and moved away.

"Gianluca! You can't… I have to…"

I felt his smirk against my hip and then his finger brushed up, replacing his tongue. It was such a sharp change. His tongue had been silky and soft. His finger was stiff and the pressure he applied was just what I needed. I rolled my hips forward to meet him, and he rewarded me by slipping his finger inside just enough to hit my most sensitive spot. He pressed in deeper and I tightened my grip on his hair, *showing* him that I needed more.

He added a second finger, delicately teasing them both into me as I exhaled a shaky breath. My stomach quivered.

By then I was so turned on, he could have leaned forward and *breathed* on me and I would have come apart on his lips.

He knew it too. There was no end to the torture I endured before he let me come. He dragged his fingers in and out and swirled his tongue around me. He used his other hand to keep my hips still so I couldn't rock against his mouth, not until he'd turned me absolutely mental, not until my pleas were slipping out, over and over. I begged him to give in and let me come and then when the fireworks trickled down my body from head to toe, and his mouth was on me and his fingers were fucking me, I shook like my life was ending, like that orgasm was the last thing I'd ever experience on Earth.

There was no more waiting.

I was done.

I told him to get a condom, ignoring the shaking in my voice, the way I was covered in sweat and rain and lust as he opened his bedside drawer and tore open the wrapper.

I didn't let him lead us onto the bed. My appetite had turned carnal. I wanted to push and shove him, make him pay for torturing me like that, but any punishment for him would be worse for me. I gripped his shoulder, dug my nails into his skin, and pushed him to the floor. He was confused. Why would we fuck on the floor when the bed was right there, within reach?

Why?

Because I couldn't stand it for one…more…second.

Because I needed him inside me and he'd oblige me because I deserved it after what I'd just endured, because he was about to come apart the way I had, and I wanted to straddle him on the hardwood floor with the rain pouring down until our tea candle burned out.

I tugged down his jeans, heavy and wet. When he was naked in the dark, splayed out on the floor, I brushed my palms from his ankles up to his chest, careful to avoid his hardness. I wanted him to experience the pain of anticipation, as I had. I kissed his chest and dragged my teeth down his abs. His muscles tightened and his hand reached up to grip my bicep. It was a warning to proceed cautiously and it lit a fire inside me.

I unrolled the condom and slid it on. He inhaled through his teeth when my small hand wrapped around him, stroking up and down, ensuring he was more than ready for me. I moved up onto my knees and hovered over him. I held him there beneath me, so close I could have slid down onto him, pushing him inside.

But I held off, tempting him through my panties. He was so hard, unmistakably long and thick. He let out a hoarse moan and I smirked, feeling powerful as I took more control, rolling my hips in a soft circle as I continued my little lap dance. I used the silky material I wore to slide back and forth along his length. His hands found my hips and squeezed, trying to still me. He stayed silent, but I heard every word he didn't say in those heavy breaths, in his soft moans, in the deep growl as I finally brushed my underwear aside and positioned him at my entrance. I'd come to know his body these past few weeks and he knew mine, but this, him slowly sliding his length into me was wholly earth-shattering.

It was then that he stole the reins from me once again. I'd have pushed down onto him completely, felt him stretch me until I broke, but he teased me with shallow, deepening thrusts. I stayed sitting up, propping my hands on his chest as he lifted his hips off the ground. Each time he pulled back, he sank in another inch deeper, until finally our hip bones met and I felt him inside of me, *every delicious inch*. He let out a pained sigh and we fell into an erotic rhythm.

My second orgasm came quicker than its predecessor. The fire had already been set, and with him inside me, there was no shortage of fuel. Slow thrusts turned quicker. Hands dug into flesh. Moans turned hurried and wild. With me on top, I should have been in control, but he stole the show. I collapsed on top of him, breathing heavily against his neck as he held my hips and thrust into me, faster and harder than before. I could only grip his shoulders and cling on. He moved too fast for me to keep up and then he made it all but impossible when he started to whisper delicious things against the shell of my ear, moaning about how tight and warm I felt around him, how good I made him feel. He wanted me to come again like that, with him rocking up into me, and when he let go of my hip with one hand and dropped it between my legs, I knew I would. It only took a few brushes of his thumb against me, hardly half a dozen circles and I shattered on top of him.

To come against Gianluca's mouth was amazing, but with him unraveling inside me, there was no going back. I'd never stop chasing that high.

We eventually moved to the bed. He tossed aside the used condom. We told each other we would lie still for a few minutes and rest, but those promises barely left our lips before Gianluca's hand brushed up to cup my breast. He made it out to be romantic. He said he just wanted to *feel* me, but I couldn't stop the wildfire from erupting once more.

It wasn't long before he took me again, this time with my face turned down into the pillows so they could muffle my cries. Gianluca positioned himself behind me and reshaped a position of one-sided dominance into an intimate act of lovemaking. He took his time spreading my legs, dragging his hands up over my hips and down the curve of my bottom. He caressed every inch of my skin until he hovered right over the center of me. He leaned back and I knew he was just looking at me. I was glad for the pillow so he couldn't see how red my cheeks had gone. It was such a personal gift to let someone see every inch of you. Eventually he moved closer, teasing me with his fingertips, spreading my thighs just enough for him to position himself between them. His chest pressed against my back and his fingers laced through mine beside my ribs. He propped himself up on his knees and gently fucked me like that until I was writhing beneath him.

It was the most delicious night of my life and though I was sad when exhaustion started to overpower my desire to have him for a fourth time, he didn't let me wallow. I was lying flat on top of him with my eyes closed, half-asleep with a pleasant little smile lingering on my lips.

Gianluca was drawing circles on my back when he asked if I was still awake.

"Barely," I whispered. "Don't even think about moving those hands lower though."

I could feel his smile against my shoulder.

"I won't, for now…"

I let out a greedy sigh and settled back into him, glad for the extra warmth. Even though my body was ready for sleep, my mind needed a few minutes to wind down. I listened to the rain clattering on the tile roof, Gianluca's steady breathing behind me. I thought he'd already drifted off when he spoke again, his voice hardly more than a whisper.

"Do you remember me telling you about the winds when we were out on the boat?"

I hummed, sure that I was asleep, in a dream. "The ones from Africa that bring the rain."

"And the ones from the north? They clear the skies. Do you remember that?"

"*Tramontana*," I replied, quite proud of myself for remembering the name.

He squeezed me tighter and pressed a kiss to my neck.

Chapter Twenty-Six

Georgie

THE NEXT MORNING, I awoke alone in Gianluca's bed to the sound of chatter downstairs. I recalled him kissing me earlier, trying to draw me out of sleep. I'd groaned and pulled the covers up over my head, begging for a few more minutes. He'd obliged, and I had no clue how much longer I'd slept after that. The level of noise downstairs made me think it'd been a few hours.

I stretched and pushed the covers down, turning to Gianluca's bedside table to find a clock. There was a stack of books and a turned-down picture frame. I reached to flip it over and then jerked away as if it'd burned me. The frame clattered back down onto the bedside table and I bristled at the sound of glass cracking. I'd accidently split it down the middle.

Allie's beaming smile stared back at me through the splintered glass.

The photo was from their wedding day, and Allie was

dressed in a fitted lace gown. Her blonde hair spilled down around her shoulders, long and angelic. Her eyes shined with pure joy, and her smile was the most real thing I'd ever seen.

She was beautiful and in love and suddenly, I felt ill.

I pushed off the bed and reached down for my dress. It was still wet; I'd never hung it up to dry the night before. I groaned and turned toward Gianluca's closed closet door. I'd find a t-shirt and pull it on for now. I didn't want to be naked anymore. I suddenly felt vulnerable and raw after the night I'd had with him.

I whipped the door open and flipped the light on, sucker-punched by the sight in front of me. Dresses, scarves, high heels—they took up most of the modest space, even invading some of Gianluca's side. It was Allie's stuff. Her shoes looked like they'd just recently been kicked off and piled in the corner. Her laundry sat untouched beside it. There was a bright yellow dress hanging up right at the front. I reached out and felt the silky material, rubbing my thumb over the fabric. The lemon print would have looked silly in London, but it was the perfect dress for Vernazza, light and cheerful.

I let the fabric slip out of my fingers and I spun from the closet to inspect his room through new eyes. The night before it'd been dark and romantic, nothing but him and me. In the light of day, there was no ignoring the signs of Allie strewn everywhere: her robe hanging on the back of the door, her books stacked on the nightstand right next to where I'd slept, her unused medicine in the bathroom cabinet. There were two toothbrushes sitting in a cup on the bathroom counter. One was new, blue, and clearly belonged to Gianluca. The other was purple and faded, its bristles dried and split. I reached forward to touch it and then pulled back. What would Allie think if she knew I was in her house, sleeping with her husband, touching her belongings, staring at her smiling face on her wedding day?

I was going to be sick. My stomach squeezed tight and I pressed a hand to the back of my neck, willing the nausea to pass. I couldn't be sick in her bathroom. I felt her there, judging me, *condemning* me for sleeping with Gianluca.

Allie might have passed away five years earlier, but inside Gianluca's house she still held court. He hadn't lied to me all those weeks ago when he'd told me he wasn't ready for a relationship. The man was still completely in love with his wife. *A ghost.*

"Georgie! Are you awake yet?"

It was Katerina, calling me from the bottom of the stairs.

"We were going to go get breakfast now that the rain has stopped!"

I wiped at tears I hadn't realized were falling. I jerked the back of my hand across my cheek, angry with myself for being emotional. *Get it together.* I'd pushed for this relationship or *non-relationship.* Whatever. I'd told Gianluca I was perfectly content with no strings, but this was different. This felt dirty. *Wrong.*

I met my reflection in the mirror, seeing myself through the eyes of Allie's ghost. I looked so different from her, nearly her polar opposite. She was fair-skinned with bright blonde hair and light eyes. Maybe that's why Gianluca fancied me—I wasn't at risk of replacing the love of his life.

"Georgie! Come on!"

It was Gianluca shouting then. His feet were on the stairs; he was coming up to drag me out of bed. I ran out of the bathroom and snatched up my dress off the floor. I shivered as the cold, wet silk settled into place on my body. My underwear were nowhere in sight, but there was no time. I couldn't see Gianluca in this room again; it would be too much with the *three* of us in the cramped space.

I combed my fingers through my hair, wiped at my cheeks one last time, and left the room. Gianluca was just cresting the top of the stairs and when he saw me, he beamed.

"There you are. I was worried you'd never wake up."

I laughed—it sounded tight and awkward—and then I brushed past him to trot down the stairs.

"Georgie?"

"Yeah?" I called over my shoulder, trying to keep my features neutral.

"Do you need some of my clothes to wear? Your dress is still wet. I don't want you catching a cold."

I was drowning there, trying to keep it together and breathe and pretend he and I were okay.

"No thanks. Actually, I'm going to skip out on breakfast. I feel like heading down to do a few things at the B&B. We've only got a few weeks before Taylor arrives."

"Do you need my help?"

"No! No," I repeated myself again, trying for a calmer tone.

If he thought my answer was strange, he didn't say anything as I continued down the stairs, putting distance between us. The living room was full of people. Everyone from the party was still there and they called out to me when I slipped into the room. I plastered on a fake smile and skirted behind the couch to snatch my shoes. They were still stashed by the door in the kitchen, muddy and soggy, but that didn't matter. I'd clean them at home.

Katerina tried to catch hold of my arm as I ran for the

door.

"Hey, what's wrong? You sleep late then don't stay for breakfast?"

"She has work to do," Gianluca answered for me with a cold tone.

I nodded and forced one more massive grin. It felt more genuine than any of the others had that morning and I figured it was because I was so close to freedom, so close to fresh air.

Katerina promised to bring round a bottle of wine later. I offered up a sort of noncommittal nod then pulled the front door open and made a run for it. In the end, I wasn't even very angry with Gianluca. No. Witnessing his love for Allie was a good thing because it made me realize what I wanted: for someone to love me the way he still loved her.

Chapter Twenty-Seven

Gianluca

ALLIE HAD BEEN right and I didn't think it was possible. A few days before she died, we were lying in bed and I was reading aloud to her from a book of short stories by David Sedaris. I was just getting to the good part when she moved her hand to block the words from my view and turned her face to me.

"Promise me you'll get married again one day."

She said it just like that, totally out of the blue, and it felt like a punch to the chest.

"Allie, I don't want to talk about—"

"*Swear* to me," she insisted, her voice never wavering.

I brushed her hand from the page and tried to continue reading.

"I'm scared to die, Gianluca, but even more than that, I'm scared that this cancer is going to kill both of us. From the moment we met, you've loved me so fiercely that I worry you'll never recover."

"I won't."

"You have to! I'm making it my final wish. You have to live and grow and fall in love again."

I shook my head and stared at the words starting to blur on the page. "No."

Her small hand clutched mine, so weak by that point. "I promise that by the time you're twenty-eight, you'll be happy again. You'll have moved on and I'll be nothing but a distant memory."

I disagreed. That was only three years. Even if I lived for another lifetime, I'd never get over her.

"Twenty-nine then," she countered.

"*Never*."

"Fine. Thirty. By the time you're thirty, you'll be happy again and madly in love. I promise. I'll work some kind of cosmic magic to make it happen, just you wait and see."

At the time, I'd insisted she was crazy, but now, a few weeks before my thirtieth birthday, I wasn't so sure anymore.

I followed Georgie down the hill that morning. She'd acted so strangely, running off as soon as she woke up. I'd given up trying to decipher the meanings of most of Georgie's words and actions, but she'd run out of there like a bat out of hell and I wanted to know why. The door to the bed and breakfast was locked by the time I arrived. I pulled out my keys, unlocked it, and flipped the light switch in the common room.

Georgie was in her bedroom with the door closed. I could see a small shaft of light spilling out from the beneath the door. I leaned forward and knocked gently.

"Georgie?"

"Oh bloody hell," she cursed under her breath.

"Are you okay?"

"No! Feeling a bit ill actually, better stay away so you don't get it."

"Stop being ridiculous and let me in."

I heard footsteps moving toward the door and then she spoke again, louder this time. "Now isn't a good time, Gianluca! I think I've come down with that cold you were talking about earlier."

I rolled my eyes and turned the door handle. At first she tried to hold it closed, but she eventually gave in and stepped back. The door flung open and Georgie stood on the other side with a red nose and puffy eyes and a sad frown tugging at my heartstrings.

I wanted to step forward and comfort her, but she took a step back, keeping a healthy distance between us.

"What's the matter? Why did you run off like that?"

"Please could we talk about this another time? I'm really tired and I just want to sleep for a little bit."

"I just want to know what's going on. Is this about last night?"

She groaned, flinging her eyes past me as if she was deciding the best method of escape. "Please, Gianlu—"

"Stop it. Stop pushing me away and tell me why you ran off like that."

There were several long moments of silence, with her gaze on the doorway and her fists clenched by her sides. It was such a long pause, in fact, I assumed she would never speak up, so when she did, it hit twice as hard.

"You love her still, don't you?"

Allie.

I didn't even have to pause. "Of course I do. I always will."

She nodded and turned away, trying to hide her tears.

"Is that why you're upset? Because I love Allie?"

"You keep her up there in that house, Gianluca! You love her like she's still alive. Her toothbrush, her pills, her clothes—it's not healthy to hold on to her like that!"

I'd heard the same argument from Massimo and Katerina more times than I could count and my rage nearly boiled over now that Georgie was laying it on me as well. I was sick of people telling me how to mourn and when to move on. No one knew what it was like to lose Allie the way I did, what it feels like to watch, powerless, as death slowly robs you of the person you love most in the world. There was no clean break, no tragic accident, here one day and gone the next. No, I was there watching as she struggled for her last ragged breaths, crying and terrified. There was no closure. There was only the end.

No one could possibly tell me how to move on from that, not even Georgie. That's why I had secluded myself for all these years.

"You'll never have room for love as long as she's there."

"If you're asking me to choose you over her, I won't do it, Georgie. I can't do it."

She squeezed her eyes closed as if in pain. She had to know this was the case. I'd been nothing but honest with her from the start. Things were developing between us, but I couldn't turn off my love for Allie.

"Get out of my room, please."

Her voice was small and defeated.

"Georgie…"

"Just leave!" she bellowed, shoving past me and wrenching the door open so wide it collided with the wall behind it. She reached forward and shoved me, *hard*. "JUST GET OUT!"

That time, I listened.

"ARGH!"

I tossed myself back on my bed and stared up at the ceiling. I wanted to hate him. I wanted to call him a selfish cow and go on about how he'd led me on and forced me to fall for him, but the words felt hollow. He was kind and loyal, with the rare brand of devotion that didn't just run skin deep, the sort of man who'd do anything for those he loves and more than anything, I wanted all of that—but for me. That's what hurt—the fact that I'd fallen so fast for a man who'd warned me away from the start.

"Idiot," I groaned, covering my eyes with my hands. I wasn't being melodramatic. I'd been stupid, and now I was paying the price, holding up a solitary candle at a vigil for my dearly departed heart.

He told you not to fall in love with him.
He said he still loved his wife.
You told him you could do no strings.

I was still lying there in a puddle of soggy tissues and self-loathing when Katerina turned up with two bottles of wine and takeout from one of the sandwich shops down in the square. My stomach couldn't handle food, but I greedily accepted the bottle of wine, uncorked it, and sipped straight from the bottle.

"I'm sorry, G."

I peered at her over the wine bottle. There was no mistaking the pity in her gaze.

"I take it you know Gianluca and I have been sleeping together?"

She frowned. "I guessed there was something going on a few weeks back, but I didn't want to jinx it."

"You didn't want to be the bearer of bad news, you mean."

She looked away. "I honestly wanted you to prove me wrong about him being unsalvageable. It's not like you'd have listened anyway, right? The heart wants what it wants."

"What exactly would you have said to me?"

"What do you mean?"

"When you found out we were sleeping together, would you have told me to go for it with him?"

She looked down and twisted her thumbs.

"Be honest," I goaded.

"No. I would have told you to go for *any* other man in Vernazza. Gianluca doesn't know how charming he is; he doesn't realize how easily women fall for him. He probably thinks this thing between you two could stay casual and easy, but I doubt any woman on Earth would be able to casually sleep with a guy like Gianluca without developing, you know…"

"Stronger feelings." I swallowed down my tears.

"Right. It's why I kept my mouth shut. You wouldn't have wanted to hear that."

"And what if it's too late? What if I'm already half in love with him?"

"Be thankful for the half that's not. As for the half that is…I suppose I should have brought more wine."

• • •

I managed to stay away from Gianluca the next day. I woke up before the sun and took the train into La Spezia. I sat facing the window, watching the sea whip in and out of view. The sun poured in and heated my legs. I leaned my forehead against the warm glass and enjoyed the sensation. I ended up missing my stop and had to double back, finally forcing myself to step out. Compared to Vernazza, La Spezia might as well have been New York City. There were proper grocers and tons of restaurants, fast food chains I hadn't seen in months. I stopped in for breakfast and took my time, trying to fill my day with as much activity as possible so that by the time I returned to Vernazza, I'd only have time to brush my teeth and collapse into bed.

I walked through the streets, dipping into shops that seemed interesting. There was a stationery shop with old calligraphy pens and parchment paper. I snatched up a few postcards and dawdled at a café, writing to my brother and sister-in-law. I hadn't started to miss my family until that moment. They'd have known how to comfort me…well, perhaps not, but at the very least, they would have distracted me with their own problems. I wrote to them and told them how much I loved Italy, how I'd choose never to

239

leave if I didn't have to. I wrote that I intended to explore other destinations soon, but for right now, Vernazza felt like home.

It was a lie. Vernazza didn't feel like home. Gianluca felt like home. Our relationship, the ease and beauty of it was the comfort I craved. He was so lovely. I thought back to a perfect day a few weeks earlier and realized there had been nothing extraordinary about it. We'd been painting one of the upstairs bedrooms, working together. Gianluca would come up behind me and touch up the patches of wall I'd been working on, never pestering me about my sloppy technique. He swore I was a brilliant painter—*the Michelangelo of Vernazzan bed and breakfasts*. He never sought out conflict over inconsequential things like painting plaster walls. Instead, he encouraged me and said I could make a real job of it if I wanted to.

I didn't want to be a painter and I told him so. He grinned and wrapped his arms around my waist, tugging me against his chest.

"That's good, because you're pretty shite at it."

I laughed. "For all you know, I've just been making intentional errors so you feel as if you're contributing."

He squeezed my hips and spun me around, bending low to kiss me softly. "Fair point. So let's do something where we both contribute."

With a soft smirk, he dragged me down to the floor of that abandoned bedroom and stripped off my stained painting clothes. The sounds of the square—laughter and chatter and clinking glasses—filtered up through the open window and we added a chorus of our own.

• • •

Gianluca hadn't come round Il Mare since our confrontation. Two excruciatingly long weeks and still no sign of him. His tools were littered around the place, but I sidestepped them, careful not to dwell on his presence in the building for too long. It wasn't a very efficient use of time, to cry and mope around like the world was ending. I kept busy, always on the move. I went to sleep early, cutting my days short so I'd have less time to dwell on the twisted feeling in my stomach.

I'd go for afternoon swims in the sea, stopping only when my arms and legs became too exhausted to move. It was like I was trying to sweat the sadness out of me. Afterward, I'd flop onto my back and float in the waves, closing my eyes to the Italian sun and letting it warm me from above. Out there, I couldn't tell if it was tears or the sea water running down my cheeks, and neither could anyone else.

I was heading home from one of those swims when Katerina caught up with me. She'd been lingering outside Il Mare, trying to catch me. I hadn't eaten much and I knew I'd have to force down a decent dinner or I'd pass out from all the exertion. I tried to tell Katerina that, but she insisted she had a solution. We were going to meet up with friends at a bar and then go for a proper dinner. Have a real "fun night out".

Italians all seemed to believe that a few drinks and a good meal would cure any ill. Fat chance.

I tried to talk her out of it, insisting that I was too tired to get tarted up, but she was deaf to my excuses. She dragged me inside and all but carted me into the shower. When I'd finished rinsing off with my favorite lavender-scented body wash and shampoo, she plopped me down in front of my small vanity and started to blow dry my hair. I sat in silence, content to let her do what she wanted.

When she finished, my brown hair was long, straight, and silky. Even in my sad haze, I thought it looked nice, and I told her so.

"And I'm not even finished!"

She produced a red dress from her bag and tossed it at me.

"Put that on and then I'll do your makeup."

The only thing harder than sitting there and allowing Katerina to make me over was the idea of fending her off. I had no energy for it. I was drained and numb. If she thought the red dress made my legs go on for days and cinched my waist to nothing, that was nice, but it seemed like mowing your lawn during the apocalypse—what did it really matter?

The group had decided on a bar in Corniglia since they were having drink specials. I hated that I'd have to catch the train to get home instead of just walking the short distance back from the bars in Vernazza.

"I know it's a little farther, but it'll be better. Busy and full of locals and tourists. Tons of happy people to distract you from—c'mon it'll be fun!"

She didn't say his name, like she was scared I would lapse into a fit of tears over the mere mention of him.

"Gianluca," I said. "He's not Voldemort, you can say his name. It's not a big deal."

She smiled ruefully, not quite believing me. "Right, okay. Well this place will be so packed, you won't even remember him!"

She wasn't lying. Even before we'd turned down the narrow street toward the bar, noise spilled out into the quiet night. It was tucked on the bottom floor of a three-story building, hardly the size of the common room back at Il Mare.

All the tables outside were claimed already, but Katerina insisted that the rest of the group was already inside. They'd snagged a space near the small bar and when we joined, Massimo smiled at me, putting on a real show of feigning ignorance that anything was wrong.

"Cheers!" he said, handing me an ice-cold beer.

I tried a smile on, hated the way it felt, and decided not to force my emotions the rest of the night. The group was big enough that no one minded if I sat quietly, observing the scene without being an active participant. Everyone appreciates a tragic loser hanging about to remind them how much better their life is, comparatively. Tonight, I would fill that role.

It was nice to be in the noisy bar with everyone. Paolo told football stories that made us all laugh and Massimo made sure I always had a drink in hand, though I didn't choose to imbibe. I didn't want to be sloppy drunk and start crying to everyone about how much I missed Gianluca.

God, I missed him though.

It'd been two weeks since I'd seen him, which felt like centuries after such an extended period of closeness. I felt overwhelmed by the idea that this would be the new normal.

My throat felt tight and my eyes burned with stifled tears.

Katerina nudged my side. "You all right?"

I swallowed and took a deep breath, relieved when the tightness in my throat eased a bit.

"Yes, fine. I always get a bit choked up when they play Britney. Her comeback and all."

A new song came on over the radio and Sofia, one of

243

the Italian girls with Paolo, squealed and stood up to dance. She was so confident, spinning in the center of our circle. She convinced a few more people to join in and then eventually, we'd all stood and pushed our chairs back. Massimo and Katerina wouldn't allow me to mope in the corner while everyone else danced. They took turns forcing me into spins and entertaining me with truly heinous dance moves.

"You've got two left feet, Katerina!"

She turned back to me and I realized I had a genuine smile on my face for the first time in days.

"Hate to say it, but you're not much better!"

I laughed and tried to shimmy my upper body, doing a few silly moves to jokingly convince her of my dancing ability. I truly was terrible. Other girls knew how to move their bodies so well. I moved around like a stiff gran, scared to slip a disc.

"Drinks!" Paolo shouted over the group, holding up his empty glass. "Who's thirsty?"

"G and I will get this round!" Katerina said, taking my hand and dragging me through the crowd. We weren't far from the bar, but it still took us a while to cut through everyone. It was loud and overwhelming, but I liked it. Being in the bar overwhelmed all my senses, temporarily drowning out the sensation of a broken heart.

Katerina was leaned forward over the bar, shouting her order to the bartender when a cool breeze forced the hair on the back of my neck to stand on end. I shivered and looked over my shoulder, scanning the crowd. There were dancing couples and rowdy groups of tourists. I watched a few girls shout in unison, clink their shot glasses overhead, and then down them with looks of mirthful disgust. Their groans and shudders made me smile.

Katerina nudged my arm to alert me that our drinks had arrived, but I was frozen in place, staring at the front where the bar spilled out into the street. There, standing in the fringe, was Gianluca, cast in the hazy yellow light of the street.

Chapter Twenty-Nine

Georgie

HE WAS AN absolute dream in his black t-shirt, jeans, and boots. His hair looked dark and damp, his eyes a few shades darker. His hands were stuffed into his jean pockets and he was staring straight at me, his expression indiscernible from that distance.

My stomach squeezed tight as I blinked, just to be sure it was him that was attracting the stares of every woman he passed. He'd begun to weave toward us through the crowd and I felt sick. I wasn't ready to see him; I hadn't collected my thoughts and composure. I had been hoping to have a few more days for my head and my heart to compare notes.

Katerina shook my arm, pointing to the drinks on the bar. She needed help carrying them. She hadn't spotted Gianluca yet and she was complaining that I'd gone catatonic on her. I opened my mouth to tell her he was there, but I couldn't seem to form the words.

My hands shook as I grabbed the three beers. I focused

on them as we weaved through the crowd, so anxious that Gianluca would come up behind me I jumped out of my skin when a girl accidently bumped into me. In the end, we reached the group at the same time. Everyone cheered when they saw him, excited to see their friend. I couldn't force myself meet his eyes.

Having finished dancing while we had been away, they were back to sitting in a circle and chatting. I handed off the beers and took my seat beside Katerina again. Someone found a seat for Gianluca and he sat down across from me, so far away I'd have to shout if I wanted to talk to him.

I could feel several eyes trained on me. Katerina and Massimo's flicked over to me repeatedly like I was a teetering Jenga tower ready to crumble. I straightened my spine and forced a smile in a concerted effort to disappoint them, then turned to Paolo and goaded him into telling another story.

Gianluca and I were neck and neck in a competition for who could be the quietest in the group. Sofia tried several times to bait him into conversation, but he offered up one-word answers and sipped the beer Katerina had passed to him.

Tonight calls for beer.

It felt so miserable sitting there and pretending Gianluca and I were complete strangers. We were acting as though nothing had ever happened between us, good or bad, and the longer the night continued, the angrier I became. Why had he even bothered coming? Surely Massimo had told him I'd be here. He couldn't come round to collect his tools, but he could come out and ruin the mood of the entire group? Well, I suppose he was only ruining *my* mood, which was admittedly not filled with sunshine to begin with. Everyone else was continuing on with their night like there wasn't this massive elephant in the room, but I couldn't do it. I handed my still-full beer to Katerina and went to find the loo. I suspected Gianluca might follow after me, but he didn't. I queued forever, went in to wash my hands, and then went back to the group. Gianluca wasn't there when I returned; Katerina pointed to the bar, where he and Massimo were talking animatedly.

"Are you upset that he's here?" she asked in a hushed tone. "Because we can leave if you want."

I shook my head, trying to play the role of the cool girl. If Gianluca could sit in a group and face me, then I would show him that I wouldn't go running off either.

A little while later everyone decided to migrate to a restaurant down the street for a late-night meal. I stuck close to Katerina and Paolo pulled Gianluca ahead, going on about some work that needed to be done at the farm. I wanted to shout at him, shake him, shove him, *something*. I needed to know what he was thinking, how the last few days had been for him. Was he missing me or was he glad to have the separation?

There was only one restaurant in Corniglia still open and they didn't have much room for a group our size. They put us at a few tables outside, pushing them together so we'd all fit. I took a seat in the middle, silently daring Gianluca to take the seat beside me, but Paolo and Katerina swooped in first and I stifled a groan. Gianluca pulled out the chair at the head of the table and an overwhelmed waiter went round to pass out menus to everyone. I ordered an orange juice, too anxious to munch on anything of substance, but Katerina promised me I could nibble on her pasta.

Every few minutes, I'd work up the courage to glance over at Gianluca, and going on looks alone, he was as miserable as I was—*beautifully* miserable. His brows were furrowed and his lips were pulled into a tight frown, like he was trying to work something out in his head. He noticed me staring once and I whipped my head to the other side of the table quick enough that I hoped he hadn't noticed. No doubt I'd strained something in my neck.

"Georgie, how is the building? Il Mare?" Sofia asked from across the table. Her English was clouded by a beautiful Italian accent, and though her words were a bit choppy, it wasn't hard to decipher what she meant.

"It's nearly finished. We have our first guest coming tomorrow."

Her eyes lit up. "*Stupefacente!*"

I could feel Gianluca's attention on me just before the food arrived, and everyone turned to their meals, eating as though they'd starved themselves all day. There was talk of continuing the party at Katerina's flat, but I was exhausted from wearing a mask for the last few hours. I stayed noncommittal, planning on taking the train back with everyone but escaping to my room when we reached Vernazza. Gianluca kept silent, and I suspected he was planning on going to the after-party and would be glad when he realized I'd bailed. But then, when we all piled into the last train back to Vernazza, Gianluca took the seat beside me before anyone else could. I stiffened and stared out the window, desperate for an escape from the harsh fluorescent lighting of the train.

"I think we should talk," he said, bending low to whisper the words against my hair. His voice sent a shiver down my spine. That voice had driven me to highs more times than I could count and I squeezed my eyes closed, willing the memories to pass. I swallowed down the emotion bubbling inside of me, but it was futile. He was so

250

close to me then, his thigh pressed against mine, his scent wrapped around me.

I nodded, reviewing the conclusions I'd arrived at in the days since we last spoke. I knew Gianluca wasn't ready for love—would never be ready for love—but that didn't erase my feelings, *my* love. I could pretend things were casual. I could tell him he meant less to me than he really did if it meant things could go back to the way they were before.

I couldn't go on like this, pretending I was all right. I needed to have him so desperately I'd accept whatever he had to offer. I'd take his body and his time and allow Allie to reign in his heart. I'd keep my judgements to myself. I'd laugh and smile and give him a happy-go-lucky version of myself if only it meant I could drag him back to that room at Il Mare and feel his weight on top of me again, his mouth on my thighs, his hands on my breasts, his moans against my ear.

There was a sort of power in deciding to keep things casual. It meant there'd be no more surprises. He wasn't meant to be my forever, but forever was a long way away. I could live in the moment and soak him in while I was still able to, right?

I stayed quiet the rest of the ride home, trying to work out my words in my head. We waved goodbye at the train station and I promised to see Katerina for dinner the next day. Gianluca and I set off and there was thick silence in the air. Eventually, as we rounded the corner into the square, I just dove right in, as if we were in the middle of a conversation.

"We got so heavy so fast, didn't we? We were cooped up in that bed and breakfast so long, and we both had needs, and we just didn't give ourselves enough time to define the boundaries. There was no need for me to freak

251

out like I did when I woke up and found Al…Allie's stuff."
I wasn't sure what it would feel like to talk about her
openly with him, to say her name. I didn't like the taste of
it, but I tried to keep my face neutral. "I'll admit, I had no
right to freak out like I did. You—"

He tried to cut me off, but I trudged on, forcing my
point.

"She was—*is* the love of your life. I don't want to
replace her, and I don't want you to have to pick me over
her." I paused and turned back to him. "This thing between
us is wonderful, but we've agreed that it's temporary, so
let's keep it like that, yeah? I won't be in Vernazza forever
and I'm sure I'll eventually find someone who's a little
better suited to me." I smiled to emphasize my point,
though the idea of meeting someone else overwhelmed me
with an immense sadness.

He looked torn. "I don't want it to end either, but I also
don't want you to waste your time on me. You're beautiful,
Georgie. You've got this thing about you, a real magnetism
that everyone can see. I don't want you to wait around for
me to move on, because honestly, I don't know when these
feelings are supposed to pass. I can't give you a timeline."

No, *no*. I wanted to be with him. I *needed* to be with
him. It wasn't wasted time, not at all.

"Right now, I don't want anyone else. How's that? I
want to be with you—warts and all."

He smiled and my heart skipped a beat. I felt a bit wild
standing there, exhausted from the past few days and drunk
with the selfish need to have him take me back. My
breathing kept catching short of a lungful and my stomach
was in knots, waiting to drop. I felt like sinking to my
knees and begging him, pleading with him to forget about
our fight, to forget how I'd reacted. I was calmer now,

more levelheaded. I could share him. I could contain my greed this time. He would be the wound and the bandage.

"I'm sorry. About the other day…what I said, I didn't mean that. I just got so angry when you brought up Allie—"

After everything, it still hurt when he said her name, like he was grazing my heart with the point of a dagger.

I shook my head and reached for his hands. "Let's drop it, yeah? Let's go back to the bed and breakfast and I'll make us some tea. You can tell me if you like the furniture I added yesterday and we can pretend like this never happened, right?"

God, I was starting to sound desperate. I needed to pretend like there was no Allie and that Gianluca was the type of man who could love me if only I gave him enough time.

Sad, right?

To still pine for a man who'd told me time and time again that he didn't fancy me like that. All my life I'd imagined myself a strong woman. I'd never let a man rule my life, had always been the one to walk away. I kept myself at a cool distance, and now suddenly I was more than happy to take any scraps Gianluca could spare, like a hungry stray.

He looked a bit pained as he nodded, like he wasn't quite convinced, but it was

decided then. On the surface, Gianluca and I would stay the same. He'd tease me and I'd give it right back. He'd come around to the B&B and we'd spend our days together. We'd never go on official dates, but we didn't need to. We had something better: a life together.

"Georgie, what's that?"

I hummed and followed the path of his finger. A tiny

white kitten sat on the steps of Il Mare, waiting for me. I'd seen it a few times over the last few days. The first time was the morning after Gianluca and I had our massive fight. I had thought it was a sign then, but I'd kept my distance in case it had a home. Several stray cats lived well in Vernazza, after all. But the day before, after struggling with what to do, I'd set out a bit of water and food, just in case. He hadn't been there when Katerina had come round to drag me out for the night, but he was there now. He hopped up and started twisting in circles as we drew closer, excited to see me. I bent down, scratched behind his ear, and then picked him up in my arms.

"What are you doing?"

"I'm going to let him in for the night. It's chilly out here, and he hasn't got as much blubber as the others."

"You can't, Georgie. He's got fleas."

"No, I promise you he doesn't." I didn't tell him I'd bought special shampoo and bathed the kitten the day before in the kitchen sink. "Mopsie just wants a warm place to sleep for the night."

He didn't bother fighting me as I opened the door and carried the cat inside. He was too focused on the name.

"*Mopsie?*"

I smiled. "He needed a proper name."

"So let me know when he's found one. How's he supposed to go around and pick up lady cats with a name like *Mopsie?*"

"Why does he need lady cats when he's got me?"

Gianluca laughed and shook his head, at a loss for words.

"You can keep him for a day or two, but then you'll have to see about getting him a home somewhere else."

I nodded, knowing by his retreat that Mopsie was as

good as mine. Neither of us was alone in Vernazza anymore.

"Is that a litter box? Have you already been keeping this kitten with you?"

"Why isn't that a coincidence…" (Yes, there was technically a litter box set up on the first floor, but I was going to move it somewhere away from the guests before Taylor arrived in the morning.)

"And there are toys everywhere…"

Just a few trinkets. Kittens need stimulation, after all.

"*Georgie…*"

"Hey, don't look at me—Mopsie picked everything out himself! Now come on, let's go to bed and we'll talk it over in the morning."

Really, I couldn't bear another argument. I needed Gianluca to follow me into the bed and breakfast and come into my room. I needed tangible proof that we were back to normal. I set the kitten down with a few toys inside my room and then dimmed the lights. Moonlight streamed in from the window as I tugged my dress overhead. Gianluca was there immediately, stroking his hand up the side of my body, over my waist and ribs. His touch was feather-light, as if he were nervous to scare me away. I was glad to be facing away from him so he couldn't see my eyes squeeze shut or the look of heartbreak on my face. His fingers gripped me tight and pulled me back against him. There was no better feeling than being wrapped in his arms and I could almost convince myself he was about to make love to me.

It truly felt like it. He swore he missed me, saying it in English and Italian so many times that I believed him. His mouth and hands were everywhere, moving over me with a sort of greed that convinced me I'd done the right thing. I

255

couldn't stand how good it was, how excruciatingly painful it felt to have his mouth on mine again. He kissed me slowly and passionately as I dragged my hand up to cradle the back of his neck. I pulled him closer and his mouth moved over mine, kissing me hard and not pulling away until I was nearly breathless. We weren't good at everything together, but we'd mastered *this*.

He pushed me back onto the bed, pulling my panties down with a sharp tug. He worked on his jeans, unzipping them quickly and then spreading my thighs on the bed. He crawled back on top of me, using his knees to keep my thighs split as he slid inside, spreading me as I cried out.

It was different than before—*frenzied*. He pulled back and held my hips and thrust back into me. I'd never been taken like that before, over and over. It was pain and it was bliss, agony and ecstasy. He held me hostage, possessing me body and soul.

I clung to his shoulders and let out soft moans when he thrust back in all the way. His fingers found their way between my thighs as my legs wrapped around his waist. The position offered no reprieve; I was at his mercy as he circled his fingertips, faster and faster.

"I...*Gianluca*—"

I was so close to crumbling. My hands fisted his hair. He sped up his rhythm, dropping his mouth to capture my lips. His tongue swirled with mine as my legs started to convulse. Tiny sparks started to spread and I knew he could feel me come around him. He pumped into me a few more times, finding his own release with a powerful shudder and a soul-stealing kiss.

After, we stayed there, him still inside me as I struggled to catch my breath.

I kept my eyes squeezed closed and I could sense him

doing the same, clinging to the moment for as long as possible.

Eventually, I tried to move, but my muscles ignored my brain's commands. It was with loads of effort that I eventually sat up. Gianluca pulled back, kissed my cheek, and pulled me to stand. We washed up and got ready for bed in sated silence. I met his gaze in the mirror while we were brushing our teeth and he offered up a guarded smile. We weren't yet out of the woods, but there was hope for us, I thought.

Chapter Thirty

Gianluca

I HADN'T EXPECTED Georgie to push the idea of keeping things casual between us. After our dramatic blowup, I'd been a wreck, trying to decide how to proceed without hurting her. The way she'd looked at me after she'd found Allie's things…it was as if I'd been cheating on her. She'd wanted to make me feel guilty for keeping Allie's things and I'd jumped down her throat, angry with myself more than her.

The truth was, I couldn't offer her my future. Pinning it on some undying love for Allie was an oversimplification: in reality, things were much more complicated. Sure, I still thought about Allie on most days, and I did love all the memories we'd made together, but the reason I couldn't move on had very little to do with eternal devotion to my dead wife. It was more like I was trying to climb a new mountain when I'd left all my ropes and harnesses on the previous one. I just wasn't equipped with any of the tools to safely ascend, which led to the inevitable fall with Georgie.

Things might have been simpler if I knew how to get it all back, how to free my heart from its prison, but I didn't have the key and I didn't know the sentence. The more I tried to make sense of my feelings for Georgie, the more confused I became. I needed a bit more time with her. We'd only known each other for a few months, hardly any time at all.

Just a short time before, I'd never wanted a Georgie in my life. I'd been perfectly content living out my days on my own. I had the villa and my repair work. I loved to fish and tend to the garden around my home.

I had no need for love in my life. I'd experienced an abundance of it already, more than most people can hope to have in their entire lives. I'd counted myself lucky and I'd pushed the idea of finding someone else so far into the back of my mind that Georgie had taken me by utter surprise.

Forgetting Georgie was clearly the easiest way forward. It was a well-worn path, flat and featureless, and I knew it by heart after five years of traversing it. I wouldn't need to climb, wouldn't need to fall.

But it was too late; I already loved Georgie. So, I found a solid foothold, and I climbed.

• • •

I knew Georgie well enough to see that things had changed since our discussion the night before. Mopsie aside, she wanted to try to put the cat back into the bag, and I was too selfish to tell her it wouldn't work. I wanted things to go back to the way they had been as badly as she did. No pressure, no future, no ultimatums, just an easy sort of life together. There was something off about her though, like I was watching a flickering projection of the way things had been before. She still smiled and laughed. She kissed me when I bent low to greet her hello in the morning, but her smile stopped at her cheeks and her eyes betrayed her unease. She'd pulled away and I was too scared to bring up the reasons why.

Fortunately, our first guest's impending arrival meant Georgie was flitting around making sure everything was set. For the time being, a discussion about our relationship (or lack thereof) would have to wait.

"Georgie, it looks great. You can relax," I assured her.

She glanced over at me, as if only then realizing I was there.

"I just want to check one last time!"

She didn't need to worry; the place was spotless. From the entryway to the bathrooms, every square inch of Il Mare had been fixed up and redesigned as a contemporary, clean space. She'd brought in new furniture for the downstairs common room and even purchased a massive oak table from a carpenter in Monterosso. With it on one side of the room and a couch and coffee table positioned on the other, she'd transformed the space so that it was functional and open. I was impressed.

There was still work to be done, of course. I was outfitting a balcony on the top floor and touching up a few spots in the bedrooms on the second floor, but I promised Georgie I'd only work when our guest had gone exploring for the day. I could have rushed and finished up the work quickly, in a week or two, but I wanted to stretch it out as long as possible. If nothing else, it meant I had an excuse to spend my days as close to Georgie as possible.

I adjusted my tool belt and was about to take the stairs

up to the second floor to start working when the front door opened. It was our first guest, arriving a few minutes earlier than expected. I spun to greet her and then stopped short when my gaze caught on a man strolling through the doorway and lugging a heavy suitcase behind him. Georgie had said the first guest was a woman, *hadn't she?* This was some posh bloke wearing trousers and a button-down with brown leather loafers. He had a well-made laptop bag hanging off one shoulder and a duffel bag clutched in one hand. With that amount of luggage, it looked like he was planning on staying on a while.

He glanced up and saw me, letting out a puff of air.

"This is Il Mare, right?"

I realized I hadn't greeted him, just stood there staring at him in disbelief.

"Right, yeah. Are you Taylor?"

He grinned. "That's me."

"Taylor is here?!" Georgie called from the top floor. Her light footsteps hit the stairs and then she was there, gliding into the space like a breath of fresh air with Mopsie following after her. She was wearing a light blue dress that morning and it complimented her skin so well. She looked radiant.

"You must be Georgie," Taylor said, stepping forward with an appreciative smile.

"I am! It's so good to finally meet you. Did you get in all right? Here, let me get that duffel bag for you."

He protested, insisting that he could carry it.

She laughed. "Right, well, let me get you checked in then."

She moved around the front desk and started typing on the small laptop she must have purchased sometime in the last two weeks.

"You're actually my first guest, so you'll have to bear with me here."

Taylor didn't seem to mind. He moved right up to the other side of the counter and beamed down at her. "No problem. I'm more than happy to be your guinea pig."

She glanced up at him through her lashes. "You're from the States, right?"

She'd picked up on his accent.

He beamed. "Seattle."

"Oh right! I remember you mentioning that in an email. I've always wanted to visit there."

He never took his eyes off her as she worked through the list of things she needed to collect: a credit card to put on file, a copy of his passport…it seemed to drag on forever. I could have left, but I was rooted to the spot, watching their exchange. I tried to see him through her eyes, something I wasn't very accustomed to. I supposed he was decent looking. He'd done his blond hair like I used to when I worked for the finance firm, all slicked back and unnatural. He had a crooked smile and expressive eyes. He seemed like the type of man girls usually fancied, but what did I know?

"Oh, here, let me find it," he said, digging into his laptop bag for something she'd requested. He pulled out his wallet and a worn paperback, setting them both on the counter to continue digging.

"Is that *Oliver Twist*?"

"Yeah. Favorite of yours?"

She blushed. "Haven't read it. It's on my list."

"I'll loan it to you after I'm finished. Everyone should read it at least once."

"I'd love to borrow it. It's actually a mandatory part of British citizenship to read all of Dickens, and that's why

263

I'm here—I've been exiled," she joked.

The American bloke was enamored by her, and why wouldn't he be? Georgie was more than any man could hope for in life. To have her love and attention was like standing beneath the scorching sun on a summer day: suffocating and sustaining all at once.

He handed her a piece of paper and she started typing something into the computer.

Mopsie meowed by my feet and I glanced down to see the kitten pawing at my jeans.

"He really likes you," Georgie said, eyeing me from beneath her lashes.

Taylor frowned. "Oh. Is it a resident?"

Georgie beamed, proud of the kitten we still hadn't agreed she could keep.

"Yep. His name is Mopsie."

His mouth twisted in a sort of frown. "I'm allergic to cats."

Brilliant, I thought. It was decided: we'd keep the cat.

"Oh." She frowned. "I should have anticipated that. We'll keep him out of the common areas and all that. If you feel your allergies kicking in, we'll move him to Gianluca's villa for the duration of your stay."

He seemed fine with that compromise and went on, saying he wasn't really *that* allergic, though I'd caught a few sniffles. *Good boy, Mopsie.*

She continued checking him in. I had work to do, but instead I watched this odd exchange take place, trying to squash the burning feeling in my lungs.

"Well if you'll follow me, I'll show you to your room!"

"Great. The place looks fantastic, by the way. Did you design it?" he asked, lifting his bags and flexing the bicep on her side. Bloody hell, what a wanker. I'd seen enough.

"Let's go Mopsie." I clicked my tongue and patted my thigh like I was dealing with a dog. Surprisingly, Mopsie listened, following after me as I took the stairs two at a time.

TAYLOR WAS A food critic for a prominent American magazine. He'd told me the name, but I'd promptly forgotten. He seemed eager to explore Vernazza and told me as I finished checking him in that his plan was to spend a few weeks in Vernazza and use it as a home base to explore the surrounding towns and villages.

He was working on a restaurant guide for the Italian Riviera, which sounded so posh and exciting. I told him about Massimo's restaurant. He seemed keen on profiling something outside the square and a little off the beaten path.

"I'm always on the lookout for hidden gems. Should we go there for lunch?" he asked, his face lighting up with boyish charm.

"I'd love to! Let me go see if Gianluca could join us. He's just up working on a few last minute repairs upstairs."

"Oh? Gianluca?"

I nodded. "Yeah he is…well…" It took me a second to realize he wasn't asking me to define my *very* confusing relationship; he just wanted a general idea of who Gianluca was in relation to the bed and breakfast. "He's the man who was here when you walked in. He owns this place actually. I think you'll really get on with him, and as a local he'll be able to recommend loads more restaurants than I can."

He nodded eagerly. "Sounds great."

It was settled after that. I showed Taylor up to his room to let him get unpacked a bit and then I agreed to meet him downstairs in half an hour for lunch.

Gianluca was in the second-floor bedroom and just before I reached up to knock on the door, I heard him on the phone with someone.

"We don't need to make a big show of it. I'd rather just go to dinner."

The person on the other end seemed to disagree.

Gianluca sighed. "Listen, if you're set on celebrating my birthday, we'll go out for drinks or something. Nothing major, right?"

Birthday?

He hadn't said anything to me about it.

He offered a quick goodbye to the person on the other end of the line, who I now suspected was Massimo, and then I knocked gently.

"Come in."

"Hey." I poked my head past the door and saw him hunched over a can of paint, mixing it as Mopsie played beside him, clawing at a wooden stirrer of his own. "Taylor wanted to go grab some lunch so I was going to take him up to Massimo's restaurant. Could you manage to take a short break and come with us? He's a food critic and I told him you'd know of all the good places to eat in Cinque

Terre."

He frowned and glanced down to Mopsie and then to the open can of paint. "I ought to stay here for now. I just started and this paint will dry out if I leave it like this."

I almost asked about just putting the lid back on it, but I knew better. The paint was just an excuse.

"Oh. Okay. Right. I'll tell Taylor we'll go another time then."

I made to back out of the room and he shook his head. "It's okay if you go on with him by yourself, if you want to."

The fact that we were still on unclear terms made such a simple proposition seem wildly fraught with complications. We'd only made up the night before and I quite liked the peace between us, even if it was a bit fake.

"Yeah, right. Still..." I didn't finish the second part of my sentence: *I'd rather not go without you.*

• • •

I did end up going to Massimo's restaurant that day, but it was by myself and for an entirely different reason: to plan a birthday surprise for Gianluca. It was his thirtieth, after all; drinks and a quick dinner wouldn't do. He deserved a proper celebration and Massimo was fully on board with my plan. He promised to phone everyone and arrange the details. All I had to worry about was getting Gianluca to the train station on time.

Easier said than done.

The morning of his birthday surprise, I woke up feeling like I needed another ten hours of sleep. I could barely pry my eyes open and when I did, I spotted Gianluca across the room, pulling on jeans and buttoning them at his waist. What a beautiful, *beautiful* sight. His tan skin was on full display, and his hair was all mussed up from my hands the night before. Still, the sight couldn't rouse me from bed. I felt like a ton of bricks were weighing me down. I'd stayed up the night before tossing and turning, worrying over every little detail of his birthday. I wanted it to be special for Gianluca, but now I found myself wishing I'd managed a minute or two of actual rest. I needed it for the day ahead.

"I've seen you staring at me. You can't go back to sleep now."

I'd managed to pull the sheets back overhead, burrowing myself under the covers. I felt kitten paws on my stomach and glanced down right as Mopsie circled round and curled into a ball.

"Mopsie and I have reached a majority decision that we deserve a bit of a snooze."

"Is that right?"

"Mmhmm. Also, Mopsie has requested a hot cup of tea with two sugars."

Gianluca laughed and finally managed to pry the blanket from my hands, tugging it down to expose my naked torso. I always started the night with a full pajama set, but Gianluca somehow managed to strip me as soon as I hit the bed. Very inconvenient, really, as it got quite cold at night.

"Rise and shine, both of you."

I grinned. "I know what today is."

"Oh?"

"It's your birthday," I said with a wide conspiratorial grin. "I heard you chatting about it on the phone a few days ago and I have an entire day planned for us."

His brows arched in surprise. "Have you?"

I grinned and sat up, reaching to the side table to pull out a little paper birthday crown I'd made for Mopsie the day before. I had one for me as well. We put them on (Mopsie chewed on his) and then I sang Gianluca "Happy Birthday" so loudly and off-key that a shout came from the square in Italian.

"What'd they say?" I laughed.

"That your singing is beautiful and they'd like you to continue all morning."

"Well sorry for them because we've got to be at the train station in"—I glanced at the clock beside my bed—"ten minutes!"

"What? Are you mad? I haven't even had breakfast."

"It's all been taken care of, birthday boy. Now get on and get dressed in something more outdoorsy. No jeans!"

A few minutes later, we were on our way. I still felt a bit off, tired and achy, but my head felt fine. I knew some caffeine would help, and fortunately, Massimo was standing on the platform with two cups of espresso for Gianluca and me. Surrounding him was our small group of friends. We'd invited Paolo and Matteo, Sofia, Massimo, Kat, and even Taylor. I hadn't expected him to show up, passing along an invitation as an afterthought, but he reached out and gave Gianluca a big pat on the back as we arrived, excited to be included in our activities for the day. I felt glad I'd invited him. I knew firsthand how lonely you can get traveling by yourself.

"You've done all this?" Gianluca asked once he'd gone around and greeted everyone in the group.

I smiled. "Massimo helped as well."

"Where are we going?"

I'd planned a hike between two of the seaside villages in Cinque Terre: Riomaggiore to Manarola. There was a

271

popular trail between them called The Way of Love that wound right along the coast. It had amazing views and wouldn't be too much of a trek. We'd stop for lunch in Manarola and then spend the afternoon wine tasting.

Unfortunately, I was shite at planning and hadn't thought to confirm that the trail was indeed open. Apparently during the massive storm a few weeks earlier, a good bit of the trail had become impassable. They'd closed the whole thing for repairs and the group of us were left at the entrance, facing the *DO NOT ENTER* sign and then turning to one another with awkward smiles.

"It's no problem. Let's take the trail through the national park," Massimo said, pointing back toward the train station. "It'll still take us to Manarola and it leads right through the mountains. It's a bit harder and most people prefer the easy stroll along the lover's trail, but we're all young and fit. It should be fine. Plus, the views are second to none."

I looked to Gianluca; after all, it was *his* day. He nodded and smiled. "I haven't done that trail before. It'll be fun."

Oh how very, very wrong he was.

We started out on a lovely path, winding along old houses and blooming hydrangeas. We even stopped for a group photo or two with the sea at our back, but while the Via dell'Amore forked off and remained relatively flat, this trail was laid directly up the steepest part of the mountain. A quarter of the way up, I genuinely wondered whether scientists had missed this peak when deciding that Mt. Everest was the world's tallest.

And then we hit the first set of stairs.

Yes, stairs. On a hike.

They'd been carved from the mountain and they

stretched up as far as the eye could see, like some kind of sick analog StairMaster.

"It won't be bad," Gianluca promised, coming up behind me and pressing his hand to the small of my back. It was meant to be encouraging, his hand there, but in the end it was more of a nudge than anything else. I should have bowed out from the start. I'd worn Converse instead of proper tennies. I'd assumed we'd just be walking, y'know, on a flat surface, but by the time we'd made it up a hundred or so stairs, the backs of my heels were already rubbed raw.

Lovely.

Paolo and Matteo lead the group at the front, taking the stairs two or three at a time like they were part mountain goat. I had a feeling they were trying to impress Sofia, who was right behind them with Massimo and Kat. Gianluca, Taylor, and I made up the rear, and the longer we hiked, the more distance fell between the three groups. I couldn't even see Paolo and Matteo anymore. Taylor and Gianluca were doing their best to hang back and wait for me, but I felt embarrassed and told them to go on.

They swore they didn't mind hanging back with me as I rested, but I knew they were both wishing they didn't have me as a dead weight. I'd always assumed I was pretty fit. I'd swum a ton since arriving in Vernazza and walked everywhere, but I'd yet to train my body for this.

We'd started early, when the sun was still hidden in the clouds, but not long into the hike, the sun made its appearance, scorching us from above and making the hike just *that* much harder.

I could *hear* the sizzle against the back of my neck and legs. Cicadas welcomed the heat, humming louder than ever in the short trees dotting the trail.

Halfway through the ascent, Gianluca, Taylor, and I

reached a sort of plateau in the center of a shady tree grove. The group was sitting there in the shade, resting and drinking water. Paolo and Matteo had reclined back on their hands with their legs outstretched. It looked as if they'd been there ages, waiting for us to show up, and I reddened, embarrassed at how much longer I was taking than the rest of the group.

Fortunately, Sofia and Katerina looked near death as well.

"I think I'll hang back with you guys for the next leg," Sofia said, still trying to catch her breath.

I nodded and accepted the water bottle Taylor handed to me.

"Thanks."

"You're doing great," he said, coming to take the seat beside me.

"Not quite what you had in mind visiting Vernazza, right?" My words were dotted with my measly attempts to catch my breath.

He narrowed his eyes, thinking over my question, and then he turned his full attention to me. "It's actually really great. They have trails like this back in Seattle. It's not quite as sunny, but the views are spectacular."

"Oh? That sounds lovely. The sun is the part that's getting to me, actually. It's been so cool down in Vernazza, I didn't realize it could get so hot up here in the mountains."

He turned to dig into his backpack and pulled out a little red handkerchief. "Here, this bandanna has been wrapped around my water bottle. It's ice cold and you can wrap it around your neck."

I nearly sighed with relief when the chilled fabric hit my skin. I tied it around my neck and grinned.

"Thanks."

"You look like a cowgirl," he said with a funny little smile. It was then that I realized Taylor was flirting with me. Up until that point, I'd been smiling along, content to have a chat, but then I realized Taylor was looking at me the way blokes did when they fancied a girl: hopeful, swoony, a bit overeager.

I blanched and stood, wiping the dirt from the back of my denim shorts.

"Are we ready to head on?" I asked.

Gianluca came up beside me and together, we took up the lead at the front of the group. We trekked on in silence for a bit, the only sound coming from our feet crunching against the dirt. I could feel his attention on me and I turned to glance at him from beneath my lashes.

He was wearing a little grin.

"Don't even say it."

"What?"

"I can see the wheels spinning in your head, Gianluca."

"I was just going to compliment you on your fancy red bandanna."

"He was just being nice," I hissed right before properly tripping over my next stair. "See! You were having a go at me and made me trip."

He reached down and hauled me back to my feet, brushing the dust from my bare legs. Even when I was clean, he didn't remove his hand from my upper arm. He took some of the weight for me and half carried me up the next few flights of stairs. It was all a bit *macho man* for my taste, but honestly, it felt good. At that point, my feet were just two massive blisters.

"I know I shouldn't, but I haven't felt this jealous in a long time, Georgie," he said, his tone low enough that the others couldn't hear.

I arched a brow. "Scared I'll run off to *the new world* with a hunky American?"

His eyes narrowed. I'd pushed a button and I liked it.

"Maybe I will. It worked for my brother; he found a nice American girl."

He shook his head, having had more than enough of me for the moment.

"How're your feet?"

I supposed he could tell they were aching.

"They've been better."

"Should I put you on my back? I could carry you the rest of the way."

I grinned. "My own personal Sherpa."

He didn't think that was as funny as I did.

"No, it's okay," I continued. "It's the only way I'll learn."

I still felt a bit ill, not quite sick, but I thought the sun might have been getting to me a little. My stomach felt a bit queasy too, but I didn't want to tell him that. It was his birthday and nothing was going to ruin it.

Matteo and Paolo suggested the guys go on ahead, race up the hill against one another, and we encouraged them. Honestly, I needed a bit of a break from Taylor and Gianluca. The two of them doting on me like that was going to go straight to my head, and I'd soon start believing even more than I already did that I was god's gift to mankind.

"Finally," Katerina said, linking her arm through mine. "Let's let them go on ahead and we'll go at our own pace."

Sofia agreed, muttering in choppy English mixed with Italian about how torturous the hike was.

We laughed and continued on at a snail's pace. With the

boys gone, it was much nicer. We walked slow and took breaks in the shade when we felt like it.

"Sooooo…" Katerina said, shaking my arm. "What do you think of Taylor?"

"Hmmm? He's nice."

She rolled her eyes. "No, I mean, what do you *think* about him? He's a nomad like you, G."

I opened my mouth, confused about what she was getting at, and then I realized I'd never filled Katerina in on Gianluca and I reaching an armistice. We'd rewound our relationship, but Katerina still assumed I was heartbroken over him.

"On paper, he's everything you're looking for. Georgie, I saw that he was reading *Oliver Twist*! He had it in his backpack. It isn't *A Tale of Two Cities*, but what are the odds? You named that *exact* author when you talked about the kind of man you wanted for a future husband."

Had I said that? Funny.

"He's cute too, and polite. Most importantly, I asked and he has no girlfriend, no wife, no skeletons in his closet."

"Right."

"That's all you have to say?" She was shocked, maybe even a bit annoyed with my lack of enthusiasm. "You've been waiting for a man like Taylor since you arrived here and you're not even going to give him a chance?"

"Katerina, I'm not interested. Okay? He's not for me. No chemistry. He chatted with me for a good ten minutes back there before I realized he was trying to lay on the charm."

"Give him a chance. He's probably just nervous."

"Why don't you date him if you're so keen on him?"

"Don't be ridiculous."

"You're the one being ridiculous!"

We walked on for a bit longer then, in brooding silence.

Then, finally, she turned and grilled me.

"What happened with Gianluca?"

I hesitated before telling her the truth. Her words flashed through my mind—she'd warned me to keep away from Gianluca, to protect my heart against him. She'd said that out of every man in Vernazza, Gianluca was the last one I should I fancy. What would she say if she knew we were sleeping together again? That I was still so in love with him it blinded me to all logic and reason.

I sighed before replying. "We talked and neither one of us wants to throw in the towel just yet—"

"Oh good GOD!"

"What?!"

"Nothing." She shook her head and tried to move past me. "C'mon, let's just catch up with the others."

I reached for her arm to tug her back. "No! Say it!"

"You're fooling yourself, Georgie! You're being so *bloody* stupid!"

It felt as if she'd just slapped me cross the face. "No I'm not!"

"You're telling me you won't even give a lovely guy a chance because you're 'not ready to throw in the towel'? HOW ROMANTIC!"

"Oh, just *sod off*. That's not how it is."

"Then tell me! How is it? You're okay with just being Gianluca's fuck buddy?!"

I shoved away from her then, so hard she fell back against the brush beside the trail. "You have no idea what you're talking about! How dare you judge my choices. You think I should walk away from the man I love because some other guy walks up and says hi?"

278

"Oh bloody hell. You *love* him?! What about all the crap you wanted?! You had a list a mile long of all the things you cared about! You're going to toss all that away?"

"I don't care about any of that stuff! I don't care if Taylor reads *every miserable book on the planet!* I want Gianluca and I want him enough to deal with the baggage. So, if you'll excuse me, I've got to continue on—it's my *fuck buddy's* birthday!"

Chapter thirty-two

Gianluca

I HEARD KATERINA and Georgie shouting at one another—
actually, we all heard them. The mountain, like most
mountains, was deserted, and sound carried readily. We'd
stopped to wait for them and then I listened carefully,
bristling as Katerina tried to push Taylor on Georgie. My
mates had the good sense to pretend they couldn't hear it,
but it was no use. Taylor wouldn't meet my eyes, Massimo
was watching me with pity, and Matteo and Paolo, the
arseholes, were doing their best to contain their snickering.
Apparently they enjoyed hearing the girls shouting about
fuck buddies.

I didn't.

I felt for Georgie in that moment. Having to defend her
choice to be with me was hard to hear, especially when I
hadn't given her much to use in way of defense. I was
angry with Katerina for assuming I wasn't good enough for
Georgie, for trying to convince her to give Taylor a chance.

I was angry because she was right. I wasn't good enough for Georgie, but more than anything, I wanted to be. I wanted to change. I wanted to be the man Georgie Archibald deserved to marry.

To marry.

I stared up at the sky and laughed a sort of crazy chuckle at how correct Allie had been.

"By the time you're thirty, you'll be happy again and madly in love. I promise. I'll work some kind of cosmic magic to make it happen, just you wait and see."

I guess you win, Allie.

You win.

"You want to go on, Luca?" Massimo asked, coming up to drop his hand on my shoulder. "We can give them a bit of privacy?"

Just then, Georgie crested the top of the mountain. Her cheeks were red with rage and her fists were clamped by her sides. I knew her feet were killing her, but she rushed past like she was on a mission. I reached out to stop her, but she tugged her arm free and shook her head.

"I'm continuing on the trail. I'll see you at the finish line."

Chapter thirty-three

Georgie

I'D BECOME THE type of woman I loathed: a spineless git. For months, I'd followed Gianluca around like a sad little puppy, hoping he'd eventually soften his heart and take me home. A part of me had known this all along, but I'd been living in blissful denial up until Katerina had dropped that truth bomb on me in front of everyone.

Did everyone pity me?

Did they all think I was delusional for pining after Gianluca?

God, how embarrassing.

I hadn't realized I'd become a sideshow attraction, the latest in a long string of women who thought they could sway the cranky recluse. How many had come before me? How many had left Vernazza brokenhearted?

I couldn't face the group. I didn't wait for them at the base of the trail; instead I headed straight for the train station and went back to Vernazza. I felt bad, not giving

283

some sort of explanation for where I'd gone, but they'd probably guess I'd gone home.

My emotional torture had momentarily overshadowed the pain from the blisters on my feet, but by the time I unlocked the door to the bed and breakfast, there was no denying it: my body ached as much as my heart.

Mopsie was waiting for me on the other side of the door, offering up a furry toy mouse for me to take. I scooped him up and walked straight to the bathroom, drawing a nice, hot bath. I opened the window, the small one that faced the back alley; it let in the sounds of the sea without compromising my privacy. After a candle was lit and enough lavender-scented bubble bath poured into the warm water, I stripped and stepped in, setting Mopsie down on the tile. He had no desire to get in the water, but he was happy to lie on my warm clothes and resume his main mission in life: sleeping.

I kept the water going until I was nearly submerged, everything in the water but my face. I stared up at the white plaster ceiling and tried to make sense of my situation. Now that I had a bit of distance from her, I didn't think Katerina was wrong. Her delivery was a bit harsh, but she was being a good friend, trying to watch out for my heart. She wanted me to stay away from Gianluca because it was obvious that I was going to get hurt, and she didn't want that.

It was too late though. It was like being told to watch your step when you've already missed the stair. I should have listened to her earlier because now I was in the worst spot imaginable. I was stuck, so in love with Gianluca that I couldn't sleep, couldn't *breathe* without him. I felt it eating away at me. I was so desperate to keep him that I didn't pay attention to the warning signs: the sick feeling in my stomach, the tight tug of my heart when he walked out of a room, the twisted thoughts in the back of my mind. I'd completely lost myself in him. I no longer wanted a simple kind of love. I'd settle for nothing short of crazy in love, and the moment Gianluca realized how serious I was about him, how shattered I'd be by the end of us, he would walk away. He had to; he was too much of a good guy to lead me on.

I was due for an explosion any day and the anticipation of it was worse than anything, the slow-rolling despair settling over me. I squeezed my eyes shut and slid farther into the water, wondering how long I could stay before I transformed into a prune.

Argh. I didn't want to be this in love. It felt like a sort of abuse, and the signs were there. I'd had a row on top of a mountain with my best friend in Vernazza. There were bags under my eyes that never disappeared. I'd lost the will to eat, to care about anything beyond keeping Gianluca. In recent days, I'd been shedding pounds as if I had a few to spare. My emotions were brittle and frayed. I hated who I'd become.

Something had to give, and I was afraid it would be me.

• • •

I wasn't in that bath long before I heard the muffled sound of Gianluca calling out to me in the front common room. I'd ruined his birthday, absolutely shat all over it, and he was there, pushing open the bathroom door with a soft knock.

I sat up and turned to look at him over my shoulder, my skin prickling with goosebumps from the cool bathroom air.

"I'm sorry."

He shook his head and stepped forward, tearing his shirt off overhead. His shorts and boxer-briefs followed, and then he was stepping into the large bath behind me, nearing overflowing the water. We drained a bit, added more hot water, and then I settled against his chest. The nearness killed me: his skin against mine, his lips pressed against my shoulder, his words in my ear, promising me I hadn't ruined his birthday, that I could *never* ruin his birthday.

He wiped a tear from my cheek.

"Please don't cry. *Please*."

His kindness tore at me.

I had to tell him the truth.

"I don't think I can do it, Gianluca. What I said the other night, about keeping things casual…"

"No. No. You and I, we're more than that, right? I promise. Please don't listen to Katerina."

I wanted to believe him. I really wanted to sink into his words and let them swirl around me like the warm bath water, to let them blanket me from the outside world.

And then it sort of clicked: this was how it continued. I would get upset, he would keep stringing me along with little promises of more. A year from now, I would look back on all the tender moments when I'd cowed to him, and I'd wonder how I'd let myself fall into such a one-sided love affair.

He gripped my biceps and twisted me to him so I was straddling him in the bathtub. We touched everywhere, so intimately fused that the nature of our discussion broke my heart.

"Don't you remember what I told you? You're my northern wind, my *tramontana*."

His words weren't enough; when your heart is set on love, anything less seems paltry.

I didn't want to talk anymore. A part of me realized this would be the last time we touched like this, the last time our two bodies moved like one. I leaned forward and kissed him, slow and sweet at first. He responded right away, tilting my head back and softly gliding his tongue past my lips. My chest pressed against his and my breasts glided across his wet skin. It was all so deeply erotic—our minds were slaves to caution, but our bodies were free. His touch turned me on like never before.

He tilted me back, peeling my chest off his so he could bend down and take my right breast into his mouth. His tongue swirled around my sensitive nipple, working it to a peak before switching to the other. His hand moved to the velvet skin under the curve of my breast, bringing the warm bathwater up across my chest, heating my flushed skin.

I tried to lean forward and touch him, but he had such a gentle, commanding grip on me. With his hand on my waist, I couldn't move over his hard length. The best I could do was string my fingers in his hair, gently moaning when he continued to seduce me.

I knew his body more than I knew my own, but this time was different. I tried to memorialize every fleeting moment. When he picked me up and positioned himself at my center, I squeezed my eyes and focused on every delicious inch sliding into me. He gripped my neck and his touch sent a ripple of sensation down my spine, numbing my toes.

"Open your eyes," he told me when I'd pinched them closed.

It was hard to take it all in. With mine open, I was compelled to stare into his dark eyes, to witness our exchange. I didn't want to see the incredible potential for love there.

Is that adoration in his eyes?

I knew my mind was playing tricks on me. Like a mirage, the promise of Gianluca's unbridled affection was too good to be true.

I squeezed my eyes closed and gripped his shoulders as he picked me up and slid me back down onto him. It went on like that, painfully slow. I shuddered as the first waves of pleasure started to spread, but then he turned me around so my back was flush with his.

"Be here," he said, leaning forward and dropping his lips to my neck.

He gripped my thighs and spread them beneath the bath water, sinking back into me as I let my head fall against his shoulder. His hand traveled down the front of my chest and I watched its descent. It was hidden beneath the bubbly bath water, but I felt him slide past my navel and my hips. He circled so close to my center that my toes curled and my fingers dug into the nape of his neck.

His lips found the shell of my ear and then at once, he was everywhere, circling his fingers beneath the water, right across the most sensitive part of me, and whispering in my ear, his breath warm, his words confident. His other hand sought my breast, thumbing my nipple in time with his circles. It was all too much; I couldn't hang on.

"Gianluca..."

I felt vulnerable, utterly *exposed* to him. He could see my nerves starting to fray, my body shuddering from the rush of climax. He continued his rhythmic teasing with his finger as he sank deep inside me, all the way to the hilt. My breaths came in short, weak cries against his neck. My teeth grazed him there, and then finally he picked up the pace,

288

pumping in and out of me, and I was writhing in agony and pleasure, climaxing so high I thought I'd split in two from the pleasure of it.

I was in a daze, vaguely aware of his orgasm combining with mine. I luxuriated in the blissful claim he laid on my body. Vaguely, I registered him sliding out of me and forcing the two of us to stand. He held up my weight as he bent forward and pulled the drain open. The spray of the shower collided with my back and we lathered each other up, taking our time and being lazy about it.

He bent down and kissed my cheek as I lathered up his chest. Before I'd even finished, he hauled me up against his body. He was soapy and warm, a human shield I used to block the shower's spray as well as the depressing reality that would await us when the water eventually turned cold.

Chapter Thirty-Four

Gianluca

ALLIE HATED THE sea. She'd watched some nature program about sharks as a little girl and subsequently, she wouldn't go near the ocean. She said it was too unpredictable for her taste. She liked pools, nice lovely resort pools with umbrellas in the drinks and complimentary towels. It was a bit funny that we'd moved to Vernazza for the last year of her life because she never once touched the water. She'd sit up on the pebbled beach, reading while I swam laps. I'd try to entice her, drag her to the edge of the water. It was crystal clear, no fish in sight, but Allie would scrunch her nose and retreat, slipping back to her spot in the shade or ordering a drink from one of the seaside vendors.

I hadn't ever let myself consider it, but in the last year of her life, Allie had been incredibly hard to love. I couldn't blame her for it. I'd placed her on a pedestal, treated her like a princess, and she'd grown accustomed to the role. It made sense. If she only had a finite number of days, what was the point of compromise, in forcing herself to do something she didn't want to? That last year, and even the years before (if I really wanted to consider it), my world revolved around pleasing Allie. If she wanted pasta for dinner, I'd have Massimo deliver a special dish just for her. If she fancied a massage, I'd hire someone and bring them in from La Spezia. If she needed more sleep, or extra pain meds, or anything at all, I'd oblige. What choice did I have? I'd have cut my arm off to please her and she deserved to be a bit selfish, didn't she? Only recently had I come to realize that in the five years since her death, I'd only remembered the good, the fun, the rose-colored.

I was up in my bedroom with boxes and packing supplies. I had hefty bin bags filled with things I should have tossed ages ago: her toothbrush, hairspray, makeup. Anything that could be reused I stowed away in donation boxes: jewelry, shoes, dresses. My house was filled with her things; I'd realized it long ago, I'd just preferred to live in denial. There was less guilt involved.

Even now, as I let myself mull over Allie's few unsavory qualities, it didn't make it any easier to put away her things. I'd loved Allie fiercely and eternally, and I'd lost her.

Now, I was doing the unthinkable: loving someone new.

I had been to rock bottom and grown accustomed to the comfort it provided. Leaving it gave me hope for a future, but also a fear for the unknown. Loving Georgie took courage I hadn't known I still had, courage that at times seemed like an act of sheer folly.

"Am I dreaming right now or are you packing Allie's stuff?"

Massimo was standing in the doorway of the room. I'd called him and asked for help, but I'd forgotten about it until he was there, thumbing through a box of Allie's shoes, wearing a look of disbelief.

"You're not dreaming," I said, tossing a marker to him so he had to think fast to catch it. "Label that one, will you? Then tape it and take it down to the others."

"I passed the boxes downstairs. You're really doing this, aren't you?"

I didn't meet his gaze; I continued working. "What? Getting rid of her things? It's about time."

"No. It's more than that, I can tell."

I sighed and stared down at the empty box waiting to be filled.

"Yeah. It is."

Chapter thirty-five

Georgie

THREE DAYS AFTER Gianluca's birthday, I was hunched over the toilet in the first-floor bathroom getting rid of everything I'd eaten for breakfast that morning—not by choice, mind you. Apparently I was so miserable that even my oatmeal wanted nothing to do with me.

In the days since our hike, I'd felt like utter crap. Tired and queasy. Emotionally and physically drained. Everything ached: my head, my body, and worst of all, my heart. I chalked it up to the stress of living a life I knew might come crashing down around me at any moment. I wasn't sleeping well, and I felt close to tears at every moment, so emotionally fragile that I knew I couldn't keep up the charade much longer. I'd walk around the bed and breakfast, trying to focus on a task, but would get distracted, suddenly so overcome with sadness that I couldn't do it.

Taylor knocked on the bathroom door. "Georgie, are

you all right?"

I jerked up and flushed, scared he'd barge in and see the evidence of my sickness.

"I'm fine!" I shouted, feigning cheeriness. "Just cleaning up in here a bit."

"Really? Because it sounds like you're cleaning out your stomach."

Oh god. I wanted to shout at him to piss off. What was I thinking bringing on a guest at the bed and breakfast? The place was better when it was empty.

I forced myself to stand and wash my hands, splashed water on my face, and patted it dry. By the time I whipped the bathroom door open, Taylor looked genuinely worried.

Nausea hit me in another wave, but I refused to acknowledge it as I brushed past him.

"How are *you*, Taylor? Hungry? I could put on some tea for you?" My plan was to continue talking so he could never get a word in edgewise. "I think we've still got a bit of bacon and eggs. I'll whip you up something to eat."

"I'm fine, really."

I waved him away. "Nonsense. This is a bed and *breakfast*, right? We can't have you going hungry!"

I could hear the slight hysteria in my voice, the edge that told him to handle me with caution. I was moments away from crying or throwing up and he had enough sense to keep a wide berth.

"How about a double breakfast tomorrow? I'm heading off for a hike and then I'm reviewing a restaurant in La Spezia later."

I nearly cried with relief. He'd be gone and I'd have a few hours of peace and quiet.

"Oh, right then! Well, good luck. I'll see you when you get back then, yeah?"

I was already heading toward my room, waving to him over my shoulder. I locked the door and sat on the edge of my bed, listening to him leave. I reached for the crackers I'd set on my bedside table and nibbled on one, forcing it down.

I needed to talk to someone, *anyone*. I felt so alone sitting in that quiet bed and breakfast, sad and sick and lonely. I tossed the crackers aside and reached for my mobile. My sister-in-law would know what to do.

Andie answered on the second ring.

"Georgie! That you?"

Like a warm hug, her words broke the dam I'd been struggling to brace for the last few days. I sniffled and cried real sobby tears that were more painful than anything else. I hadn't realized how much I'd been missing my family until I was on the phone with Andie, listening to her on the other end of the line, trying to get a word out of me.

"Are you okay? Dear god, are you hurt?"

I managed a weak no.

"Should I call the police? Georgie?"

"No. No, I'm okay."

"It doesn't sound like it."

It took a few more minutes for me to catch my breath, and then finally I started to speak through soft tears.

"I've gotten myself into real trouble in Italy."

"How? Have you gambled away all your money? Broken the law? Murdered someone?"

"Worse. I'm in love."

She laughed. "I...well, that doesn't sound all that bad, to be honest."

"He doesn't love me back, Andie! Keep up!"

"Oh, Georgie. *I'm so sorry.*"

I groaned. "It's so bloody complicated, Andie. The

297

worst sort of situation, and I can't keep anything down. I think I'm lovesick, *truly*, vomitously so."

"So you've been throwing up?"

"For the last few days."

"What else is going on? Do you have a fever?"

"I don't know. On an emotional level, I feel very cold, so probably not."

"Do you feel flu-ish?"

"Maybe. I've had headaches and I feel like I'm always on the brink of tears. I'm tired all the time, even when I get a few decent hours of sleep. Just yesterday I walked into a room to grab something and I couldn't remember what it was. My brain isn't working, I *swear* it. It's like I'm a zombie."

"Sounds terrible, Georgie."

"Oh well, I guess there's not much to be done now."

"Do you want to tell me about him?"

I pinched my eyes closed. "Imagine the most gorgeous, thoughtful, lovely man in the world and then multiple that by ten billion. *That's* Gianluca."

She hummed. "Sounds like the type of man you could talk to about this sort of thing. Have you tried explaining to him how you feel?"

"I can't go near him. You see, we have a very 21st-century relationship, where even though he doesn't love me back we still frequently…*shag*. But at the moment I couldn't bear it because my breasts are bloody tender. Do you think it's possible my heart ripped in two, and that maybe the pieces have lodged themselves into my boobs?"

"Georgie…"

"I can't do it. If this is love, it's too much. I can't go on like…like some—"

"Georgie!"

298

"What?!"

"When did you last have your period?"

"I don't know, but that hardly seems relevant when I'm dying of a broken heart. And anyway—"

"I think you might be more than lovesick. Those sound like pregnancy symptoms."

WHAT?!

I threw my mobile across the room so fast it collided with the wall and clattered to the ground, screen split in two.

No.

No. Not possible.

CRAP.

I stood and ran for my mobile, trying to turn it back on. It was bloody broken. *That's what I get for swimming so many laps and toning up my arms—I can now throw with the force of Wonder Woman.*

I slapped it against my palm a couple times and then held down the power button for a solid minute. Nothing.

R.I.P., you useless piece of shite that is actually quite useful when navigating a foreign country.

I turned on my laptop, something I'd rarely done since arriving in Vernazza, and worded a quick email to Andie. She replied within minutes.

To: AndieArchibald@Yahoo.com
From: Georgie08@Gmail.com

Dear Andie,

Thank you for your advice regarding my sickness. You are—*sadly*—very, very mistaken, possibly delusional. Just because *you* possess the fertility of ancient Mesopotamia doesn't mean the rest of us are baby-making machines.

As you are barking mad, please refrain from giving any more advice to others until you seek professional help.

Your Concerned SIL,
Georgie

———

To: Georgie08@Gmail.com
From: AndieArchibald@Yahoo.com

Georgie,
I know it's a lot to handle, but you need to think it over. Seriously. Fatigue, morning sickness, tender breasts. I'd be willing to bet you even missed your last period...

Don't freak out. Call me back.

Your EVEN MORE concerned SIL,
Andie

———

To: AndieArchibald@Yahoo.com
From: Georgie08@Gmail.com

Dear Andie,
What a rapid reply, have they let you bring your computer into the asylum? What's concerning is that you think pregnancy is even an option. ARE YOU PREGNANT? I took one semester of

psychology, and I remember learning about your condition. It's called *projecting*. Is that what this is all about?

I've attached a few names of proper therapists in London. Please do give them a call.

Will pray for your speedy recovery,
Georgie

———

To: Georgie08@Gmail.com
From: AndieArchibald@Yahoo.com

Ha ha. Just take a pregnancy test. Once you know for sure, you can decide what you'll do. Until then, you'll drive yourself crazy worrying.

-Andie

———

To: AndieArchibald@Yahoo.com
From: Georgie08@Gmail.com

Dear Andie,

Let's entertain your sick fantasy for a moment. What'll I do?! If I am in fact pregnant (*massive eye roll*), I'd be so completely lost I would simply pop out of existence and cease to exist. Due to the fact that I do, indeed, *exist*, it stands to reason that I therefore could not possibly be preggo.

I think therefore I am (not pregnant),
Georgie

I slammed my laptop closed and reached for my box of crackers. Now that I thought about it, when Andie was pregnant and had suffered from morning sickness, she'd sworn having an empty stomach made it worse. But...that didn't apply here...since I wasn't pregnant.

I was on the pill, mind you. I took it every day—well I had forgotten once a few weeks back, but the chances that I'd happened to miss a day *and* had begun to ovulate had to be astronomical. The odds were on my side. My stomach, however, was not.

I munched on another cracker, letting it dissolve in my mouth as I stared off at a point in my room, right at the corner. I wanted to freeze time, to live in denial as long as possible. I'd never been pregnant before; maybe this was just a simple stomach flu? I did feel a bit lightheaded.

Oh bloody hell.

If it was true, my brother was going to freak out.

My mum would moan on and on about me being an unwed mother. The scandal would likely do her in and then I'd have to shoulder the weight of having killed my own mother. How's that for grief, Gianluca?

Oh god, Gianluca. I dropped back onto my bed and shielded my eyes with my forearm. I had absolutely no clue what he would do if it was true. The worst part of me feared that maybe he'd assume I'd done it on purpose, like it was some twisted plot to trap him into staying with me forever.

I knew it was silly, he would never truly think that, but how could I not worry?

He'd been busy the last few days. He hadn't come to work at Il Mare and had mentioned a bit of work he had to

302

do up at his villa. I'd gladly shoved him out, telling him to take as much time as he needed to sort out whatever it was he was doing. I needed time away from him, time to think and wrap my head around my feelings.

Now, I had this *thing* to think over…this massive, impossible, 100% unlikely…yet maybe possible *THING* Andie had just torpedoed at me.

It was all too much. I tried to take in a deep breath, but my lungs constricted, fighting me. I couldn't breathe. I thought I was having a proper panic attack. I had to get out. I couldn't die in a bed, alone, with saltine cracker crumbs scattered across my chest. Too pathetic even for me.

I stood and reached for the jacket on the back of my door. I slipped on a pair of sandals and left. Evening had rolled in and the air was chilly outside. I had nowhere to be, but it felt good to get out and walk. I went up to the train station and bought a ticket to La Spezia. I sat alone and stared down at my fingers twisted together on my lap.

We passed village after village and the train filled up. I listened to the sound of the passengers, more attuned to the children aboard than ever before. A mom and infant even took the seat in front of me, and I thought it was a real sign from God—up until the infant saw my face and started to wail.

Oh baby Jesus.

I was doomed.

Chapter Thirty-Six

Georgie

AFTER A LONG walk around La Spezia the night before and loads of sleep, I'd really come to my senses about things and had concluded that everything was fine, whether it wanted to be or not.

Sure, I'd strolled into a pharmacy in La Spezia and picked up a dozen pregnancy tests, but they were more for drama than anything else. The real problem was that my brother had married a mental patient, and I thought it was best if we all focused our energy on getting her the help she needed.

She'd emailed me a few more times overnight, but I didn't read them. Instead, I munched on a few crackers—which were really helping with my *stomach flu*—and sat back on my fluffy pillows with a paperback cracked open. In the last hour I'd only managed to scan half a page, but I'd heard that literacy tends to come and go in adulthood. I wasn't worried.

Another email from Andie pinged on my laptop and I read the subject line:

PEE ON A STICK, YOU STUBBORN IDIOT.

See what I mean? Shockingly unstable, that one.

Still, she might have had a point. I had literally bought out the village's supply of pregnancy tests. I could have sat outside the lone pharmacy, waiting for a couple to go rushing in, then price-gouged them on their way out. Since I owned a monopoly, I figured it wouldn't hurt my position to get rid of one or two.

I thought I really might take one then. I opened my bedside table and reached for the pink and white box, but then I heard footsteps in the common room and Gianluca's voice filled the bed and breakfast.

"Georgie?"

Oh god.

I slammed the drawer closed and jumped up to conceal it. Gianluca opened the door after a gentle knock and I feigned a big, easy smile.

"HEY-OOO there."

He furrowed his brows, clearly suspicious. "Wow. Hi."

"Hello again."

He laughed and shook his head. "What are you doing in here?"

At once, both of our gazes fell to the open crackers sitting on my bed.

"Are you feeling all right?"

"Yes. I was just reading…and I wanted a snack."

It was the truth, *technically*.

"Right well, c'mon. I've got something to show you."

I frowned. "Where? Honestly, I've got to stay here and…"

He shook his head and reached out for my hand, all but

dragging me from my room. My stomach flu had flared up earlier, but the crackers had settled my stomach for the moment; I just had to hope they would last for a while.

Massimo and Katerina were waiting for us outside. I hadn't seen Katerina since our blowup on the mountain, but one look at her told me she wanted to make up. I didn't lay into her—I regretted the way I'd shouted at her as well—and without a word, I stepped right up to her and held out my hand for her to shake.

"Truce?"

She grinned, bloody relieved, and pulled me into a hug. "Truce."

"Sorry I was an utter cow. Pun intended."

"That makes two of us."

"Well that was fast." Massimo laughed. "I thought we'd be standing here for at least a half hour while you two had another go at one each other."

"We're very ma-tour," Katerina laughed, looping her arm through mine and tugging me into the square.

Everyone seemed to know our destination but me.

"Where are we going?"

"To finish that hike we started a few days ago."

Oh, murder me. They expected me to climb mountains in my state?

"Let me at least go change into some proper shoes."

Katerina shook her head and kept walking, forcing me toward the train station. We hopped on and headed toward Manarola. Out of the five villages in Cinque Terre, I'd spent the least amount of time there, hardly any at all, in fact. It was where I'd stormed off the other day, so I was familiar with the train station, but the group led me down a stone path toward the sea.

I was concerned about my sandals and sundress, but I

looked around and noticed no one else had their hiking gear on either. Gianluca was wearing shorts and a white linen shirt. Katerina carried a hefty straw bag stuffed to the brim with what looked to be beach towels.

We continued down the stone path until we arrived in the center of Manarola, an area I'd never ventured to before. There were pastel buildings and restaurants bustling with tourists, but unlike Vernazza, Manarola was positioned high up on cliffs, giving us a spectacular view of the surrounding sea. Tourists were crowded at the iron railing at the edge of the main square, posing for photos and dipping over the edge to look down. That's where Katerina dragged me, right to the edge. I looked down and gasped.

There was a massive, naturally formed swimming grotto just below. Crystal clear water surrounded a jagged central rock formation that children were climbing on and then jumping off of. A few fish darted around the edges, staying out of the way of the swimmers. Sunbathers relaxed around the grotto, making use of the smooth granite rocks, worn down from use over the years.

"Are we going down there?"

Gianluca had come up behind me, boxing me in against the railing. "We're going to swim."

"I didn't bring my suit."

"I know."

They told me it was a rite of passage to take a hike from Riomaggiore to Manarola, strip off your sweaty clothes, and jump into the water as a reward for all your hard work. Since I'd stormed off the other day, we hadn't had the chance.

Now, we were going to make up for it.

Gianluca led me down a steep staircase cut out of the

granite rock. We carved out a bit of space for ourselves, sliding out of our shoes. The boys tugged off their shirts and I glanced up, aware of all the tourists watching us. I had on a pair of blue underwear and a matching bra, nothing more scandalous than the majority of the bathing suits I'd seen in Italy, but I still felt self-conscious tugging my sundress overhead.

Massimo was already in his skivvies, about to jump into the water. Katerina had stripped off her clothes and was folding them beside her beach bag.

"Nervous?" Gianluca asked, glancing back at me over his shoulder.

For a moment, I just looked at him standing there with the sun shining overhead and the turquoise water at his back. He had beautiful tan skin. Broad, muscular shoulders. Heavy lashes. Thick brown hair and a devilish smirk. He was the most romantic-looking man I'd ever seen, and at times it hurt to look at him. In another world, he would have been an arrogant asshole. No man is that good looking without taking advantage of it, but Gianluca wasn't like that. He had a heart of gold, a gentle soul, and I knew that once he loved, he loved forever.

He reached his hand back for me. "Come on, we'll go in together."

• • •

Later that night, alone in the bed and breakfast, I finally worked up the courage to take a test.

Chapter thirty-seven

Gianluca

THE DAY AFTER we swam in Manarola, I finished gathering Allie's things from my house. I shipped a good bit of her stuff to her parents back in London, passed on a few lightly worn dresses to Katerina so she could resell them in her shop, and kept a few photos and trinkets in a small shoebox, sealed with tape, for myself. My house felt empty. My closet was half-bare, my medicine cabinet had been depleted of her old prescriptions, and my walls were blank canvases once again. I'd taken down every hint of her and rather than the guilt I'd expected, I felt relief. After all this time, it felt good, right.

I'd build a new life with Georgie in that villa. She'd fill the place with color and laughter and life. And while I feared loving someone else, knowing I could lose them just as easily, it wasn't strong enough to override the new sense of optimism Georgie had infected me with.

Georgie was youthful and vivacious. She spoke her

311

mind and rarely let anyone else get a word in when she really got going. She was bold and beautiful, adventurous and so full of life, she made everyone around her feel it as well.

I was in love with her.

I knew it now, but the trouble came in the fact that it might have been too late.

In the days since my birthday, she'd been distant and aloof, not quite cold, but guarded. Her smiles came slower, more forced. Her thoughts were somewhere else, and though I tried to pull her out of her quiet moods, I knew it wouldn't work. Georgie was too stubborn for it. Even swimming in the grotto, she'd tried her hardest to keep her distance.

The next day, I went into Il Mare early and spent the day working up on the third floor, but Georgie was M.I.A. I saw Taylor when he arrived back home in the evening.

"Have you seen Georgie around?" I asked.

"Oh, we had breakfast this morning and then she was heading to swim, I think. Did she not tell you?"

I swallowed down my anger that Taylor seemed to know more about the woman I loved than I did.

"No." I shook my head. "She didn't tell me."

I waited for her. I had a plan. The moment I saw her, I would lay down my heart for her, plead with her to stay in Vernazza and share her life with me. I wanted to make up for lost time, to explain to her that my heart wasn't split in half anymore, that she owned it all.

When darkness fell and I still hadn't heard her come in, I started to worry.

Why hadn't she come home?

Why was she trying to avoid me?

I packed up my tools and decided to head up to the villa

in case she might have been waiting for me there, though I knew it was a stretch.

During the walk home, I overanalyzed our last few encounters. What if Georgie had finally realized I wasn't worth the trouble after all? I'd been assuming she'd jump into my arms when I finally told her about moving on from Allie, but what if it was too little, too late? My imagination ran wild with dark thoughts of what my life would turn into if Georgie left. Everything would go back to the way it was before. I'd have Massimo and Katerina, sure, but there was little else.

I grabbed a beer out of the fridge and stood outside, watching the waves crash against the breaker.

In truth, it'd taken me five years to fall in love again. I didn't let people in easily, and now the woman I wanted more than anything was pushing me away. *For good reason*, I reminded myself. In recent weeks, I'd taken my sweet time unraveling my feelings, keeping her at arm's length, trying to work out my baggage before unloading it in her lap.

After that thought, I went back inside for a second beer, then thought better of it and pulled down a dusty bottle of whiskey. I'd stayed away from alcohol after Allie's death, too scared I would spiral out of control. Now, I needed it. I relished the burn, the physical symptoms that accompanied heartache.

A few shots later, when the edges of my world started to blur, I finally noticed a light on in Georgie's room at Il Mare. She was home, safe, and though I longed to see her, my drunken state promised disaster if I ran down and tried to explain myself now.

No, I stayed up there, fixed on the hazy yellow glow from her window, preparing for the next morning. There was no way in hell I would just let Georgie walk away from us without showing her that I was ready to move on. At the crack of dawn, I'd march down to Il Mare and make the promises she'd been so desperate to hear from me. I could prove to her that I was ready to move on.

I was ready for strings.

GIANLUCA LEFT AND I couldn't sit still. I'd been hiding in my room at Il Mare like a coward all evening, even keeping the light off so he wouldn't know I was there. Pathetic, I know, but now my chocolate reserves were running low and Mopsie was clawing at the door, angry with me for keeping him away from his coveted plush mouse. *We all have needs, Mopsie.* Mine centered around avoiding Gianluca at all costs.

Tomorrow was a big day.

The biggest day of any big days.

"All right! *All right*, I'm letting you out," I said to Mopsie after he'd shot me what could only be described as a menacing glare. I slid off my bed and stood on atrophied knees, pried the door open slowly just in case Gianluca was still hiding somewhere.

He wasn't, and even Mopsie was a bit sad about that.

Il Mare was eerily quiet and I had half a mind to go up

315

and ask if Taylor fancied some company, but he'd brought home a girl a few hours ago and I doubted they wanted me to join in their love fest. I was shite enough at managing one lover; I didn't need to add two more.

Truthfully, I had a lot on my mind. Too much. Tomorrow was a big day. Had I mentioned that? Big. Decisions loomed heavy in the distance, and instead of focusing on them like a healthy adult, I cleaned my room. Top to bottom, every single floorboard, every nook and cranny.

I found a leftover lemon candy wrapper in the closet and teared up, even stuffed it into the tiny pocket on my pajama top for safekeeping. *Who's the hoarder now?*

I did a load of laundry, and then another. I packed my bag for the next day, wanting to ensure I brought enough things to entertain me. I stuffed a paperback inside, and then thought better of it and put them all in there. No point in leaving any. The lemon candy wrapper went right up at the top. It was a poor substitute for Gianluca himself, but it was better than nothing.

I straightened up the common room, fluffed the pillows, and arranged a vase of flowers on the coffee table.

Everything was set.

At 8:15 AM the next morning, I'd catch a train out of Vernazza, and my whole life would change.

Chapter thirty-Nine

Gianluca

THE NEXT MORNING, I peeled my eyes open and blinked twice, trying to pinpoint where I was. I'd never made it up to my bedroom the night before. I was sprawled out on my couch with empty beer bottles littering the floor around me. I sat up, instantly regretted it, and then leaned my head back against the cushion, overtaken by the sharp ache of my hangover.

"*Merde,*" I moaned, pressing the heel of my hands against my temples, massaging gently. Nothing helped. I eventually forced my way into the kitchen, guzzled a glass of the water, and then filled it again. I downed a few painkillers and splashed water on my face. I needed a decent shower, maybe two. My face needed a good shave, but there was no time.

I needed to find Georgie.

I changed my clothes and dragged a hand through my hair. I shoved my keys into my pocket and ran for the bed and breakfast, fearing Georgie wouldn't be there, and as I suspected, she wasn't. The front door was locked. Her room was empty. Her bed was made and the rest of the place looked spotless, as if she'd spent the entire day before cleaning it from top to bottom. The stack of books she usually kept on her nightstand was gone, and I didn't want to think about what that could mean.

I headed to Katerina's shop, prepared to drag information out of her, but she wasn't there when I arrived. I knocked on her door and held my hands up to the glass. The lights were off and a sign beside the door said the shop wouldn't be open for another two hours.

Fuck.

I turned and caught sight of The Blue Marlin on the edge of my vision. I needed coffee to clear my head, and it would be a good place to wait. I'd be able to spot Georgie if she walked by and I'd catch Katerina before she made it into the shop.

Antonio looked up when I stepped inside and offered me a smile.

"*Buongiorno.*"

I nodded and asked for a double espresso and a croissant.

"That early bird of yours already stopped in for hers this morning," he said with a soft chuckle.

I whipped my head up. "What? Georgie's been by?"

He nodded and pointed up the path toward the train station. "Just a few minutes ago. She asked me to wrap a few things to-go, said she had a long day ahead of her."

I cursed under my breath, turned on my heel, and ran as fast as I could to the train station in disbelief. The road was deserted that early and it only took me a few seconds to reach the stairs. I took them two at a time, surfaced at the top of the platform, and spun in a circle. There were a few hikers waiting for the next train, but no Georgie.

"Have you seen a girl with brown hair?" I asked them.

I held my hand up to my shoulder to show her height, but they shook their heads.

"Sorry, mate," one man replied, shaking his head. "The platform was empty when we arrived."

I tugged my hands through my hair, turned in circles, and then ran down the train platform to see if maybe she was sitting down somewhere. I checked the small tourist shop, but it was still locked up. The tracks were empty. Another train arrived, everyone loaded on, and then I was left by myself.

She was nowhere and I couldn't breathe.

I hunched over and tried to suppress the vomit rising in my throat. My catastrophic thinking from the night before seemed to be coming true.

It made sense that she would leave Vernazza as suddenly as she had appeared.

"Man, are you okay?"

It was the guy from before, concerned. I was still hunched over, trying to catch my breath.

"Anything we can do to help?"

I shook my head.

How could anybody help?

Georgie was gone.

Chapter Forty

Gianluca

ON GEORGIE'S FIRST day in Vernazza, she had fainted. On what seemed to be her last, I was the one feeling lightheaded. I couldn't believe she'd gone.

Even when I tried to be logical and assure myself that she was probably off shopping or clearing her head in a nearby village, the pessimist inside me would counter, arguing that even if she wasn't leaving for good this time, eventually, she would. She was in Vernazza on holiday. It was absolutely mad to think she'd stay on forever. Unlike me, Georgie had a life back home in London. She had somewhere to go.

I sat on a bench at the train station waiting for her for ages. I watched families load in and out of the train, keeping a careful watch for a brunette girl with a wide smile and just a little bit of crazy lurking behind her gaze.

I confirmed she wasn't at Il Mare or my villa, and then finally sick of pacing around the village, I threw up my hands and took my boat out to the middle of the sea, far enough away that Vernazza was nothing but a dot on the horizon. My boat was too small to be out this far, but I took comfort in the waves rocking me up and down. I'd come out with hopes of fishing, but I couldn't work up the will to prepare my line.

Instead, I entertained ideas of chasing after Georgie. If I loved her as much as I thought I did, wouldn't I follow her to London? We could start over and date like normal people. I could try to get my old job back at the finance firm. They'd been sympathetic when I needed time off for Allie, and even mentioned I could always come back when I was ready. I still had my flat there. I could get my things out of storage and settle back into my old life.

Those thoughts didn't last long though. Vernazza allowed me to be the man Georgie loved. She could have any miserable sod in a suit in London if she wanted.

I stayed out on the water, rocking in the boat until the sun had started to set. It didn't seem right to have spent all day on the water with nothing to show for it, but the water was getting choppy, and I knew it was time.

The pastel buildings came into view first. Lights twinkling behind shuttered windows. Clothing hung on lines, flapping in the evening wind. Sound carried out on the water, the usual clinking of glasses and speckled conversation. Tourists were everywhere, filling the tables outside and spilling out onto the breaker to take photos of the sunset. It was right at the beginning of the golden hour and the entire village was basked in gentle, warm light.

I maneuvered my boat around a buoy and looked onto the granite boulders. They formed the first breaker for Vernazza, and they also offered the best view of the setting sun. On them, it felt like you were sitting on the edge of the world with nothing but sea and sky stretched in front of you. There were tourists lingering around them, even a few brave enough to venture out and take a seat.

I'd seen Georgie sitting on them before—the memory was so sharp that as I closed my eyes, I could see it as clear as day.

When I opened my eyes, the image remained: Georgie sitting on the boulder in the very center of the breakers, just a foot or two out of reach of the waves. She was kicking her feet back and forth like a child. I blinked a few times, trying to work out if it was really her or just a figment of my imagination.

My boat brought me closer and she stood, waving to me from her perch.

She was a siren calling out to me. Her brown hair was loose, long, and whipping in the wind from the north. Her blue sundress fluttered around her legs and her lips split into a wide grin when I rounded the side of the breaker and slowed my boat to a crawl. There was a fellow boatman unloading his catches of the day; he helped me anchor and then I jumped back onto land, looking around for Georgie. She was still standing on the boulder, waiting for me to join her. It was a precarious path, with boulders jutting in every direction, but I'd journeyed there enough times to know a quick way to get to her.

I stepped onto the boulder and took her in. The sun was setting behind her and the sea stretched to infinity. Her brown eyes sought mine and I realized we were both standing there silent.

I bent to kiss her cheek, enveloped by her warmth...her scent...*her*.

God, I missed her. It'd been days since I touched her and I missed her so much.

"I thought you'd left Vernazza for good," I admitted.

"And leave Mopsie in your care? Never."

"He likes me."

"Not without me around—he's fiercely loyal."

I grinned.

"Why'd you think I left? For good?"

"Your room was cleaner than I've ever seen it before. I thought it was a sign."

"Ah. I can see how that might have been alarming."

"It was quite a sight. I didn't realize you had a proper floor in there."

She laughed and glanced away; I could feel her nerves radiating off her.

"I was watching you out there," she continued, pointing out to the patch of sea I'd come from.

"Sorry I took so long."

She shrugged. "I didn't mind waiting."

We weren't talking about my time on the water.

I wanted to cover her mouth with mine so that the conversation ended there. I didn't need to hear any of the thoughts swirling in that stubborn head of hers. I didn't want her to continue to push me away or talk of her plans to leave Vernazza.

She reached for my hands and squeezed. "I actually have something really important to tell you."

"So do I." The words came out in a rush, one after another until I couldn't stop them. I had to speak first. "Stay here with me. Stay in Vernazza and move into the villa. I don't want to lose you and I should have told you earlier, but I only realized a few days ago. I love you, Georgie. There, see? I love you and I need you to stay. Please say you'll stay."

She let out a high-pitched, hysterical laugh.

"Does that villa of yours have a spare room?"

A spare room?

I wrapped my hands around her waist and pulled her into me. "I think we're beyond having separate rooms. You'll be in mine. With me. I'll get used to the clothes on the floor."

"It's not *for me*."

"For who then?"

She turned to face the sea and it was only then that she let her face start to crumble. She furrowed her brows and tugged her bottom lip between her teeth. Whatever it was she was about to say, she was nervous, maybe even *scared* of my reaction.

"Tell me. What's wrong? Are you still thinking of leaving?"

"I'm pregnant."

The force of those two words nearly sent me flying backward.

"Say again?"

She pinched her eyes closed and turned back to me, letting her forehead drop to my chest.

"I'm...*with child*. I've got your *bun* in my *oven*."

I laughed, though it sounded a bit hysterical. "Georgie. Look at me."

I tilted her chin up, but she kept her eyes closed.

"Are you serious? Open your eyes."

"I can't."

I laughed and tugged on her eyebrows. Finally, she opened her eyes, but she stared at a spot just to the side of my forehead, refusing to meet my eye.

"It's yours—*obviously*," she continued. "I went into La Spezia to see a doctor today. That's why I've been gone all day. They confirmed the pregnancy and did an ultrasound.

They printed out a little polaroid I can show you, though really it doesn't look like anything quite yet, just a black and white piece of abstract art. Still, it made me cry all over the nurse's scrubs. I think they felt a bit bad for me—being a blubbering mess and all. They said in two weeks I can go back and listen to her heartbeat, Gianluca! It'll be this whirring little sound. And I can show you the picture if you'd like. It's quite boring, but I love it and I'll show you if you want to see it."

"Georgie—"

"Don't think you have to stay with me for the baby. I'm quite prepared to be a single mum if I have to—I think I've got the temperament for it and I do think I'll secretly relish seeing people look on at me with pity. Besides, I'm quite good with kids. We enjoy a lot of the same things."

"Georgie, stop talking."

"Oh god, you're so sad that you're crying."

I supposed I was—crying, that is.

"You're ridiculous," I said, cradling the back of her neck so she couldn't pull away from me.

"You can't call a pregnant woman ridiculous. It's in the rules."

I kissed her to shut her up and when I pulled back, her lips were parted and her eyes were wide as saucers.

"I suppose I've got to marry you now."

If possible, her eyes went even wider.

"What do you mean—*marry?!*"

I grinned. "It's really the only option we have."

"Don't toy with me, Gianluca."

"I wouldn't dream of it."

She started vehemently shaking her head then, trying to push away from me. "No, I won't allow you to propose just because you feel obligated to—by this." She pointed at her stomach.

"Didn't you hear the bit where I said I loved you?"

"You said that?"

"Earlier."

"Oh." She touched her lips, thinking it over. "I suppose I was caught up in my own world, trying to work out how to tell you about the baby."

"Well it's too bad you missed it. I poured my heart out to you and it was bloody romantic."

"No, no, go on, say it again and I swear I'll listen properly this time."

"It really wasn't much, just a little speech about me really loving you and all that."

"Oh. Wow. That does sound good."

"The real proposal will be better."

"So you're going to propose with a ring and all?"

"I'm not a brute, Georgie."

"Sometimes you really act like one."

"You shouldn't call the father of your child a brute."

Her lip quivered then.

"We're having a baby, Gianluca."

My heart swelled and I leaned in to kiss her again, and this time it was soft and slow. I could hardly break it off.

"You could start calling me Luca now, don't you think?"

She grinned. "I suppose I could." Then she proceeded to try it out. "*Luca*."

I loved the sound of it coming from her.

"Does this mean we're friends now?"

"We'll see."

• • •

It was nearly amusing to look back on the last few days with a fresh set of eyes. Ever since the blowup on the mountain, Georgie had been acting strangely. What I had interpreted as her pulling away from me was actually her panic at the thought of having conceived a child with a man she couldn't rely on. I kicked myself for taking so long to give her the assurance she needed, but I knew it didn't matter anymore.

Now she knew how much I loved her and I planned on ensuring she never forgot.

I moved her things to the villa that night.

I couldn't wait.

She didn't have much more than when I'd moved her in, just a suitcase and a few bags. She had more sandals than any one human needed, but I didn't care. Georgie was moving into my villa and I wore a shit-eating grin as I carried her things up the steep hill. She was lying on the couch, listening to the record I'd put on as I carried in the last few things. Mopsie was curled up at her feet, and I couldn't resist the temptation to join them.

"Don't move."

I kicked the door closed, dropped her bags by the door, and stole Mopsie's spot, pulling Georgie's legs up onto my lap so she didn't have to shift at all. I sank into the cushions and glanced over to find Georgie spilling life into every nook and cranny of that empty villa. She smiled at me and wiggled her toes.

"You're the best moving man I've ever hired." I smiled. "My own personal Sherpa, after all."

"Yeah, a shoe Sherpa. That's quite the collection you've got going."

"Just doing my part to stimulate the local economy."

I arched a brow. "Oh, so you enjoy stimulating things?"

"Oh, ha ha, very charming. How could I possibly love you?"

"You do then?"

"So much it feels like torture at times."

She pointed to the bare wall behind her.

"You've taken away Allie's things."

I nodded. "A few days ago."

She turned back to me with a small frown. "You don't have to, Luca. Not on my account."

"I didn't do it for you. It was long overdue."

I needed her to know I wasn't using her to get over Allie. Georgie wasn't my second love. She was my only love.

"You should know I never intended to fall in love again. I never imagined I'd have a reason to move on, and when you came along, I wasn't prepared. I didn't know how to handle you. You were...*a lot* to take in at once. I tried to keep my wall up, but you blew right past it."

She grinned. "*Tramontana*." Her Italian accent had improved dramatically.

"Exactly." I leaned forward and cupped her cheek, stroking my thumb across her skin. "You're the woman I love now, Georgie. The *only* woman."

She mashed her lips together and nodded, trying to keep from crying, I thought. I didn't pester her about it. She'd had a long day and I didn't want her getting too stressed out. Apparently the doctors said she needed lots of rest and relaxation, though Georgie also went on about needing a daily allotment of prenatal chocolate and circulation-improving foot rubs. I didn't mind giving her everything she wanted. I'd spoil her and in a few months, I'd spoil our child just as much.

It'd been too long since I'd been this happy, this full of hope for the future, and I knew it was no coincidence. Something had brought Georgie to me, and whether it was fate, or God, or Allie working the cosmic magic she'd promised, I knew I'd spend the rest of my life loving Georgie Archibald here, in our place in the sun.

Chapter Forty-One

Georgie

EPILOGUE: ONE YEAR LATER

IT MIGHT SEEM odd, but I would have given anything for one conversation with Allie. There was so much I would have liked to tell her, and more that I wanted to ask. She was Luca's first love, an irreplaceable part of his life. She'd taught him what it meant to be a man, to grow and love in spite of life's hardships. Given the chance, I would have thanked her, pulled her close, and promised to do my best to love him. When I'd first arrived in Vernazza and had struggled and fought with Luca, I wasn't upset by the idea of sharing his heart with her; I was concerned that he was still wearing his tragedy like a stiff mask he refused to take off. A part of me feared he would never emerge from the veil of mourning.

Allie, who had lost her own life at such a young age, would have hated to know that she'd cut Luca's short as well.

In the year since I'd moved into the villa, I thought of her often. I felt her presence during the birth of Julianna. I'd held my newborn baby in my arms and I'd cried, first with happiness, and then for Allie, for all she had lost. Handing off Julianna to Luca and seeing him step into fatherhood was a gift I never once took for granted. I wanted Allie to see it, to know that more than any role he'd tried on before—financier, husband, widower, recluse—he was meant to be a father. His love for Julianna eclipsed all else.

There was even a moment, a few months after Julianna was born, when my imagination fooled me into thinking I might get the chance to have that conversation. Luca, Julianna, and I were eating breakfast at The Blue Marlin. Our addiction to their croissants was as strong as ever—not to mention, Julianna seemed to enjoy waking up at the crack of dawn, so Luca and I were mostly functioning off espresso and the sheer stubborn willpower only available to new parents.

We took our favorite seats outside on the wooden porch. Antonio brought us a few pastries that had just come out of the oven and I tore one in half, handing a bit to Luca while he bounced Julianna on his knee.

She looked so much like him. She'd inherited his long, dark lashes and thick hair, his olive skin and pouty lips. Her eyes were like mine though, light brown and round.

She started to giggle, watching her dad while he talked to her.

God, she was putty for him. He could do no wrong in her eyes, and though I couldn't prove it, I swore she purposely saved her spit-up for me.

"I was thinking we could go on a hike later?" he asked. "Nothing too far."

I hummed in agreement, eager to enjoy the good weather.

"I just have a bit to do at Il Mare. I need to see that Elena is managing everything all right."

He nodded and turned back to Julianna, but she was focused on me now. She'd locked onto her *mamma* and I bent forward, rubbing the bottom of her feet until she lapsed into a fit of giggles. There was no better sound.

"Katerina asked about dinner tomorrow."

He nodded. "That'd be nice. We'll have to see them at Massimo's. I doubt Katerina would want to trek all the way up to the villa."

She was just beginning her seventh month of pregnancy.

"True—although, I did it."

"Sure, though I seem to remember quite a bit of moaning about it."

I grinned. "Only there at the end, when I was more beach ball than woman."

Antonio came round with our espressos and we settled back into our seats to enjoy them. The street was busier than usual. It was Tuesday, so the open-air market would start soon and vendors were bustling around getting everything ready. Katerina wasn't there—she was too tired to manage the shop and the market so close to the end of her pregnancy.

I reached into our diaper bag and handed Luca a toy for Julianna. She jingled the colorful, oversized keys in her little hand and for a few minutes, I sipped my drink and watched her playing, content to enjoy the slow morning.

A train pulled into the station and we heard the first lot of tourists chattering and winding their way down the main street. In a few minutes, Vernazza would be flooded like it was every day during the summer months. I loved sitting back and people-watching, and that's what I did, taking in all the different people coming to enjoy a little slice of heaven. I loved hearing their shocked sighs when they got their first proper view of the village and the sea.

One particular family stuck out to me: a mom trying to corral her children away from the cakes and cookies on display at the market. I followed their journey down the main road until a flash of fabric caught my attention. It was on a woman walking alone, and my flipbook view of her was dependent on the motion of the swirling crowd. She was wearing a dress I recognized. It was bright yellow and had lemons printed all over it. It was light and cheerful and I had *absolutely* seen it before.

I muttered to Luca about wanting to check out a new vendor, jumped out of my seat, and took off down the street after her, trying to dart around groups of tourists stopped to shop in the market. She'd gotten so far ahead that I thought I'd never catch her. I picked up the pace, all but sprinting.

"Excuse me! 'Scuse me!"

I pushed past a man, offered up a weak apology, and then continued down the road. I shouted her name above the crowd, but she never turned. She rounded the corner into the square and I lost her. There were too many people on the streets. Too many people had come in on the train all at once. I spun in a circle, looking around the square, and then I spotted her standing near the granite boulders, looking out to the sea.

I knew in my gut that it was Allie.

It was her long pale blonde hair. Her delicate profile. Her lemon dress. It whipped in the wind around her legs as she propped her hands on her hips. For a year and a half I'd longed for this moment, a chance to walk up and tap her shoulder, to have her turn and offer me a gentle smile.

I wanted to step closer, and yet, I didn't.

There was no need.

I wasn't fooling myself—I knew it couldn't have been Allie—but what else is left of a person on this earth after they've died except their old clothes, their memory, and the loose strings they leave the rest of us holding on to? By that rationale, it *was* Allie, and seeing her standing there on the boulder with her head tilted to the sun told me everything I needed to know. More than closure, it was assurance that Allie was at peace now. She knew her magic had worked.

Acknowledgements

Thank you to Lance for working on this project with me. I know I didn't make it easy, but without you, this book would be half as funny and probably still in the plotting phase, hah.

Thank you to my friends and family for their unwavering love and support. Thank you also to my fellow author friends. You guys all know who you are. Thank you to my readers, especially the Little Reds. This book is for you guys.

Thank you to my editor, Caitlin, and my proofreader, Jennifer. You're both such a pleasure to work with and I know how fortunate I am to have you both on my team.

Thank you to my agent, Kimberly Brower!

Thank you to all of the bloggers who help spread the word about my books! Vilma's Book Blog, Book Baristas, Angie's Dreamy Reads, Southern Belle Book Blog, Typical Distractions Book Blog, Natasha is a Book Junkie, Rock Stars of Romance, A Bookish Love Affair, Swept Away by Books, Library Cutie, Hopeless Book Lover, and many, many more! You all have been such a cheerleader for me and I am so grateful to each and every one of you!

Find other R.S. Grey Books on Amazon!

Behind His Lens
With This Heart
Scoring Wilder
The Duet
The Design
The Allure of Julian Lefray
The Allure of Dean Harper
Chasing Spring
The Summer Games: Settling the Score
The Summer Games: Out of Bounds

Made in the USA
Lexington, KY
22 September 2018